GUARDING HIS ROYAL BRIDE

C.J. Miller

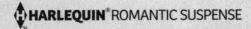

Recycling programs
for this product may
not exist in your area.

ISBN-13: 978-0-373-27973-9

Guarding His Royal Bride

Printed in U.S.A.

www.Harlequin.com

"Are you trying to antagonize me?"

Iliana smirked. "Yes."

"At least you admit it," Demetrius said.

"I want you to apologize."

"If I say the words, will you stop being upset?"

"You have to mean them. Then I'll see how I feel."

"Iliana, I haven't been more attracted to another woman than I am to you. What I know about the king of Valencia being related to you has nothing to do with that attraction."

"But you married me because of it."

"I would have married you one day. I moved up the timeline because of the king's health problems."

"You could have been honest with me."

"I told you about the king when the time was right."

"Do you think the man who tried to kill me was after me because of my connection to the king of Valencia?"

"I suspect someone else knows who you are and wants you dead because of it."

"Going to Valencia seems like a patently bad idea, then, if someone wants to kill me."

"No one will kill my wife."

"You're not invincible, Demetrius."

"I would sooner die than let someone harm you."

***

Be sure to check out the next books in this miniseries.

Conspiracy Against the Crown: Ally or foe? No one can tell in this fight for power...and love.

If you're on Twitter, tell us what you think of Harlequin Romantic Suspense! #harlequinromsuspense

Dear Reader,

Welcome back to the Mediterranean! Demetrius DeSante and Iliana Kracos were introduced in *The Secret King* (Harlequin Romantic Suspense, September 2015). Both are spirited individuals, but Iliana is a dreamer and Demetrius is a realist. His every move is to further his personal and political goals. Iliana follows her heart.

Demetrius's secrets are a necessary burden. Needing Iliana's help means sharing those long-buried secrets and letting her inside his private thoughts. That's hard for a man whose history is peppered with lies and betrayal. Iliana thinks her love will be the answer, except that word is far more difficult for Demetrius to accept—or to speak—than Iliana realized.

When Iliana learns that Demetrius has been keeping secrets about her past and a family she never knew existed, she has to decide whether to forgive him or walk away and destroy everything Demetrius has worked for.

I hope you enjoy the second book in the Conspiracy Against the Crown series.

Best,

C.J. Miller

C.J. Miller loves to hear from her readers and can be contacted through her website: cj-miller.com. She lives in Maryland with her husband, son and daughter. C.J. believes in first loves, second chances and happily-ever-after.

Visit C.J.'s Author Profile page at Harlequin.com, or cj-miller.com, for more titles.

To my dear friends, Jen, the level-headed realist, and Christy, the daydreamer. Here's to 28 more years of secret keeping.

Chapter 1

The king of Valencia was dying and leaving behind a hell of a mess.

Emmanuel Floros had two ex-wives, five spoiled children who had grown into self-centered adults and a wife who was as controlling as she was stupid. The eight of them were squabbling for land and money, but the fighting was pointless. After the king died and his will was read, all would be revealed. Some might be cut out; others may have inherited a treasure trove.

Fortunately for him, President Demetrius DeSante of Icarus had a knack for turning disasters into opportunities. In this case, the opportunity had a name: Iliana Kracos. It wasn't like him to care about a woman this much, even a woman as beautiful as Iliana, but she was special.

He wouldn't allow a little obstacle like her fury at him to stand in his way.

Demetrius had to take his pursuit of Iliana to another level. No more casual phone calls, flower arrangements, gifts or dropping by the castle to see her. She was giving him the old-fashioned silent treatment, and maybe he deserved it. She had been angry with him when he had refused to back down from a fight brewing in the Mediterranean, but since war had been averted, she should have moved past it and forgiven him. Yet she'd rebuffed his calls and communicated only through intermediaries. During his infrequent visits to Acacia, she'd been away from the castle on business.

He was outside Iliana's home, fist hovering in front of the wood door, prepared to knock.

Why was he nervous? He had nerves of steel, which had been tested many times over on the battlefield, and courage in spades that he displayed every time he faced difficulties head-on. But one fiery, green-eyed goddess had the power to reduce him to an anxious mess. Much more was on the line than Iliana's significance in Valencia. She was the most fascinating woman he had ever known—feisty, smart and sexy, all wrapped up in a spicy package.

His servicemen were behind him, and he wouldn't show fear in front of them. Though their loyalty was unconditional and challenged on a regular basis, he wouldn't give anyone one shred of a reason to doubt him. He maintained control by showing power and strength. His careful decisions had pulled Icarus back from ruin and had changed it into a productive country for the first time in a century.

He heard a crash inside the house.

His protective instincts roared, and he pounded on the door. "Iliana! Open the door!"

Iliana's terror-filled scream rang out. Demetrius kicked at the door handle. Once, twice and the door splintered under his weight. He rushed into the house, his servicemen on his heels.

He followed Iliana's screams and the sound of breaking dishes.

She was at the back of the house, in her kitchen. Her hands were gripping the counter behind her, and a man was pointing a gun at her. Demetrius's own gun was in his hands in milliseconds. His guards would be brandishing theirs, as well.

Demetrius didn't recognize the man, but it wouldn't be the first time he'd be forced to kill a stranger. "You are outgunned and outmanned. Drop your weapon, or I'll kill you."

The intruder looked from Iliana to Demetrius. The coldness in his eyes and the firepower in his hands indicated this wasn't an armed robbery. This wasn't personal. This was a would-be assassination. The man was likely a hired gun who knew his trade well. The hit man didn't know Iliana, and that worked in their favor. He wouldn't make reckless decisions based on emotion.

Demetrius would have killed him on the spot for threatening Iliana, but she didn't like violence. And if the assassin was dead, they couldn't find out who had sent him. "Last warning."

Three more seconds and Iliana's aversion to violence would come second to keeping her safe.

The assassin set his weapon on the kitchen table and raised his hands. The man didn't have a death wish after all. Lucky for him. Demetrius took the gun and gestured to his servicemen to deal with the assailant.

After holstering his gun and handing the hit man's gun to his guard, he strode to Iliana, who was still clutching the countertop, her face white, her body shaking. His rage for the assassin was renewed. He should have killed the man for upsetting her and found out who'd hired him another way.

His woman shouldn't tremble from fear, and whether or not she chose to recognize it, Iliana was his woman.

White-hot anger sliced through him, and he reached for his gun. Any man who harmed Iliana would pay, and he'd set the precedent now.

Iliana set her hand on his, her soft fingers sending a jolt of lust and desire through him. "No, Demetrius. Don't kill him. Please."

She knew him too well. She had read the intention in his eyes. It wasn't the first time she had stopped him from killing a man. If it were any other woman, he would have ignored her plea.

"He hurt you." Translation: he deserved to die.

She shook her head. "He scared me. He didn't hurt me. I threw dishes at him."

Scaring her and hurting her made little difference to him. "It's the same." But he had to admit, her fight and her resourcefulness impressed him.

"My gun is in that drawer," she said, pointing to a cabinet a few feet from her. "I was trying to get to it."

Surprise and admiration washed over him. "Since when do you have a gun?"

She stabbed her slender fingers through her red hair. "Since a few months after my cousin and uncle were gunned down at his birthday party."

Demetrius had attended the late king of Acacia's birthday party. Tragic scene, catastrophic consequences. "You didn't mention your interest in owning a gun. I could have taught you to use it."

"I took lessons." She shook her head, still seeming dazed. "What are you doing here?" Her voice sounded faint. He wasn't used to that. Usually everything Iliana said was accompanied by an energetic, playful tone, occasionally marked with a little sass.

Except during the last conversation they had, the conversation he didn't like to think about. She had been hurt and angry with him.

"I came to speak with you." She had pulled her hand away, and he was desperate to reach for her. He didn't. The number of times he had touched Iliana could be counted on one hand. Their relationship, though far more intimate than any other he'd had with a woman in years, was lacking in the physical aspect. Not because he wasn't interested. He was very interested. What held him back was the fear he would mess this up. He needed it to work in order to follow through with his plan.

"Did you arrange this attack in an attempt to win my forgiveness by saving me?" she asked.

The idea was repulsive, and it burned that she thought so low of him. "I have told you before. It is not my intention to hurt you, ever. I would never send a man here to kill you or threaten you so I could step in and save you. The timing was fortuitous, and you can confirm with your queen's husband that I am in Acacia at his invitation. We met earlier today." King Casimir, one of the few men Demetrius trusted, had invited him to Acacia to discuss some outstanding political issues, among them, trade arrangements in the Mediterranean.

Iliana nodded once swiftly. She believed him and she should, because he spoke the truth. Demetrius made it his policy not to lie to her outright. But secret keeping was necessary, and as a member of the royal family, she should understand that.

"You're here. Say what you need to say," Iliana said. She set her hand on her hip, and he liked that her sass was back.

He had practiced the speech many times, but now he felt words were inadequate to express his thoughts. "I'm sorry that politics interfered in our relationship."

Iliana quirked a brow. Demetrius kept his eyes locked on her face, but it was tempting to peek at her generous curves. For a petite woman, she was shapely in the right places.

When he had first learned of Iliana's existence during a poker game with Emmanuel the First, the king of Valencia, Demetrius had been intrigued. Locating her had been a simple matter, as had been confirming her identity—one even she wasn't aware of—by taking a strand of hair from her hairbrush. What had not been simple was his attraction to her. She was take-his-breath-away gorgeous. Although he was regularly hit on by sexy women, those drawn to his power and money, Iliana intrigued him like no one else did.

She fascinated him in all the right ways. He found it refreshing that she didn't seem to care about his position or his wealth. It had been far too long since a woman liked him for him.

"It wasn't politics that came between us. You didn't

listen to me. You did what you wanted without any consideration for my thoughts and feelings."

Demetrius checked his temper. Iliana could push his buttons like no one else. Fighting with her made his blood run hot. Because she mattered to him. She had then, and she did now. "I had to do what was right for Icarus. I believed that war could be avoided, but I could not appear weak by backing away from provocation from Rizari."

Iliana's eyes softened. Was he winning her over? "I couldn't explain everything to you with the queen close at hand, and, after that, you refused to speak to me," he said.

She dropped her arms to her sides, hands unclenched. She was considering the matter.

He went for broke. "You've been through an ordeal today. Please stay with me until things settle down and we know more about this incident." Such as who the assassin was and why he had targeted Iliana. Demetrius could venture a few guesses, but vocalizing them would only scare her or anger her further.

She inhaled deeply, seeming to consider his proposition. "I will be fine. The police will be here soon, and it will be over."

Demetrius didn't want to frighten her, but he knew this would not be over until she was dead or the person who wanted her dead was stopped. "Could we speak in private?"

Iliana glanced over his shoulder at her attacker. "Outside?"

He hadn't swept the outside to see if another killer was lying in wait. "Upstairs would be better."

She swallowed hard. "Okay."

Demetrius followed her up the stairs, taking in the details around him, paint color, the pictures on the wall, all canvas paintings, and the flooring: soft but worn. He hadn't been inside her home before, and he noticed how much like her it was. Inviting, modern and comfortable.

When she reached the top of the stairs, she took one more step and turned. "There are only bedrooms and a bathroom up here. We can talk in the hallway."

Was she worried about being alone with him in the bedroom because of what may happen when a bed was close by? The idea thrilled him because it meant she still felt their attraction. For him, it was a constant thrum in his veins.

Being attracted to her was an unexpected bonus of the larger, more important task at hand—to win her over. He would have had to seduce her no matter what he felt for her, but being that she was gorgeous and smart, it made the job that much more pleasant.

He needed to be honest with her and give her the right motivation to stay with him. He could keep her safe as no one else could. "The man in your kitchen meant to assassinate you. Whoever sent him won't give up after one attempt."

Iliana shot him a look of disbelief. He loved that about her. She wasn't a simpering woman, quick to burst into tears. She rallied quickly in the face of hardships. "Perhaps there are a lot of people who have reasons to kill you. No one has reasons to kill me."

She knew so little about her life. It was too soon to tell her all he knew. He had to disarm her, marry her and then show her how she fit into the chess game.

"If you will not stay with me, please call your dear cousin and arrange to stay in the castle."

Since a massive corruption conspiracy had been uncovered within the queen of Acacia's ranks, she had cleaned house. New security measures had been put in place, and Queen Serena kept her thumb on everything and everyone in the Acacian government. It helped that her husband, King Constantine Casimir Warrington IV of Rizari, brought his skills as an experienced military man to the table.

Iliana wrinkled her nose. "I don't want to stay in the castle. It's big, but Serena and Casimir are still in the honeymoon phase and I'd be the third wheel there."

Demetrius knew the feeling. Those long looks and the constant touching between Serena and Casimir nauseated him. "Then, my home it is."

Iliana hesitated.

Shouting below them had Demetrius reaching again for his gun and pushing Iliana behind him. If more hit men had arrived, they'd have to shoot him dead to get to Iliana. He'd been shot four times in his life and had survived without any loss of major body functions. He'd cheated death and tempted fate before, and he would do it again.

The police had arrived. Demetrius surveyed the scene before bringing Iliana downstairs with him.

A detective strolled up to Iliana. "We found another man lurking outside. This address is on the queen's watch list. Ms. Kracos, you'll need to come with us."

"I've invited Iliana to stay with me. I think we should let her decide where she'd feel safest," Demetrius said, banking on Iliana choosing him. It was risky, but Iliana couldn't be cornered.

* * *

As bad days went, this one was tops. Iliana hadn't even had breakfast yet and her home had already been invaded by an assassin and Demetrius DeSante.

It was the second time that Demetrius had saved her life. She was capable of protecting herself, but being around him made her feel like batting her eyes and flirting and giggling. Not the tough image she wanted to convey.

A woman didn't flirt with the president of Icarus. He would find that behavior appalling. He was so serious and stern and powerful. Darkly good-looking, a fact he seemed unaware of, which made him that much more attractive.

Instead, Iliana kept her wits about her and reviewed her options.

She could stay in her home, she could stay with Serena and Casimir at the castle or she could run off with Demetrius DeSante.

Her heart had an obvious preference, given that it almost beat out of her chest at the idea of being alone with Demetrius. The safest place, in more ways than one, was the Acacian castle. Yet she would be loath to intrude on her cousin and her new husband. Her home felt unsafe and the police would likely insist, to the point of forcing her, that she leave. Demetrius's home held appeal.

She had a history of being brash and wild with men, so she would exercise some caution this time. "If I go with you to Icarus and wish to return to Acacia, you'll allow it?"

"This is not a kidnapping. You are coming with me of your own volition and may leave whenever you wish. I will arrange safe transportation for you to return to Acacia at your request."

His voice was liquid honey, and her knees felt as if they might give out. "If I come with you, it doesn't mean that I forgive you."

His eyes darkened. "Of course not."

But he knew that he'd won. The silence between them had been broken. Her anger had already been lessened by the fact that war between their countries had been averted months earlier. By the time the smoke had cleared, Iliana hadn't been sure how to talk to Demetrius or where they stood.

When she shut him out completely, she could keep her distance. But if she let him in a little bit, he seemed to get in all the way. When he was close, her desire for him intensified and she wanted him in— inside her, in her life, in her heart.

Given Iliana's position on the queen's staff, it divided her loyalty.

Yet she yearned for Demetrius DeSante. No other man ignited her blood as much as he did. Queen Serena had said she was fine with Iliana seeing DeSante. Granted, that was before the dictator had decided war was the only way and had shown he was willing to go to the mat over any infraction against Icarus.

Iliana didn't want to be in a relationship with someone who didn't think her opinion mattered. Could she give him another chance? Was that what was already happening?

Maybe her emotions had shifted away from anger when their hands had touched. Iliana wanted to touch him, but he rarely reached for her. Demetrius could light her up with a look, and that was power. They hadn't slept together, not even close, and yet she was hungry for him.

She felt a sudden burning need to explore the part of their relationship that was a mystery to her. "I'll need to inform Serena we're traveling to Icarus."

Demetrius didn't smile, but his eyes gave him away. "Come, then. No time to waste. As we drag, someone could be arranging to send another team of assassins. Perhaps the second squad will not be as incompetent as the first."

Iliana hadn't traveled to Icarus before, and its capital city of Daedalus, where the president's home was located, wasn't what she had expected. She had seen pictures of Icarus, but witnessing it in person told a different story.

The pictures in the media of Icarus were of filthy slums, dirty children running wild on the streets and a general sense of desolation and despair. Icarus, or at least Daedalus, was nothing like that.

The streets were hectic, but they were lined with businesses that seemed clean, bright and industrious. Sidewalk easels announced the sale of food, clothes, trinkets and even skateboards.

"You seem surprised," Demetrius said. He was seated across from her in the back of the extended town car. He had his tablet on his lap, but his intense dark blue eyes were locked on her.

She wouldn't lie. "This isn't what I expected."

"I've been inviting you to visit for months. It took someone trying to kill you for you to take me up on my offer."

He was blunt, but he didn't sound upset. "I have my

reservations about being involved with a war-hungry leader."

He smirked. "I am not war hungry. If I wanted a war, I wouldn't have backed down from the fight with Rizari."

"You backed down because the new king of Rizari is your best friend."

"I have no friends when it comes to protecting the interests of my country. Casimir is a man I respect. We are close like brothers."

She flinched. "If you don't have friends, what am I to you?" A question she had pondered often.

"A woman I am interested in pursuing. A woman who I would like to marry."

"Marry?" The word sent shock waves through her. A man hadn't brought up marriage before, at least, not a marriage with her. She had once discovered a man she was dating was married and had ended the relationship, but that was her and marriage in a totally different context.

Iliana didn't dwell on past mistakes. It was typical of the men she met to want to sleep with her and have fun with her. Maybe it was a vibe she was giving off.

To have a powerful and desirable man like Demetrius speak those words to her made her ego purr.

"I assume you wish to be married?" he asked, leaning close, his piercing navy eyes seeing into her soul.

She calmed her racing heart. Demetrius was intense and direct, and she couldn't overreact. He'd see fits of hysteria or giggling as unattractive, and, inexplicably, it was important to her to be seen as desirable by him. "Yes. One day. To the right man."

"Tell me—who exactly is the right man? What makes him worth waiting for?"

"Do you have to ask so many complex questions?" She was deflecting, but she didn't want to talk about her future husband and the man she hoped he would be. Demetrius would see that he was wrong for her, and the relationship would be over before it began. She definitely had the sense something was starting now. A fling or a one-night stand maybe, and a hot, passionate and fun one at that.

"You are avoiding answering my question," he said.

"Because the man I want to marry is not a checklist I'm looking to fulfill. It's a feeling. I want to be swept away."

She was grateful he had the decency not to laugh at her. Iliana had a fanciful side that had landed her in trouble with men before. She'd been inspired by her parents' relationship. They had met on a blind date, had a whirlwind romance and had been inseparable until the day they'd died. Older and wiser now, Iliana knew not to project what she wanted onto a man. She had to have her eyes open to who he was and accept him, flaws and all. Who was the man in front of her? A violent dictator—ruthless, blunt and drop-dead sexy.

Demetrius's home was another surprise. It was a large, rambling three-story house, not as ornate as she had expected. It looked well maintained but in need of softening. He had no flowers in the garden, no curtains in the windows, nothing to add contrast to the gray stone exterior.

The sedan circled to the back of the house. To her

right was what might have been a beautiful, lush garden many years earlier. Some plants were overgrown; other patches of the garden were bare. A large stone wall surrounding the space was beginning to crumble. Didn't that bother Demetrius? He was detail oriented and precise. Wasn't he concerned about the state of his home? As president of Icarus, his residence should reflect his power and wealth.

They parked behind the house, and Demetrius opened the car door and climbed out. He took her hand and helped her out of the black sedan. Heat surged between them. Now that they were out of the public eye, could she step closer, rub against him, make it clear she was interested in moving their relationship forward, at least the physical aspects of it?

She lost her nerve. He placed her hand on his arm and led her into the house.

Much like the exterior, the inside was plain. Little furniture, white walls, clean, but it didn't look occupied. "You live here?" she asked.

"Yes."

This was his primary home? "It looks bare." No knickknacks, no artwork and nothing on the table or sofa.

"I haven't had time to decorate. I'd like my wife to do that."

It wasn't the first time he had commented about tasks he wanted a wife to perform. She was certain he didn't mean to offend her, although it struck her as presumptive to assume a woman would have time or interest in remodeling a home. "What if your wife doesn't want to decorate your house?"

He shrugged. "Then, she can hire someone to do

it the way she likes. Don't misunderstand me. I don't view my wife as my servant or believe that her role is to please me. My intention in allowing her to decorate is for her to find our home comfortable and pleasing."

It was all she could do to keep from swooning. Though she and Demetrius had trouble communicating, sometimes his words blew her away. Her parents had put her first in their lives, but since they had died, no one made her the top priority. No one went out of his or her way to please her.

"Show me your favorite room in the house," Iliana said.

Demetrius's lips twitched. She half expected him to deny her request. "Follow me."

She followed Demetrius up two flights of stairs to the top floor. At the end of the hallway, he opened the double doors. This had to be his bedroom. His favorite room was his personal sanctuary, and she was inside it. A surge of happiness swept over her and she was genuinely pleased he had brought her here.

Unlike the plainness of the rest of the house, this room was beautiful. It was him. Dark wood furniture, blue bedding and geometric-patterned curtains worked together and made the room flow. It was charming and distinctly Demetrius.

She sat on the bed and gave it a few test bounces. "Harder than I like."

"I'll have it replaced," he said.

He was nothing if not confident. "I don't plan to sleep here," she said.

"I don't plan for you to sleep there, either, but I do intend to have you in my bed," he said.

His words made her hot and excited. Her insides clutched with yearning. "Come here. Please."

He strode to her and knelt on the floor in front of her. He took both her hands in his and kissed her palms. To have a powerful man like Demetrius acquiesce to her made her, in turn, feel powerful.

He watched her with such absolute focus that she felt like the only person in the world who mattered to him in that moment. Maybe she was. "I've fantasized about having you in my bedroom and about what I would do to you when I finally got you here."

They had flirted, they'd had long conversations, but they hadn't allowed their relationship to cross over into a physical one. Their attraction was the one part of their relationship that had been consistent. Consistent and persistently drawing her to him. She had daydreamed about him, about this moment, and now she couldn't think about anything except him. "Then, do it to me. Show me." He would be confident and talented in bed. She knew it.

His eyes blazed sex. Taking the relationship from zero to sixty was rash, but Iliana didn't know how long this would last. She had kept his attention, and he had pursued her. They were alone together in his room. Why fight it? Iliana knew the difference between sex and intimacy, and while she preferred the latter, in this blistering moment, she wanted the former with Demetrius.

"When I've thought of you at night, when I'm alone, I've imagined you touching me and I know you will be very, very good," she said.

He grinned. "You know right, but I will show you."

She expected him to pounce on her, but instead he

stood and drew her to her feet. He walked her to the large window overlooking the gardens.

He stood behind her and moved her hair to the side. He pressed his lips to her neck and ran his hands down her sides. Her stomach fluttered in anticipation. He had been restrained every other time they were alone, and it made her want him that much more.

When he reached her waist, he unsnapped her pants. She had a moment of panic. What underwear was she wearing? She couldn't recall what she had slipped on that morning. She hadn't been anticipating taking a lover that day.

"Relax. What are you worried about?" he asked.

"I think I'm wearing green underwear."

Demetrius laughed and plucked the back of her pants. "Yes. It seems you are."

She felt a flush over her cheeks. Normally sleeping with a man for the first time required careful preparation—manicure, a facial and some primping. No special arrangements had been made today. But she had the feeling with Demetrius, this could be now or never. He had said the word *marriage* to her, but Iliana couldn't process that on any real level. Achy, needy desire swelled inside her. She couldn't slow the build of lust and wanting in her body. "I don't want you to be disappointed."

"There is nothing you could do now to disappoint me. Except maybe leave." He slid her pants down her legs and let them fall to the floor around her feet. She stepped out of them. He tugged her shirt over her head.

Demetrius spun her around. He growled as he swept his eyes down her body. "You are glorious and perfectly feminine." He touched the side of her face gently, tracing his thumb down her cheek.

Then he moved quickly and deliberately, bringing her against his body and kissing her. His lips seared her to the core. She moved against him, feeling his hardness through his pants, and had the intense urge to drop to her knees and take him in her mouth. The kisses turned carnal, tongues tasting, teeth clicking.

Demetrius reached between her legs and ran a finger across the V of her thighs. "Wet. Already. I like that."

She was dripping. Hungry. His hands cupped her breasts, and he squeezed lightly.

He was wearing entirely too many clothes for this to be fair. She tugged his shirt from his pants, pulling at the buttons and grappling with his belt. When his shirt was unfastened, he shrugged it off, and it joined her clothes on the floor.

His pants came next, then his boxers, and she could see everything. Every bronzed, roped muscle, his impressive arousal, long and thick, the ripple of his abdominals and a collection of scars.

She set her hand over the circular scars, one near his heart, two at his sides, one on his thigh. "What happened?"

"Gunshot wounds." He sounded indifferent.

"All of them?" He had been shot four times?

"Different occurrences. Do they bother you?" For the first time, he sounded unsure, and that warmed her. He was human. He was sweet. He had a soft side that she guessed he revealed to few people.

"Not at all. You are a warrior." To prove it, she kissed each one, tracing them and the other scars that marred his body.

"Enough," he said, and swept her into his arms. He carried her to the bed and laid her down. She let her legs fall open because she wanted him now and didn't feel the need to be coy about it.

He removed her bra with the snap of his fingers and kissed each of her breasts, laving them with attention, making her feel loved and cherished. He reached for her feet, removing her shoes and letting them hit the floor.

"Demetrius, please hurry." Her body ached for his, longed to feel his weight on top of her.

Other sexual encounters with boyfriends had been brief, a quick pounding, leaving her unsatisfied. Demetrius seemed in no hurry and intent on leaving her satisfied. She was so turned on, if she moved the right way against him, she might come from his touch.

He kissed a trail down her body and tugged her green—*ugh*—panties down her legs. "I'm throwing those out," she said.

"Keep them. I'll think of you like this every time I see them," he said.

He brought his mouth between her legs, and she involuntarily bucked against him. He set his hand on her hip to settle her. Excitement and pleasure pulsed between her legs. He took his time, licking, sucking, caressing her until she was frantic with need. He knew what he was doing, and she tried to stay calm. Watching him in that intimate position, she felt affection and warmth flood over her.

"I need you inside me," she said. "Please, Demetrius."

He moved over her and reached into his bedside table. Donning a condom, he positioned himself at her opening. With almost no effort, he pushed inside her. She was hot and wet and so ready for this. The sensation of him filling her, of him reaching deep inside her, was utterly amazing.

He moved with hard, insistent thrusts, seeming to enjoy the thump of his body delving into hers. She ran her fingernails down his back, digging them into his buttocks, and lifted to meet him.

She felt pressure building between her legs. Everything inside her spun with pleasure and desire, pushing her higher and higher until she was plummeting over the edge of ecstasy. Their eyes locked, and she felt a shudder go through his body as he spilled his essence.

As her body relaxed beneath his, he collapsed on top of her. She welcomed the weight of him. She kissed his shoulder and rubbed his calf with her foot. The words *I love you* were on her tongue, but she refused to speak them, scared of what they could mean, fearful they were coming too soon or may be an excited utterance.

Most of all, she was scared they were true and she had fallen for a ruthless dictator who would hurt her all over again.

Chapter 2

Demetrius couldn't give Iliana time to think. He was banking on her agreeing to marry him immediately. Sated by the passion and excitement of their encounter, she'd fallen asleep beneath him. He extracted himself from her. After cleaning himself up in the bathroom, he dressed.

He could read her. She wasn't a poker player. She was falling for him. He reached into his bedside table and brought out the gray-and-black marble ring box. He'd had the ring commissioned earlier that week and sized to her finger. She'd left a ring on her desk once and he'd traced it onto a piece of paper when her back was turned. She wouldn't want to be proposed to in bed. She'd want a story to tell her cousin and her friends.

He slipped the engagement ring into his pocket.

This would happen today. By tomorrow, she would be his wife and he would have what he needed to complete his plan.

He picked up his dress shirt from the floor and carried it to the bed. Sweeping her red hair to the side, he kissed her cheek. "Iliana? I want to show you something."

She mumbled into the pillow. Into his pillow. That pleased him enormously. He rarely allowed women into his bedroom. Come to think of it, Iliana was the first. The first and the last. She moved down into the blankets, her red hair spread across his sheets, the fabric showcasing the silhouette of her lithe body.

"This will only take a moment. It can't wait."

She sat up, pushing her hair back. "Why do I have to get up now?"

He slipped his shirt over her slim shoulders. For the sake of decency, he buttoned the middle buttons. She looked good. She would be a good wife—of that he was certain. "I have something to show you."

"Interesting that you want to dress me," she said.

"I don't like the idea of my staff seeing you naked."

Though his staff members would not utter a word about anything they saw in the house, especially in his private wing, he was protective of Iliana. He didn't want to share her in any way.

She pulled on her underwear, the green pair, and her slacks. She left her feet bare.

Demetrius led her outside into the garden. It needed attention, but that task had fallen behind more pressing matters. His private garden was still tended to perfection. He unlocked the green wooden gate. He had refinished the gate himself, sanded it, painted it and rehung it. Though he could have asked someone on his staff to handle the matter, physical labor helped him clear his mind after hours of meetings. The high stone walls around the garden provided the privacy he craved.

He held the door for her, and she stepped inside and gasped.

"What is this place?" she asked.

"My garden. I work here in my spare time." A source of pride and enjoyment for him.

He took pleasure in watching her walk up and down the paths. Solar lights illuminated the rows of plants and shrubbery. He walked behind her, not wanting to rush her. The timing had to be right. Much was riding on this proposal.

She had said she wanted to be swept away. He had to give her what she needed. Having her in his bed had been every bit the sublime experience he had imagined. She was responsive and active and made the most fantastic noises when she came.

"I wouldn't have guessed you would spend time on a garden," Iliana said.

A solitary activity that involved using his hands. In that way, it was ideal. "It's a productive garden. I grow food here for myself and my staff." Growing up poor, he, his brother and his mother had kept a garden, eating what they could, selling produce to neighbors. Their poverty had made Demetrius resourceful. He and his brother had often made sacrifices for each other and their mother.

She smiled. "I would expect nothing less."

He didn't want to talk about himself or his childhood. Iliana had been raised by perfectly warm and loving parents. His experiences had been different. "Looking at you takes my breath away."

She lowered her head, but he saw the blush on her cheeks. "You're embarrassing me."

"We are alone here. You have nothing to be embarrassed about. I've made how I feel about you clear."

She stepped closer, and his hands greedily reached for her.

"You fascinate me," she said.

That he had captured Iliana's interest for even this long felt like an accomplishment. Demetrius planned everything in his life. Everything. He did nothing without thinking, considering and weighing his options. But he didn't know exactly what he would say to win her over or how he would say it. He went with what felt right.

He fell to his knee in front of this beautiful, captivating woman. He took her hands in his. He kissed her wrists and then held her left hand, threading their fingers.

Why did he feel emotional about this? This was a calculated, crucial part of his plan, yet he was caught up in it and in her. "Iliana, I have been enchanted with you from the moment we first spoke. I admire your fire and passion for life. You've come to mean so much to me."

He removed the ring from his pocket and held it for her to see. She gasped and brought her hands to her mouth. He reached for her hands again, putting them in his where they belonged. "Iliana, will you be there for me in the ways that matter? Will you sleep in my bed and wake beside me in the morning? Will you be my friend and my lover and my confidante? Will you be my wife?"

Surprise registered on her face. "Why me? We don't know each other."

He shook his head. "I know everything I need to know about you. There won't be another in my life who means to me what you do."

She brought her hands to her mouth and then threw herself into his arms. He wrapped them around her. She kissed his cheek. "Yes, yes, I will marry you." Tears ran down her face.

He slipped the ring on her finger. "Tonight. We marry tonight."

Her smile faltered. "Tonight? Are you serious?"

"I cannot wait another day to have you as my wife."

She stared at him. "You are serious."

"Of course. I will not joke about our marriage."

"But I have plans for my wedding. I want Serena to be there. And Casimir. I wanted to wear a special dress and carry lilies."

If he gave her too much time to think about it, she could change her mind. The chess pieces could shift, rendering his position weaker. He had to marry her now, before she knew more about his plans and her future. "My Iliana, you will have everything you wish for your wedding. A few phone calls will make it so." He had a country of wedding planners, florists and dressmakers at his disposal. He would do what was needed to get her to the altar. If she wanted the wedding of her dreams, so be it.

She nodded and seemed to be half convinced. "I need to call Serena, then."

Demetrius remained calm. The queen could talk

her cousin out of this arrangement. Had he convinced Serena that his intentions were good? Casimir was his brother on the battlefield, but Demetrius hadn't shared with him the reasons why Iliana was critical or why he needed to marry her. Demetrius's biological brother needed his help, and nothing would stop him from providing it. "Please do. I will contact our event planner and have her come to the house immediately."

Pleased that this part of his plan had worked, he felt unsettled by the unfamiliar sensation of warmth that spread over him. Iliana would be his wife, and he would respect and honor her. But had he come to care for her? That had not been part of the plan.

Serena rushed to Iliana, hugging her close, a challenge with her ever-growing pregnant belly. Serena was expecting twins in five months. "Iliana, are you sure about this? This seems so sudden."

"It seems that way for me, too. But it also feels right." Demetrius had said the right things, he had treated her as if she was precious to him and he had given her carte blanche to plan the wedding, with the caveat that it had to be tonight. Many women would be envious of her position. She almost couldn't believe this was happening to her. Demetrius was an honorable man and would be a good husband.

"Why so fast? Are you pregnant?" Serena asked, her lips quirked into a smile.

Iliana laughed. "Not pregnant. My mother and father were taken from me abruptly, and now Demetrius is giving me a new family as suddenly. Maybe that's how my life works." She wouldn't kick a gift horse in the mouth.

"You've been tight-lipped about your relationship with Demetrius, but if this is what you want, I support you."

The event planner, a powerhouse named Eleni, rushed into the room carrying a wedding gown in a light blue garment bag. "I had to pull every string to get this dress in your size, but it's here. The seamstress is on her way to make adjustments."

Eleni hung the garment on a dress hook and removed the light blue bag. It was a dress Iliana had seen months earlier when shopping for another friend's wedding. It was simple and elegant, all flowing satin covered in lace. The top was fitted, and the skirt flared at the bottom.

Eleni and Serena helped her slip it on. Iliana was worried it wouldn't be as beautiful as she had pictured when she saw it on the mannequin. When the final button was fastened, she turned and caught her reflection in the mirror. Breathtaking. It was what she had hoped for. Demetrius was making her wedding dreams come true. She was still reeling at how quickly it was moving, but why question good fortune?

Serena teared up beside her. "Oh, Iliana, you look so beautiful. Demetrius won't be able to catch his breath."

The next hour was a flurry of activity. The seamstress measured, pinned and sewed. Iliana's hair was arranged, some gathered on her head, other pieces left over her shoulder, and light makeup was applied. Before she had time to think, Serena was leading her to the private garden where she would marry the president of Icarus.

"You know he isn't the bad person that people say

he is, right?" Iliana said quietly to her cousin. She needed her good friend to assure her that she was seeing Demetrius for who he was, as he was, and that this wasn't a mistake.

Serena squeezed her hand. "Casimir tells me that Demetrius is a good man. I questioned him the entire flight here."

"Demetrius is wonderful to me." Despite rumors and media spin portraying Demetrius as a dictator and a tyrant, Iliana saw the real side of him, the warmth, the compassion and his absolute love for Icarus. Everything he did was for his country and, now it seemed, for her. They'd had misunderstandings in the past, butted heads politically, but this was different. Their relationship wasn't professional anymore. It was on a whole other level.

Casmir came to the garden door and greeted them, kissing Serena's cheek and patting her belly.

Iliana curtsied to the king of Rizari, out of habit more than a required formality. "I'm doing the right thing, aren't I?"

Despite his royal status, he and Iliana had become close friends since he and Serena had married. "I can't answer that question. You know if it feels right."

She touched her stomach, which was fluttering with butterflies. "I feel nervous." She was fully aware of the gravity of the step she was taking. "But happy."

"Then, I think you answered your own question. He's waiting for you. Are you ready?" Casimir asked.

Iliana nodded, and Casimir opened the door to the garden.

Iliana stepped across the threshold for the second time that night. Once inside, her worries and doubts melted away, and all she could see was Demetrius waiting for her at the end of the petal-strewn aisle.

He was incredibly handsome, refined yet rugged. She liked that about him. She could envision him swinging an ax as easily as she could imagine him planting seeds in his garden.

Walking toward him, her body felt light; her feet floated on air. She was doing the right thing, allowing love and joy into her life. Iliana welcomed her future with open arms.

The reception following their intimate wedding ceremony brought several more important faces. Demetrius introduced her to generals in the Icarus army and navy and his political advisers. It seemed everyone who had a hand in running the country was celebrating with them in their home. Despite the last-minute plans and the late-night festivities, their guests were in high spirits.

A few times Demetrius seemed to be in a serious conversation with someone, but then he would find her face in the crowd and they'd share a private smile. He was the president of the country. He had work to do. But tonight was about them.

After a couple of hours, Demetrius swept Iliana into his arms. He addressed the room from the doorway. "Thank you all for coming tonight, but I bid you good night. My wife and I have plans."

The crowd roared with laughter, and Demetrius's military men banged their beer mugs against the wooden tables and cheered.

"Demetrius, everyone will know," Iliana said as he carried her toward his bedroom. Their bedroom.

"That I'm having sex with my wife? So what?"

She wasn't a prude, but some topics were private matters. "It's so…intimate."

Demetrius kissed her on the mouth. "Which is why I did not invite anyone else along."

She laughed, threaded her fingers around the back of his neck and laid her head on his shoulder. He took the stairs with her in his arms.

"Thank you, Demetrius, for tonight. For making this special for me."

"You're my wife. There is nothing I would not do for you, and I expect the same in return."

A shiver of concern coursed over her as doubts pressed at the edges of her emotions. She had given him her loyalty, her heart and her life. Though they had not explicitly discussed it, she would resign from her position as the queen's personal secretary. She would live in Icarus with Demetrius. Wasn't that a lot to give up for him? Did he expect more?

Demetrius entered his bedroom and kicked the doors shut behind them. The room was overflowing with flowers, lilies of all colors set in vases, petals strewn on the floor. Candles flickered in glass containers, illuminating the room.

Demetrius laid her on the bed. "I suppose you'll be angry if I tear your new dress. You look so lovely in it, and that makes it much harder to be patient."

She ran her hand over the soft, intricate lace. "You can't tear it. I want to use it to make baptismal gowns for our children."

He lifted his eyebrow. "Already we're discussing children?" She could tell by his expression he liked the idea.

When they were alone, he made little effort to conceal his emotions. In public, he was stone-faced and cold. This warm, spirited side of him stirred her emotions. She felt connected to him, as if she alone got to enjoy this side of him.

"Will you help me remove my dress so I might make love to my husband?"

He loosened his tie around his neck. "Yes. Absolutely. I want you naked of everything except my rings. You must wear my rings."

She touched the rings on her left hand. "And you must wear mine."

He removed her dress carefully and laid it over a chair. When they rushed together, Iliana felt the supreme rightness of being in his arms.

Iliana awoke in Demetrius's bed. Not Demetrius's bed. Their bed. Demetrius was gone. She stretched beneath the sheets and then looked for a note. But she found nothing to indicate where he had gone. She ignored the twinge of disappointment. She had wanted to wake with him beside her on their first morning as husband and wife. Perhaps it was a good thing. She was sore. Demetrius was an energetic lover, and she didn't think she could have sex with him again, which he would inevitably have wanted if she'd awoken in his arms.

She took a shower, pleased to see he had provided women's shampoo and toiletries for her. That small gesture erased the lingering disappointment of waking without him.

She dressed in the clothes that Serena had brought

for her and went in search of her husband. Just thinking of him in those terms made her shiver.

She found Demetrius on the main floor in his office. She entered without knocking. He was wearing a suit, as he often did, standing at the window and was on the phone, his headset clipped to his ear. She circled his desk and slipped her arms around him.

He was speaking French. She hadn't heard him speak it before. She'd had some basic French lessons in her youth but didn't remember enough to follow the conversation in any meaningful way.

When he disconnected a few minutes later, she kissed him. "How many languages do you speak?"

"Eight." His voice was cold, and he removed her hands from around him. "I need to speak with you about a grave matter."

He had to leave on a trip. Trouble in the Mediterranean. Concern whipped through her. "Are Serena and Casimir all right?"

"They are fine. I would have woken you if this matter involved them. This does involve your family, though."

Since her parents had died in a tragic car accident years earlier, she hadn't been able to shake the dread that someone else she loved would be taken from her abruptly. That sense of loss and fear gripped her now. "Please tell me quickly."

"The king of Valencia is dying."

Not what she was expecting to hear. "I'm sorry to hear that. I don't mean to be callous, but how does that involve me?" She knew the king by name, but they hadn't met. "Do you want me to prepare something to send to his wife and family?" Was this her duty as

Demetrius's wife? She could relate to what the king's family may be going through, and if she had words of comfort to share to ease their pain, she would.

Demetrius sighed. "I do not want you to send anything. The king wants to see you."

"Why?" Demetrius was being evasive. Where was the soft, warm and passionate man she had married the night before? It was as if she was with public Demetrius, and she didn't like it.

He didn't answer. Something dark and uneasy settled over her. "Demetrius, you need to tell me what's going on. You're scaring me and acting cold." It was on the tip of her tongue to mention slipping from their bed without saying good morning, but she didn't want to fight with him over a trivial problem and she still didn't understand what this was about.

"You are not the biological daughter of the man and woman who you know as your parents," he said.

Iliana shook her head. She was. She had pictures from the day of her birth to prove it. "That's not true."

"You are the biological daughter of the king of Valencia and his late mistress, Persephone Paphiti. She died in childbirth, and the king asked your parents to adopt you. A blood test will confirm what I'm telling you, or I can provide you the DNA results I have already run."

So many questions and so much hurt pummeled her at once. She struggled to make sense of it all. "You checked my DNA without telling me?"

"It was a simple matter to ensure I was correct about you and the king."

Betrayal pulsed through her. "I don't understand."

"What don't you understand?" he asked, this time his voice a little softer.

She retreated a step, putting distance between them. Why was he breaking news of this magnitude in such a cold manner? "How long have you known?"

"For over a year."

Her jaw slackened. As the pieces of the puzzle fell into place, they presented an ugly picture. She had ties to the royal family in Valencia. What did Demetrius want from those connections? She knew Demetrius's reputation for doing everything with meaning and for a purpose. She had been naive to think he had married her without an agenda.

She had been desperate for a family and for someone to care for her, and she had bought into his ploy. Hard to believe that five hours ago, she had been curled in his arms, moaning his name and falling head over heels for him.

His face was impassive. "I realize that you are upset. I will help you come to terms with this."

Anger coursed through her, hot and violent. "How do I come to terms with this? You just told me that the people I called Mom and Dad aren't my parents. Have you thought about my feelings?"

"The people who raised you are your parents in every way that matters. Nothing will change that. All I bring to your attention is that your biological father is dying. If you have questions, answers will only be available as long as he has breath."

Despite her rage, the words comforted her. Her parents, the people who had loved and raised her, would always be parents. This curveball did nothing to change that, meant nothing next to their unconditional and unrelenting love for her. She had felt it every day in the way they spoke to her and cared for her.

"If you want to see the king, we need to go now. His condition has worsened, and his days are numbered."

Though Iliana was furious with Demetrius and still reeling from the bomb he had dropped, she wanted to see the king. It may be her last chance.

Aboard Demetrius's private jet, Iliana sat as far from Demetrius as possible. It bothered her that it didn't seem to bother *him*. He was working on his laptop, taking calls. He didn't glance in her direction once. They were traveling with a couple of his servicemen and some of his advisers. Five other men on the plane, not including the pilot and the copilot. So much testosterone.

Iliana glanced at her outfit. A pair of simple black pants and a green top, fitted but not revealing. She was meeting a king after all. She had intended the outfit to catch Demetrius's eye. Getting his attention had been easy before, and it had pleased her how quickly he had turned his attention to her in any situation when they were together. Now that they were married, not even twelve hours after their wedding, he seemed indifferent to her and that stung.

Had it been an act? Iliana didn't have great judgment when it came to men. This latest fiasco proved it. She had made an epically bad decision. Not just a bad date, not her sneaking out of a man's bedroom in the early-morning hours with regrets. This was a whole other level of bad.

She had married the president of Icarus. He was

using her as a tool, and she hated that. She still didn't know exactly what he wanted, but when she figured it out, she would make sure he received the opposite from her.

Was she in love with Demetrius? She had thought so. She desired him. She cared for him. He occupied much of her time, and there was a warm feeling that accompanied thoughts of him—wasn't that love? Iliana wasn't sure she had ever been in love before. She loved her parents, her cousins, her family, but romantic love had eluded her. She'd confused lust and passion with love before, and it had ended badly every time.

Everything she felt for Demetrius was called into question. She had imagined their relationship to be a sweeping romance with grand gestures of affection. She'd had that from Demetrius for a short time. Now she had the awful sensation of being exploited and ignored.

Ignored like her biological father had ignored her, handing her off and pretending she didn't exist. Iliana loved her parents, and while she couldn't imagine being raised by anyone else, it hurt to know they had kept this secret from her. Perhaps they'd thought they were protecting her. With them gone, she would never have the answers.

Demetrius was telling her the truth about the king of Valencia and Persephone Paphiti. The information could be too easily verified for him to lie about it. Blood tests would be conclusive, and Demetrius didn't make mistakes. Having eyes and ears everywhere, he knew too much. He was shrewd and he was spot-on in political matters in the Mediterranean.

Demetrius's reputation preceded him. She had heard and read it all. He was cold and calculating. He killed without mercy. He rammed his agenda through by any means necessary. Iliana hadn't believed those accusations. She had seen him in another light, and she had felt special because she'd believed herself privy to some secret side of Demetrius.

But that warmth and affection was completely overshadowed by what he had done. He had lied to her. He had manipulated her. He didn't get the benefit of the doubt anymore.

She would make his life hard. She would make him rue the day he had decided to use her for political maneuvering.

Iliana stood and stretched, letting her shirt ride up a bit. She turned to give Demetrius a look at her profile. She wasn't vain, but she worked out and she knew she looked good. Demetrius was attracted to her. No way had he faked that. In her peripheral vision, she saw that she had his attention. So she bent over at the waist, touching her toes and wiggling her hips.

If Demetrius wanted to play the "married" card, she would play it, too. Let him see what he could have and what he was missing. She'd deny any advances, and she wouldn't stand for one moment of him cheating. But she knew he wouldn't. Demetrius DeSante was a lot of things, but he wasn't a cheater.

He did, however, move like a panther.

He was at her side in moments. "What are you doing?"

She smelled his cologne, or maybe it was the soap he used, light and spicy. It turned her on, but she tamped down her lust. That ridiculous emotion had ruled her the night before, and she was shutting it off from here on out. "Stretching. My schedule is off. I didn't work out this morning, and my muscles feel tight." She pretended to be unaware that he was hard beneath his pants. She tossed the question back at him. "What are you doing?"

He growled in the back of his throat. "Stop it."

"Stop exercising? Why?"

"You know what you're doing. Every man in this cabin is staring at you, and I won't have it."

She rolled her eyes. "You can't command people to stop using their eyes."

"I will remove the eyes of the next person who looks at my wife with lust." His voice was loud and clear. Everyone looked away from them.

"You are being ridiculous."

He walked to the entrance to the small bedroom aboard the plane. "A word. Alone, please."

Iliana followed him into the bedroom. He closed the door behind him. She sensed he was grappling for control. Control of his anger or his lust? She waited.

"Are you trying to antagonize me?"

She smirked at him. "Yes."

His eyes blazed. "At least you admit it."

"I want you to apologize," she said.

He loosened the tie around his neck and undid the first button of his shirt. Disheveled looked good on him. "If I say the words, will you stop being upset?"

"You have to say the words and mean them," she said. "Then I'll see how I feel." She would still be angry, but she wanted him to twist a little for what he had done.

He looked her up and down. She felt as if he had

touched her. "Iliana, I've never been more attracted to another woman than I am to you. What I know about the king of Valencia as it relates to you has nothing to do with that attraction."

"But you married me because of it."

He drew in a deep breath. "I would have married you one day. I moved up the timeline because of the king's health problems."

Surprising words, and she didn't know if she could believe them. His admission wouldn't slake her anger. "You could have been honest with me."

"I told you about the king when the time was right."

Right for his plans and for him. The encounter with the assassin the day before flashed to mind. "Do you think the man who tried to kill me was after me because of my connection to the king of Valencia?" She had thought the murder attempt had to do with Serena, or maybe even Demetrius.

"I suspect someone else knows who you are and they want you dead because of it."

Iliana wished she hadn't left Acacia. She could have stayed in the castle and dealt with Serena and Casimir's lovey-dovey behavior for a few days. Anything was better than this. "Going to Valencia seems like a patently bad idea, then, if someone wants to kill me."

"No one will kill my wife."

Low self-esteem wasn't his problem. "You're not invincible, Demetrius." She'd heard Casimir and Demetrius telling war stories, and she'd heard rumors of her husband's prowess in battle. Despite implications to the contrary, he was human.

"I would sooner die than let someone harm you."

He had spoken similar words before, and it accentuated how different their worlds were. She had never been in a physical confrontation. Acacia had never been to war. Demetrius had battle scars to prove that he had. "Let's aim for no one dying."

"We will stay together in Valencia. You will not sneak away. For your safety and the safety of anyone who may make the poor decision to harm you."

Iliana blinked at him. "I know how to be safe."

"Were you being safe in Elion last year?"

Of course he would bring that up. She had been nearly mugged, but Demetrius had rescued her. "I made a mistake. I've learned from it."

"Do you want to have sex?" he asked.

She shook her head, trying to clear her thoughts. Had she misheard him? "Excuse me?"

"You're sending me mixed signals."

He looked devastatingly handsome. Black shirt and gray pants, pressed and stylish, his dark hair brushed back from his face. Sliding her fingers into it, letting the silky strands fall between her fingers, would feel good. This wasn't the first time she had been angry with Demetrius, and the strange part was that she was perpetually attracted to him. She must have a thing for picking the wrong men, as she was clearly a lost cause where Demetrius was concerned. "I'm giving you one signal right now. I'm angry."

"Some couples counter fights with sex."

Tempting, but sleeping with Demetrius wouldn't get it out of her system. She'd want him more. "Couples have sex after the fight is resolved. This is nowhere near resolved."

"Tell me what I need to do to resolve the fight so

I can go back to making love to my wife when she needs me to."

Those words felt like a caress across her breasts and down her body. "I don't need sex." She'd had great sex with him in the early-morning hours. It should tide her over for at least a week. Given her recent dry spell, she could go six months without another man laying a hand on her.

"It would relax you, and you seem very tense right now."

"We aren't alone on the plane."

"My staff won't interrupt us in here."

She felt her resolve cracking, but she shored up her defenses. "No sex. You're still withholding information. I'm withholding sex. You have yet to tell me why you married me."

"I married you because I wanted to. You can't pretend that you don't enjoy it when I touch you. Sex has nothing to do with this fight. Let's keep the two separate."

Reasoning that would only make sense to a man. She wouldn't let him win. "No."

"Then, let's call a truce for at least the rest of the flight."

"No." If she argued with more than a simple word, he would find a way to negate it. She already felt herself giving in. "You left this morning before I woke up." She had meant to let that go, but she wanted ammunition and it was sitting right there.

"I wake early. I didn't want to disturb you."

She narrowed her eyes at him. "I wanted to wake beside my husband. Don't we even get a honeymoon?"

"In the future, I will wake you before I leave our

bedroom. I will give you a honeymoon when there is time."

"That was before. I'm mad now. I don't want either from you."

He looked exasperated. She exited the bedroom and returned to her seat.

Demetrius strode to his seat. To her surprise, he moved closer to her. Next to her. Unless she wanted to stand for the rest of the flight, occupy his previous seat next to his advisers and servicemen or return to the bedroom, she was trapped. Trapped in this plane and trapped in this loveless marriage.

Chapter 3

The king of Valencia had been battling brain cancer for two years. Numerous surgeries, chemotherapy and radiation had broken his eighty-year-old body but not the cancer. The king's imminent death was the Valencian government's worst-kept secret. Though no media outlets were reporting it, those closest to the king—and Demetrius, via his spies—knew that he had made his peace and was ready.

Emmanuel Floros the First was a man Demetrius respected. Though his personal life was a mess, the king was a fair and honorable man when it came to his politics and his decisions regarding Valencia.

As they drove from the airport to the palace, Demetrius conveyed to Iliana what he thought might be useful information about the king. He hoped to distract her and take off some of the pressure she surely felt from learning she was the king's daughter and knowing this may be her only shot to get answers from him. She seemed nervous and had been strangely quiet—due in part to punishment for him, no doubt—but given the king's condition, this visit needed to happen today. Every hour that passed, the window of opportunity closed further.

"The king has had three wives and five children. His first wife gave him three, the second two and his third wife is rumored to be barren. She has been running the country for the past several months. Though she claims she consults the king on matters of importance and relays the information, I suspect the king doesn't govern much in his current state."

"I have half siblings." Iliana sounded mystified.

She wasn't focused on the politics. She was focused on the heart of the matter. "Yes."

"I always wanted a sister. I didn't think I would have one. Are there others like me? Other illegitimate children?"

"None who the king claims," Demetrius said. The king had slept around on his wives, but it seemed he had been more careful with other mistresses to ensure they did not become pregnant. "Your father and the king were boyhood friends. The king knew you would be safe with him, and, to ensure that, he cut ties with your father completely."

Her eyes darkened with anger. "Safe from whom?"

"Your half brothers and sisters. The king's wives. Any number of interested parties would want the king's love child dead. The king has land and holdings to be divided among his wives and children. Though his first two wives were given large settlements after their divorces, they will receive small parcels of land as tradition dictates because they are the mothers of his children."

Iliana stared out the window with a faraway look in her eyes. "I should get nothing. I have no claim."

"The king has named you in his will." Her eyes swerved to meet his, and he felt the heat and passion in them. He loved that she lived so vibrantly, so fervidly.

"How do you know so much about the king's will?" she asked.

Demetrius heard the anger in her words. That he had expected, but he had not expected to care as much as he did about her feelings. He usually made decisions, and dissention was ignored. He found it harder to follow that policy with Iliana. "I have a friend in the court system who keeps me informed on these matters." Since the king had mentioned his illegitimate daughter years earlier, in passing, during a drunken poker game, Demetrius had considered how he could leverage that information to help his brother. Demetrius's friendship with the king had been precipitated by Demetrius needing influence in Valencia for Alexei.

Little by little, Demetrius had acquired the information about the king's as yet publically unrecognized daughter until he had gathered enough details to locate Iliana.

"You knew about me before we met. That's why you were so interested. All that attention you gave me, the time you spent with me and the words you said to me, it was all leading to this."

The crux of the matter. Nothing he said would convince her that his reasons for marrying her had to do with more than her inheritance. His initial interest was her connection to the king of Valencia, but after he had met her in person, it had developed into much more. "I will state again that I married you because I wanted to do so."

She frowned at him and then turned her head away again. Demetrius left her to her thoughts.

At the sight of the king's country estate, Demetrius felt his adrenaline kick up. Demetrius and his servicemen would stay close to Iliana. Though few knew of their visit, those closest to the king would, and they were the people most dangerous to Iliana.

It would have been safer for Iliana to remain in Icarus. It wouldn't have changed Demetrius's plans, except Iliana wanted to speak to the king. Not giving her this opportunity robbed her of something she couldn't reclaim, and Demetrius wouldn't do that to her. No one should lead a life of regrets.

The king's wife, Stella, was waiting at the door for them. He'd expected her interest, but Demetrius wondered how involved in the king's affairs Stella was and what exactly she knew about Iliana.

"President DeSante. I heard that you had an appointment with my husband. Surely you know he is unwell."

"I am aware of his condition. I need to speak to him."

Stella didn't move to allow them to pass. "I didn't realize you wanted to say goodbye in person."

Demetrius had met Stella on several other occasions. She was older than Demetrius by a few years and far younger than the king. Their brief courtship and subsequent marriage had been questioned by the country, but if Stella had been unfaithful, she had been discreet about it.

Stella was digging for information, and Demetrius would reveal nothing. He owed Stella zilch. Until he knew who was targeting Iliana, everyone was a possible enemy. It was a hard way to live, but he had been living with enemies at his back for decades. "The king is waiting."

Stella looked at Iliana. "You must be Iliana Kracos. I saw your name on the visitor request form."

Iliana stepped forward, extending her hand. No curtseying, though that would have been the accepted practice, and as the personal secretary to the queen of Acacia, Iliana would be well aware of it. Iliana was not playing subservient, and Demetrius loved her for it. "Iliana DeSante now."

Stella appeared surprised. "You've married Demetrius? How…interesting. I wasn't sure what to make of you accompanying Demetrius on this visit."

Demetrius wondered how much Stella knew about the king's will.

"I hope we'll have time to visit later," Iliana said. She smiled, and Demetrius hid his amusement. She was giving Stella no information, and she was playing as phony as Stella was.

Stella was standing between him and the hallway leading to the king's bedroom.

"Excuse us," Demetrius said. Circumventing the older woman, he and Iliana followed the king's steward to the king.

Iliana instantly disliked the king's wife. It wasn't only what Demetrius had told her about Stella running the country, but it was clear that the woman was a fake and would have refused Iliana's visit with the king if Demetrius hadn't been with her.

Stella seemed afraid of Demetrius, circling him and prodding him indirectly for information. In this case, Iliana was happy Demetrius was here. As much as she didn't like him right now, his power and courage were inspiring and infectious. Better for the other woman to know her place and not think Iliana was a weakling who could be manipulated.

Iliana didn't know how she felt about any of this yet, but she wasn't giving up ground this early. She didn't want the king's land or resources, and not because refusing would annoy Demetrius and spoil whatever agenda he was pushing. She didn't want to be involved in a contentious fight between siblings and their mothers. She was out of place in Valencia. She didn't belong here. She didn't know the culture or the traditions, and, aside from sharing genetic material, she had nothing in common with the king.

Her family had been the people who'd raised her. She refused to see them any differently, even if their betrayal and secrets burned hot in her stomach.

Iliana entered the king's chambers. He was sleeping on a bed in a sterile-looking room surrounded by medical equipment. There were two nurses on duty. A guard was posted by the window, and two more were at the entrance. The shades were open to allow in the sunlight, but the space was still dreary.

She smelled death and disinfectant. Iliana had been near death before. It was a heavy, stale scent, and she felt a combination of sad and nauseated.

No one had said a word. She wondered if the king was sleeping. Should she come back later?

She walked toward the king, unsure if she should speak. Had Demetrius explained why she was here? Would the king know who she was?

Demetrius knelt at the king's bedside. "My dear friend, Iliana is here."

The king's eyes opened. His nurses rushed forward to help him shift to a sitting position, moving pillows and arranging his arms and legs.

"Iliana." The king's voice was gruff. She wasn't sure what she'd expected him to say or for her to feel in response, but she felt sad and empty.

"Are you really my biological father?" she asked.

"Yes. Too late for a happy reunion or a meeting of the minds." He struggled to take a breath. "I've watched you over the years. I am proud of who you are. I was afraid for you, afraid of what those close to me could do if they saw you as a threat. I was troubled you wouldn't forgive me if you knew the truth. But I have nothing left to lose."

Not only did she find it disturbing that he had watched her from afar, but she was confused as to why. If he was so proud, why didn't he take a chance and tell her the truth before today? Time delivered forgiveness. Not to mention, why send the message through Demetrius? "My parents said nothing to me about being adopted."

"I asked them to keep the secret to keep you safe."

"Why did you want Demetrius to tell me about you?"

The king closed his eyes, and Iliana wasn't sure if he'd fallen asleep. After several labored breaths, he spoke again. "Demetrius has been a good friend to me. When he told me he had found you and had come to care for you, I asked him to protect you and to tell you the truth when the time was right."

A month ago would have been better, even two months ago.

"It would have come to light after my death, but this way I can look at you, grown and strong. It brings me happiness in my last days."

He opened his eyes, and this time he smiled at her. "You look like your mother."

A woman she had no memories of and had only learned existed today. "What can you tell me about her?"

"I met her while I was visiting Kontos. It's a beautiful and quiet seaside village. She was working at an ice-cream store."

Before he could continue, Stella swept into the room. "What is this nonsense? Another bimbo with a claim to the throne? I won't allow it. I won't allow someone to take advantage of my husband when he is failing. He's delusional and losing his mind."

Stella must have been listening at the door. Iliana resented the intrusion.

"You won't address my wife in that manner again," Demetrius said. "You will watch your tone. She has made no false claims. She is here at the request of the king."

The king pointed from his guards to Stella. They moved to escort her out of the room.

Stella shook off the guards and moved toward the door. "If you think I will let some gold digger rob me, you're mistaken."

The king coughed, and his nurses rushed to place an oxygen mask over his face. Iliana wanted the king to know she had not come there to make a play for an inheritance, no matter what Stella thought. "I don't want anything from you," Iliana said. Had he heard her?

Demetrius looked at her. "It does not matter what you want. You have been named in his will, and it is too late to change it. I fully expect Stella will do her best to manipulate the circumstances, but the law is clear. You will be given your rightful inheritance whether you want it or not."

Iliana looked exhausted. She had dark circles under her eyes and her skin was pale. The emotional drain of the past twenty-four hours had caught up with her. On the drive to their hotel, she'd fallen asleep, laying her head against the window. Demetrius gathered her against him, wrapping her in his arms. He wanted to shield her from some of the pain, but that was impossible. She had to live through it, push through the hurt and find a sense of peace.

Demetrius wasn't sure of his role. He was on thin ice. Persuading her to marry him had been part luck, part chemistry and part manipulation. He wouldn't feel bad about it. He'd done what he had needed to do.

She shifted. "I am mad at you. This doesn't change that."

He kissed the top of her head. She was allowing him to hold her, and he wouldn't question it. She was too tired to fight. He was her ally and he would protect her. He was grateful to have her in his arms.

She wasn't just a pawn in this game. She meant

more to him, and that rattled him. Caring for her made her a liability. He didn't need another liability.

They parked in the underground parking garage at their hotel and took a private elevator to the penthouse suite. The secrecy was for security. His servicemen would wait by the elevator. He was armed. Demetrius felt better when he was carrying his gun. His military training had been ingrained in him and it was hard to forget the basics: stay alert, have a weapon close and trust no one.

They entered the suite after his servicemen checked it for intruders. Demetrius took his wife's hand, and led her to the bedroom. He peeled back the sheets. "Rest." She sat on the edge of the bed, and he knelt at her feet, removing her shoes.

He was tempted to run his hand up her leg but knew she would reject him. She wasn't giving him any signs she was interested in anything happening between them. He'd need to take this slowly and let her lead. Demetrius wasn't good at handing over the reins on anything, but he'd have to learn. She lay back onto the pillow, and he covered her with a sheet.

"Why are you watching me?" she asked.

He loosened his tie and unfastened the top button of his shirt. Dress clothes weren't his style, but as the president of Icarus, he had appearances to maintain. "Because you are beautiful. It's hard not to stare."

"I want to go home," she said, her eyes still closed. She sounded tired and worn.

She meant home to Acacia. "We will return to Icarus after you've had some rest. Perhaps the king will be up for talking again."

She opened her eyes, and unshed tears shone in

them. "I don't want to return to Icarus. I've been attacked in my home, I slept with a man who is a total enigma to me, then I married him at midnight, slept with him again, found out I'm an heiress and that my biological father's wife thinks I'm a bimbo angling for the crown. I need stable and normal. The closest I have to that is Acacia."

The idea of her returning to Acacia panicked him. He felt her slipping away. Her connection to the king of Valencia was important to him and to Icarus. He needed her.

He would offer everything he had to keep her close. "I will be your rock. I will be anything you need to get through this."

She blinked, and tears slipped down her temple. "I don't think so. We made a mistake." She sat up. "Please be reasonable. Marrying you was impulsive. I was caught up in the moment."

Marrying her had been part of his careful plan. But revealing that wouldn't make things better.

"We can fix this. We can have the marriage annulled. The rumors will die in a week, and we can return to our lives as they were before," she said matter-of-factly, as if she had been thinking about it and had resolved the problem entirely with that one decision.

Their lives before what? Before he had met her? Before he knew about her? "Could you do that? Walk away from me and forget any of this happened?" He could have told her to forget about a divorce and hold that line, but he wanted to convince her. He didn't want to look too deeply into why it mattered that she accept their marriage as real.

"I wouldn't forget you. But I could move on."

Unacceptable and intolerable. "I won't pretend that I didn't marry you."

"You want my inheritance that much? Then take it. Take it and let me go."

"I can't do that." The laws of Valencia were clear. The money she'd inherit was useless to him. He needed her title and her power granted with that title. She was naive if she thought she could walk away without this following her. She wouldn't survive on her own. The person or people targeting her would succeed in killing her without him to keep her safe.

Apparently he wasn't the only one interested in Iliana's inheritance.

She wiped at her eyes and looked at the ceiling. "You're boxing me into a situation I don't want."

"Give me time to prove to you that I am the man you married. I haven't changed."

"But who is that? I didn't know you at all."

"Let me prove to you I am an honorable man."

"You have already hurt me and lied to me."

Demetrius wasn't accustomed to negotiating. He gave directions, and the people around him followed without question. He struggled to find a compromise, an offer that would change her mind about leaving. "Give me until the king's will is read. Much will be revealed, and events will be set into motion. I will keep you safe. I will protect you. If after the reading and after you understand the consequences of your inheritance, you don't want me in your life, I'll walk away and let you go." He could offer that because she would change her mind about leaving him. They'd had an undeniable chemistry and given enough time, she would fall to his charms.

"If I refuse my inheritance?" Iliana asked.

He hid his reaction to those words. "That will be your choice, but Valencia has their customs and traditions. Walking away free and clear isn't an option. The inheritance cannot be given away or denied."

She shook her head. "What if I had not been found? What if no one knew I was the king's daughter?"

"He named you in his will. You would have been found, or it would have waited for you."

"Forever?"

"Perhaps."

She sighed. "I will stay with you until the reading, then. For my safety."

Though he was pushing his luck, he set the terms. "You will give our relationship effort. You will sleep beside me, and you will behave as my wife. Give me a chance to convince you that what we have is good and it works. No silent treatment."

She narrowed her gaze on him. "You are not in a position to negotiate."

"Do you think I will agree to a quiet annulment? If you want your way, you will give me mine in this. You can trust my words."

"If I behave as your wife, then you'll give me an annulment after the reading of the king's will?"

Her words set his teeth on edge. He nodded once, reminding himself their marriage would not end in an annulment or a divorce. "Yes."

His phone buzzed, and Demetrius reached into his pocket and glanced at the display. It was the head of the National Security Service, a man who went by the name Amon. He answered. "Yes."

"Nicholas Floros was found dead, floating in the Mediterranean this morning at 11:00 a.m."

Nicholas Floros, the king's second son, born to his first wife, Kaliope. Nicholas was a playboy who partied too hard, but if the head of the NSS was calling, his death wasn't accidental. The timing alone was suspicious.

"Persons responsible?" Demetrius asked.

Iliana was watching him, her mouth pursed. He found her sexy even when she was brooding.

"No leads yet. The body had been in the water since the early-morning hours."

"Thank you for your call." Demetrius disconnected.

"Problem?" Iliana asked.

Demetrius could pretend it was a state matter that didn't concern her. But she seemed eager to flee. Despite her agreement that she wouldn't, Iliana was a fiery and passionate woman. She could take off running and find herself in danger. "The king's son Nicholas died this morning."

Iliana inhaled sharply. "How? Was he murdered?"

Demetrius needed to give her a compelling reason to stay close to him. "I suspect he was. An autopsy will determine cause of death."

"Someone wants to kill the king's heirs," Iliana said.

"Yes." He would have Amon follow up and see if attempts had been made on the other heirs or if any suspicious incidents had occurred of late that had been reported to the police or the royal guards.

Iliana shivered. "I don't want the inheritance. I don't know the king. I won't ever know him. Why should I be given anything? And at what cost? My life?"

"You are safe with me."

Demetrius's phone buzzed again. Another call he needed to take. He excused himself and stepped into the living room.

Iliana thought she might come out of her skin. She was tired and cranky and felt completely out of sorts.

She had imagined spending the days following her wedding wrapped in her husband's arms, perhaps lounging on a hot beach or swimming in the warm waters off the Hawaiian Islands. Not holed up in a hotel room in Valencia, worried about being killed because of her newly discovered connection to the king.

Iliana dialed Serena and was pleased when her cousin answered.

"How is the bride today?" Serena asked.

Serena sounded happy, and Iliana wished she had good news to share in return. "Haven't you heard? I'm in Valencia."

"That's a strange place for a honeymoon."

"Not on my honeymoon. Demetrius brought me here after he told me that my father is the king of Valencia."

Serena scoffed. "That's ridiculous. I knew your father and your mother. Was it a strange cover story for an elaborate surprise?"

She wished it had been a weird joke. "The king confirmed it's true."

Serena's silence indicated she was as bewildered as Iliana. Iliana was relieved to know that Serena, one of the people she trusted most in the world, hadn't been keeping the secret from her.

"I don't know what to say about that. Are you okay? Are you sure the king has the right woman?"

"Demetrius tested my DNA."

"That was fast."

"He tested it before we married. He knew who I was for months."

Serena swore, and since she rarely did, it had an impact. "I'll call Casimir and find out what he knows."

"Demetrius already said he told Casimir nothing about this matter."

"That's good news for Casimir."

Iliana smiled, thinking of how strong her cousin had become. Since being crowned queen, she had found confidence and happiness. "Did you learn anything about the break-in at my place?" Iliana guessed the trail would lead to Valencia, if it hadn't already.

"The police chief is looking into it. The man was a hired assassin. I assume there's a connection to this news about the king."

"I heard from Demetrius that another of the king's heirs was killed. Someone wants us dead."

"Slow down for one minute. Who else besides Demetrius knew you were one of the king's heirs?"

A great question. Since she hadn't known herself, Iliana didn't have answer. "I can't imagine."

Serena groaned. "I cannot believe I am saying this, but you need to stay close to Demetrius."

"Even after he lied to me?"

Iliana heard Serena drumming her fingers against her desk, a nervous habit she displayed when she was thinking hard. "Demetrius is a difficult man. I want to talk to Casimir about this, but I think Demetrius will protect you. If Demetrius is involved in this, he has a goal in mind and will keep you safe while accomplishing it."

She didn't want to be part of his plan, a tool to use to meet his agenda. "He only married me because I'm the king's heir. I am so angry and confused. What is it that he wants from me?" She had hoped he'd wanted to share his life with her, but now even the thought seemed ridiculous and naive.

"He wants more than your inheritance. I saw how he looked at you."

"He was playing a game." More than anything, she wanted to be convinced that Demetrius cared for her, for her nagging distrust of him to be silenced.

"I can't believe that," Serena said. "Think about how he has behaved since you met. He has a soft spot for you, and he's a man who has a soft spot for no one. Even if he had another motive, if he went through this trouble to use you for his purposes, then you are valuable to him. I can't imagine you being in a safer place. The man is ruthless." Serena paused. "Unless you think he would turn on you?"

Demetrius wouldn't physically harm her. He didn't have it in him. He was cold and calculating, but he wouldn't lay his hands on her in anger. "I am physically safe with Demetrius."

"If you want to return home to Acacia, you know you are welcome anytime, right?"

"Of course." Except, speaking the words, Iliana felt out of place. She had lived in Acacia all her life. Her memories were only of Acacia and her parents. To think that she didn't belong now because she was the biological daughter of someone else was wrong. But somehow, she felt shaken. As though a piece had been pulled from the foundation of her life and now everything on top was shifting and rocking.

Chapter 4

"Do you want her taken care of?" Amon asked.

Demetrius had his phone in a death grip, anxious to answer that question with a yes. But he had come too far to be reckless now. Killing Stella would solve one problem and introduce too many others.

"What are the chances she will succeed?" Demetrius asked.

"High. She has powerful allies in her corner," Amon said.

Stella had been trying to file a new will to replace the king's most recent one. It wasn't an easy task, but Stella had been greasing palms and clearing the way. She wanted control, land and power, and she didn't want to share it with the king's children.

If Stella had her way and inherited everything, his plan was ruined.

Demetrius needed Iliana to have influence in Valencia. She would be the key to freeing his brother, Alexei.

If Iliana would not help him, he would have no choice but to go to war with Valencia. Declaring war for the sake of saving one man was selfish and short-sighted, but Demetrius was out of options. Perhaps a covert op would do the job, but other ops had failed. One had nearly killed Alexei.

Iliana entered the living room where he had been standing at the window, looking out while he spoke to Amon. Demetrius was swept away by her beauty and grace. He ended his call. "Is everything okay?"

Iliana shook her head. She strode to the coffee table and picked up the remote control. She turned on the television.

The local news was reporting on their marriage and speculating about the reasons they were in Valencia.

It didn't matter what was being said in the media. When it came to light that she was the king's daughter, conjecture wouldn't change the facts.

"What do you want to do about this?" Iliana asked, pointing at the screen.

Demetrius didn't respond to rumors. He would make a statement when the time was right. But this was an opportunity to get back in her good graces. "What would you like me to do about this?"

She folded her arms. "I feel trapped."

Demetrius didn't like hearing her describe their relationship in that manner. But he would not give up. He would turn her around. "I assure you—you are not trapped. You have more power in this situation than you may believe." Iliana had an iron spirit.

She was strong, and he wanted to see her flourish. His wife should be powerful in her own right. It reflected well on him to have a capable woman at his side. He needed her by his side if he wanted to see Alexei again.

She narrowed her eyes on him. "Was this part of your plan? To let the world know that we're married?"

Her deep distrust of him was disconcerting. "No." He had known it would happen, but he'd done nothing to hasten it.

Iliana looked at some blank spot on the wall over his head. "Serena thinks I should stay with you."

That surprised him. "Serena is a wise queen."

Iliana laughed. The noise sounded great to his ears, even if he didn't understand the cause. "Did I say something funny?"

She turned off the television. "A few months ago, you were ready to war with Acacia and Rizari. Now the queen of Acacia is wise."

"My issues weren't with Acacia. You know that. I do what I have to for my country." *And for Alexei.*

Iliana crossed the room and stood a few inches from him. "When I'm near you, I feel as if I can't breathe."

He couldn't tell if she meant that as a compliment or a complaint. He watched her face, watched her gaze move from his eyes to his mouth and down his body. She was fighting their attraction, and he wanted her to lose the fight. "Tell me why you feel that way."

"You're hiding something from me. You have an agenda. It scares me that I don't know what it is or what it will mean for me. That makes you impossible to trust."

He had a political agenda, but he also had a few things on his personal agenda, like wooing her into his bed again. He was trustworthy, but proving that to her would take time. "My political aspirations will not harm you."

"How can you know that?"

"What I need is not in conflict with what you need," he said.

"What is it that you think I need?"

That was a loaded question. "I think you need me, your husband, to make you pregnant and give you the big family you always wanted. I think you need me to take you to bed and worship you. I think you need me inside you."

Her eyes were wide, and her mouth fell open. "No, you're off the mark."

"I will respect your boundaries. But you asked me what you need. A passionate and caring woman like you makes a good lover and a good mother."

Iliana huffed. "What you need to do is keep your distance."

"We have an agreement."

"I said I would behave as your wife. That doesn't mean I'm happy with you or willing to jump into bed with you at every moment."

Was she trying to provoke him? He wouldn't take the bait. "As you wish, wife."

She narrowed her eyes at him again.

"I have a few things I need to do before bed." She pointed to his computer on the desk. "May I use that?"

"Yes, of course." Iliana circled around him to access the computer.

"I'll wait for you to return to my bed."

"You may be waiting a long time."

As long as he had waited for Iliana and his plan to come to pass, a few more hours were nothing.

Iliana opened Demetrius's computer. Though an internet search couldn't tell her much about her biological mother, she could look for answers to questions about the king of Valencia, his wives and children.

The stories about Nicholas Floros's death dominated the news. Depending on the site, the report ranged from brief, stating the cause of death was "under investigation," to outright printing it had been murder.

Murder. Her world had turned crazy in the space of a few days.

"Come to bed."

Demetrius. He was standing in front of the desk in a white T-shirt and sweatpants. His hair was wet from a shower, and the roped muscles of his upper body drew her attention. His biceps stretched the material around his arms, and his broad shoulders outlined his impressive frame. Her attraction to him was back in spades.

None of this was fair. Iliana wanted to enjoy her new husband. They should be in the happy, carefree period of their relationship, locked in each other's arms, not locked in a struggle over the whys behind their marriage vows.

He looked good to her. He had from the first time they'd met eight months ago when the possibility of him being interested in her seemed slim. He had come to the castle to meet with the queen, and that first moment had been kismet, an instant connection. Knowing his reputation and who he was hadn't stopped her from feeling excited and giddy by the encounter—or recognizing that he was absolutely gorgeous.

Most of their interactions over the first weeks of their relationship had been via the phone. But despite his status as president and her lowly status as Serena's personal secretary, Demetrius had taken her calls directly. He had not rushed her off the phone. He had replied to her text messages and emails. He had made her a priority and had made her feel special. It had taken time for her to believe that their relationship was more than professional courtesy. He was interested in her as a woman, and that had felt amazing.

When her parents died, she'd lost the people closest to her, her family, the people she could call at two in the morning when she needed to talk. Demetrius's attention had been flattering and had healed her. He had wanted her as his wife, and now he wanted her in his bed. He was the person she wanted to call when she needed help. She didn't need a man to ride to her rescue, but she needed someone to listen to her and care about her.

She was tempted, but she held fast. She had reasons to keep her distance. She had made bad choices, and, given the emotional upset of the day, she was likely to make more poor choices if she let her heart rule. "Go to bed. I have a few more things I want to look up." She was grateful he hadn't questioned her about what she was doing. He could likely guess, but even so, she didn't want to open those wounds again. As she considered shutting down the computer and getting some sleep, her stomach fluttered at the thought of joining him in bed.

If she waited, he would fall asleep. Then she could creep into the bed next to him without causing an awkward, tense situation. Better yet, she could crash on the couch and make up an excuse later.

"I won't sleep until you do."

Demetrius was stubborn. He wouldn't back down. Well, two could play at that game.

Ignoring his comment and avoiding eye contact, Iliana stood from the computer and headed to the bathroom, where she brushed her teeth and changed into her pajamas, pondering her next move. She was small enough to sleep comfortably on the couch. That was a safer place than Demetrius's bed.

Hoping she was tiptoeing silently, she walked into the living area. She grabbed a few pillows and a blanket and lay down.

Demetrius appeared at the end of the couch. "You sleep beside me. That was our agreement."

"You are welcome to sleep next to me." She pointed to the floor next to her.

He tossed a pillow on the floor and lay down.

The president of Icarus was sleeping on the floor when a perfectly good mattress was a few feet away.

"Why don't you sleep in the bed? Sex isn't happening in any case, so you might as well be comfortable," she said.

"This isn't about sex. This is about keeping you close where I can keep an eye on you."

He was serious about protecting her. "Your guards are outside the door."

"I don't care where my guards are. There is no one more interested in your safety than me. That means you stay where I can see you. Furthermore, I do not care for the idea of my guards seeing you in your pajamas. You will sleep where I sleep."

He had made valid points about security. Feeling like a jerk, she stood and stepped over him. As long as he didn't try anything, she would keep to her half of the mattress. "Fine. You win. We'll sleep in the bed."

He had the decency not to look victorious when he climbed into bed beside her.

For good measure, she wedged a spare pillow between them. "Stay on your side."

He laughed, a deep rumbling noise that shook the mattress. "I am the master of self-control."

She said nothing to that.

As she tried to calm her thoughts enough to sleep, it annoyed her that Demetrius fell asleep instantly. Shouldn't he remain awake, worrying about the future and the problems they faced? She moved the separation pillow and poked him.

He didn't stir.

She nudged him again, this time harder. "Demetrius."

No response. Shouldn't his military training mean he woke and became alert quickly? She prodded him again.

This time, he grabbed her hand and pulled her on top of him, trapping her legs with his and holding her hips against him. "What do you need, wife? Is this what you want? My attention?"

She wiggled against him, but he did not free her. The movement of their bodies against each other was only turning her on more. "I wanted to know if you were sleeping."

He shifted, aligning their bodies, and she used every ounce of control not to rub against him.

His hand clamped around her rear end. "I was trying to sleep. Tell me what's wrong."

"I'm worried."

"There's nothing you can do now. Sleep so you can be sharp tomorrow."

Easy for him to say.

"The night before a battle, I refused to let my troops stay awake drinking and whoring because that created tired soldiers. Tired soldiers are dead soldiers."

He wasn't letting her move. She wanted to move. "I'm not a soldier."

"The principle applies."

She pushed his arms away, and he let them drop to the side.

Still on top of him, she ran her finger over his shadow beard.

"Are you trying to start something?" he asked.

His erection was pressing between her legs. How could she want him this much? She swiveled her hips in response. Bracing her hands on his rock-hard belly, she lifted and lowered her body over his.

"Iliana, if you are playing a game, stop." There was a clear warning in his voice. He wanted her, and he was trying to respect her limits.

Was this a game? It felt very real. He had lied to her. That hurt and anger was not far from her mind, but it was becoming more distant. She had lost control and was bent on touching him now. "I want you to lie still and let me do the work."

He watched her, his midnight eyes vivid with interest. She peeled her pajama top over her head and flung it on the ground. Then she massaged her breasts while he watched.

She had his full attention, and she was putting on

a show. She became hotter, wetter just thinking about it. He grew harder and bigger between her legs. She moaned and let her body and desires guide her. She ground against him, wanting release and being unable to reach it. "I can't get there alone."

He held her hips and shifted her, moving his hand between her legs but still refusing to do what she needed. "Tell me you want this. I won't help you unless you say the words."

She couldn't lie. "I want this."

"Tell me you want me." His words sounded almost animalistic.

That was harder to say, but it was the truth nonetheless. "I want you."

"Say my name," he said.

"Demetrius."

"And you, my Iliana, my beautiful, sexy wife, you deserve to come in my arms every night."

He moved quickly, flipping her onto her back and stripping her cotton pants and underwear down her legs. He threw the pillow she had been using as a wedge onto the floor. His magic fingers worked her, played with her, built her into a frenzy. She was thrashing and panting when release finally crashed over her.

As her orgasm eased, she expected he would want her to return the favor. Instead, he moved to lie next to her, dragging her pillow closer and fitting her body into the hard angles of his.

"This doesn't mean I forgive you," she said.

"I know," he said into her hair.

"Doesn't that upset you?"

"No. You will come around, Iliana. It's a matter of time."

* * *

"Iliana."

Iliana was curled beneath the blankets, tucked against her husband's body. She arched and stretched. Demetrius kept his desire on a short leash. Alexei was counting on him. He had to find the right words to convince Iliana to help him. Would she give him another chance?

He was hoping he'd have enough leverage over her that she would consider his situation and comply. She was a good woman with a gentle heart. He wasn't above playing to her compassion. He spoke her name again, setting his hand on her side. It was too tempting to reach beneath the blankets, down, down, lift her knee, enter her from behind and make slow, thrilling love to her.

But despite Iliana moving toward him and against him in her sleep, he would take no liberties. Making her feel taken advantage of or exploiting her attraction to him would only work against him in the long run.

She might not believe they had a future, but he had married her and they would work this out.

She made a noise in her sleep.

"Iliana, I have some bad news."

"No more problems. Let me sleep."

What he had to say couldn't wait. Perhaps it wouldn't mean anything to her, but it meant the world to him. For the first time in nineteen years, the strong possibility of Alexei going free existed. "The king of Valencia has died."

She tensed and rolled to face him. "How do you know?"

He'd asked his spies to alert him immediately to changes in the king's condition. "I was contacted."

"What happens now?"

"We'll pay our respects in the morning."

"His family must be devastated. They had time to say goodbye, I suppose, but I'm not sure there's any way to prepare for the finality of death." She swallowed hard, and he knew she was thinking of her parents.

He hugged her. He had lost people close to him, but he wasn't good at finding words of comfort. He was a take-action type.

She brushed her hair away from her face. "I still had questions for him."

She sounded devastated. He hated that the first days of their marriage had been disappointing for her. He had planned to court her slowly and get her to the altar in time, but given the king's rapidly declining health, the timing hadn't been what he'd hoped. "I will help you find answers."

She lowered her head into his chest. The shudder in her shoulders told him she was silently crying. Maybe for their marriage, maybe for her parents, maybe for the father and mother she would never know.

He didn't have the right words, so he held her close until she fell asleep in his arms.

"I don't belong at the king's memorial service," Iliana said.

"He would want you here," Demetrius said.

Iliana adjusted her black scarf around her neck. She had her hair pinned back and was wearing a gray dress. It was a somber look in keeping with the me-

morial service. After Demetrius had woken her to tell
her about the king, she hadn't been able to sleep well.
She'd spent the rest of the night tossing and turning.

The morning was cold and foggy. Traffic was
snarled around Saint Felix's, the largest church in Valencia, located in the capital of Abele, not far from the
king's country home. Security was tight, and she and
Demetrius were waiting in a long line of cars. Given
Nicholas's death, every car was being checked and
every mourner being patted down and waved with a
metal detector.

Demetrius was typing away on the tablet on his lap.
It seemed the man worked around the clock. Running
a country wasn't easy, but did he take time to relax?
It didn't appear so.

"What do you do for fun?" she asked, wanting a
distraction to unknot the tension in her stomach.

Demetrius looked at her and inclined his head.
"You."

She cracked a smile. At least he had a sense of
humor. "Before me. Don't say other women, because
that will make me…upset." She didn't want to think
about him being a womanizer and sleeping around.
Maybe variety and frequency made a man good in
bed, but consistency and building intimacy with one
person carried more weight.

"There weren't and there will not be other women.
There is only you. Before you, there was work."

She didn't believe that he hadn't dated women. He
was rich and powerful. That had a way of attracting
a certain type of woman. She rolled her eyes. "Oh,
you didn't tell me you were a virgin before I deflow-
ered you."

Demetrius laughed. "Let me rephrase. There hasn't been another woman of significance in my life. No other woman has had me the way you have."

That floored her. Though he was interested in her connection to the king, he was still pretending they were a couple, saying romantic things to her and acting like he had before they'd married. Demetrius had spoken nothing of love. It was an oversight so great, she wasn't sure why she hadn't seen it before she'd married him.

Had she mistaken lust for love? "Do you play sports?"

"I run. I lift."

Both solitary activities, and that didn't surprise her. She had seen him in social situations, and, while he was proficient, he kept things professional and focused conversations around others. He was secretive about himself. "Some couples golf together. Serena and Casimir play tennis."

"Hitting a ball into a tiny hole doesn't interest me. Hitting balls at you doesn't appeal to me, either."

"Come on—give me something."

"I will give you almost anything you ask for," he said.

"Tell me your favorite game."

"Chess."

"I don't know how to play that," she said. "I've played checkers." Chess had too many rules and she hadn't been patient enough to learn them.

"Checkers is a good start. I will teach you chess. It will help you."

Help her how? To think ahead? To see around

corners? "Is that how you played this relationship? Thinking a hundred steps ahead?"

"I did not play you, if that's the implication. I chose you and I pursued you. I won you. I know I am close to losing you, and I will work to keep you. That is all."

She laid her head on his shoulder, and he slipped his arm around her. He continued working on his tablet with his free hand, reading emails. Some were in English, others in another language. "Speak to me in Italian."

He did.

"What does that mean?" she asked.

"It means, 'Do not worry, wife. I will take care of you.'"

He was sweet and had a way with words. When he spoke like that to her, it was a chink in her armor. She didn't know why he had chosen to keep secrets or what exactly he wanted, but she felt close to him, a kinship, as if it was her and Demetrius against Valencia. Though Serena would have sided with her over these matters in private, as queen, Serena had to play politics. Demetrius didn't seem to care about politics. He did what he wanted and what he thought was best.

She settled on his shoulder and waited for their car to reach the front of the church. When it was their turn, Demetrius stepped out of the car. His servicemen flanked him. He reached for her hand, helping her onto the curb. The servicemen stayed close to her as well, but it was Demetrius's touch that made her feel safe.

Security checked her handbag and ran metal detectors up and down their bodies. A squawk sounded as security brushed the wand over Demetrius's hip.

"Sir, you cannot bring your weapon into the church," the security officer said.

Demetrius stared at him. "What?"

That single word had the man lifting his hands and glancing around nervously. "You're free to go inside."

Iliana pointed to his gun at his hip. "This is a church. You don't need that here."

"You can't know that. Not everyone has respect for the sanctity of this space."

She and Demetrius hurried up the stairs and through the large wooden doors to the church. Their servicemen stayed close, and Iliana was certain they were also carrying weapons.

Inside Stella was greeting guests. Standing next to her were the king's sons and daughters. Iliana recognized them from their pictures. Did they recognize her, as well? She fought the urge to turn and run. This would be unpleasant. Her siblings were hurting and grieving, and meeting them today was not ideal. She hadn't considered the family would be greeting mourners.

She wouldn't be intimidated. She was the cousin of the queen of Acacia. She was friends with the king of Rizari. She was married to the president of Icarus. She understood how to conduct herself with poise and dignity. Holding her head high, she offered Stella her condolences.

Stella was wearing a hat with a dark veil over her face and long black gloves to her elbows. She'd nailed the widow-in-mourning look. Iliana kept her snarky comments to herself. She was carrying around residual anger for the woman from their interaction yesterday. Putting herself in Stella's shoes, she imagined the other woman was deeply saddened and grieving. She didn't need extra attitude from Iliana piled on top.

Stella was standing ramrod straight. "You're still in Valencia."

"I was planning to leave today. I wanted to pay my respects to the king."

Stella pursed her lips. "You hardly knew my husband." She glanced at Demetrius, giving away that she felt unsure.

"I would have liked to know him better," Iliana said.

Beneath the black veil, Stella narrowed her eyes. "Many people thought my husband could help them or give them something. What is it that you wanted him to give you?"

"Good day, Stella," Demetrius said.

There were a number of things Demetrius could have said, and, given that he spoke his mind without regard for other's feelings most other times, he was showing remarkable restraint. Maybe he was holding back because this was a service for Stella's husband or he was tempering his bluntness for Iliana's sake.

Demetrius nudged her along, and Iliana came face-to-face with Emmanuel Floros, her eldest half brother. He had lost his brother Nicholas and his father in the span of a couple days. He didn't look well, and his eyes were red rimmed. Iliana's heart went out to him.

"My deepest condolences for your losses," Iliana said. When her cousin Serena had lost her father and sister, she had struggled to cope with the loss. Iliana wouldn't wish that hurt on anyone.

Emmanuel nodded at her, but nothing in his face

indicated he knew who she was. Iliana received a similar reaction from Maria, Emmanuel's younger sister.

But Spiro, the king's younger son from his second wife recognized her. "You're the long-lost heiress. Showing up at the end to make sure you get yours." He sneered at her.

She started and felt Demetrius's hand on her lower back, calming her and letting her know he was there to support her. "The king requested my presence in Valencia before his death. I only found out recently who I was."

Spiro snickered. "I don't buy the innocent act. Don't show up here with the president of Icarus and pretend to be doe-eyed. If you're shacking up with this guy, you know what's what."

Iliana set her hand against her husband's chest. Demetrius had kept his temper with Stella, but Spiro was pushing his luck. "I am not familiar with the terms in this region. Is *shacking up* the words you use for *married*?" Demetrius asked. His voice was flat, but there was no mistaking the danger. He was like a cobra set to strike.

Spiro glanced at Demetrius.

Theodore, Spiro's older brother, stepped in front of Spiro. "Please excuse my brother's rudeness. I am afraid you are not seeing us at our best."

"Even when times are bad, I don't take well to someone insulting my wife," Demetrius said. "I won't warn you again."

Spiro nodded and swallowed hard.

Iliana moved past her half siblings. This wasn't how she would have liked to meet them, and she was rattled by their contempt for her.

"No matter what they say to you, I am here for you. I will not let harm come to you," Demetrius said quietly into her ear.

"They would like to see me disappear."

"It's too bad for them that it won't happen. I need you around," Demetrius said.

But why did he need her? What would happen to her once he had what he wanted?

It was hard to shake the feeling of being watched. Though some eyes were on him and Iliana out of curiosity, Demetrius knew that much of the attention had to do with the looming inheritance battle. Emmanuel the Second would get almost everything of importance, according to Valencian law. After the will was read, he would take his father's place as king.

But Demetrius had read Valencian law carefully, every last word, and he knew of ways for others to make a play for the crown. He hoped Emmanuel had plans to secure his position. Having overthrown the former dictator of Icarus, Demetrius had experience in these matters. In a stable government, the lines of succession were clear. In an unstable one, the death of the king meant his position was in the air, and whoever got to it first—by jumping, shoving others or outright cheating—was the winner. Demetrius didn't care who was named king. He would find a way to get along with Emmanuel or Stella or whoever else took over.

But Iliana would be named marchioness. No exceptions and no negotiations.

Demetrius had another powerful enemy in the room, although that enemy wouldn't know Demetrius was present. Octavius Drakos, the baron of Aetos, was seated in the center pews near the front of the altar. He was wearing dark glasses and clutching his walking stick. The glasses were for vanity. The baron was blind and couldn't control his wandering eyes. He lived as a hermit, trapped by his paranoia and dislike of most others. He trusted no one, which worked to Demetrius's benefit.

The baron's fondness for torture may be the only reason Alexei was alive, or perhaps the baron wanted him alive for another purpose, like baiting Demetrius.

Demetrius's revenge against the baron of Aetos had been years in the making. When it was time for Demetrius to collect, the baron would be destroyed.

Iliana touched his wrist. "What's wrong?"

His anger at Drakos was white-hot. Were his emotions showing? "I will tell you later."

He would need to confess his past with the baron when the time was right. Though it was a topic he didn't discuss—he didn't think even Casimir knew about his ties to Drakos—Demetrius would come clean with Iliana, tell her the story and hope she followed her good heart and did what was right.

"You look as if you want to kill someone," she said.

The baron, among others. "Just anyone who tries to hurt you."

Iliana shifted. "That might be a lot of people in this room. I don't think my family was happy to see me."

"It doesn't matter how they feel. You exist and you have a claim. The king expected me to keep you safe and I will."

Deafening music from the pipe organ filled the space. Demetrius didn't like the sound; it reminded him too much of a horror movie. Demetrius had seen death many times in his life, and facing it with a bad soundtrack made it worse. When he died, he hoped trumpets and flutes played merrily. Life was too short to wallow in the deaths of others.

The procession down the center aisle was led by a minister in ceremonial robes. Clerics carrying candles on gleaming brass holders followed.

The king's casket was carried by his sons, Emmanuel, Theodore and Spiro, and dukes and barons who had been close to the king. No marquesses in the group. That title was reserved and hadn't been used in eleven decades. Iliana would be the only living royal of that rank.

Demetrius wasn't surprised he had not been chosen to escort the king "into heaven." He and the king had discussed it, and they had agreed it was better for him to keep a low profile. Though Demetrius's presence was tolerated, too many people feared him to believe him to be good and kind. Rumors didn't bother Demetrius. He did what he believed was right and he didn't need the approval of others. He was beholden to no one.

As the procession moved past him, Iliana sat still, her face inscrutable. One of the clerics moved away from the group, and Demetrius tensed. Any aberration from the norm worried him. Demetrius was accustomed to pervasive threats. Since he was born, someone had been gunning for him, someone had been trying to steal from him or someone had been trying to hurt him. Now it seemed someone had it out for his wife, doubling his readiness.

The clerics fanned out to move down the aisles, flinging holy water over the churchgoers.

Demetrius continued to watch for threats. Vigilance was key.

A cleric moved toward Iliana. He swung at her, his expression turning murderous. Demetrius tackled him, grabbing his arms.

A collective gasp went up from the crowd. In the man's hand was a syringe. He was strong, but Demetrius was stronger. Demetrius twisted the man's arm, forcing the syringe into the attacker and injecting him with whatever was inside.

The assassin's eyes widened.

"Secure the other heirs," Demetrius shouted. One of his servicemen was already with Iliana. Demetrius watched the assailant seizing on the ground. He felt nothing except disgust. The man had attacked his wife. Whatever poison he had meant to deliver would now be his death. It was a fitting end.

Demetrius and his servicemen led Iliana out of the church, Demetrius taking a post at his wife's side.

She was shaking in his arms. "Who was that? What was that?"

"An assassin and another assassination attempt."

Iliana stopped walking and took his lapels in her hands. "You killed that man."

"Yes."

"Why?"

"He tried to hurt you, Iliana. I have no tolerance for that. You should know that by now. If someone comes at me or mine, I will kill them."

Chapter 5

"We couldn't get the message to him," Amon said.

Demetrius appreciated that Amon wasn't mincing words or making excuses, but the statement frustrated him. Now back home in Icarus, he had been trying to send a message to Alexei in prison, to obtain a status on how he was faring and let him know that Demetrius had not given up. He would never give up trying to rescue Alexei.

The NSS leader handed him a file. Demetrius opened it, already familiar with its contents. It covered everything the NSS knew about Alexei: he was presumably still alive, he was allowed twenty minutes a day in the yard and no one inside the prison would provide a picture. Most of the intel had been gathered from ex-cons who had been released from the prison after serving their terms. In exchange for their cooperation, Demetrius provided them with a nice life in another country.

Demetrius assumed that his message to Alexei had been intercepted, like every message before it. Demetrius could not bribe or trick anyone working in the prison. Their fear of retribution from the baron of Aetos was too great.

The worst part of silence between him and Alexei was that his brother may believe that Demetrius had forgotten him. He wouldn't turn his back on his brother, but would Alexei hold to that and know Demetrius wouldn't give up?

A tap on his office door and Amon slipped out the office's hidden exit. He didn't like anyone seeing his face. He preferred to be unknown and untraceable.

"Come in," Demetrius said, and closed the file on his brother. He knew every word by heart.

Iliana entered, looking beautiful in a floor-length dress with narrow straps at the top. It was colorful and bright, like Iliana.

"Yes?" His tone was sharper than he intended, but it took time to shake off his distress about his brother.

"I'm planning to go out shopping for a while."

"Shopping?" Why did that sound suspicious? She'd shown no interest in shopping.

"What else is there for me to do around here?" She lifted her hands as if in wonder. "Maybe I could at least get some curtains and some knickknacks so this place would be more welcoming."

Demetrius wanted her to be happy. He was aware his home lacked a personal touch. "This place could use some improvements. If you need things to do, I can also have someone send you a list of charities that need volunteers."

Iliana nodded. "Sure." She turned to leave and then stopped in the doorway, setting her hand on the door frame and turning to look at him over her shoulder. "Are you okay?"

"Yes. Are you?"

"I'm fine. But you look upset." She turned fully around now, studying him.

He neutralized his face. "I have a lot of work."

She walked toward him and touched the edge of his desk. "Do you want to talk about it?"

"No." He couldn't discuss his brother. Not yet. She was still mad that he had withheld information about the king. She wasn't ready to consider using her title to help him.

She frowned. "Fine. If you change your mind, I'm around."

"Don't leave the house without your guards," he said.

Her shoulders sagged. "I won't."

He wouldn't change his mind. He wouldn't discuss Alexei with her until he had the conversation perfectly planned and the timing was right. If she knew what he needed from her, she might deny his request, and that was unacceptable.

It was the first time Iliana recalled seeing Demetrius upset. Deeply upset. She didn't think it had anything to do with her. When it came to her, he seemed to have an invisible level of restraint, as if he could turn off his emotions. What had happened? Had a political problem arisen? She had read the news online that morning, but hadn't seen anything out of the ordinary that would concern the president.

Iliana had a good sense of others' emotions, and she wished Demetrius would confide in her. It would show he was making an effort, and after his deceit, he needed to make a very big one.

As Iliana wandered through the home decor store, she absently picked up a few pieces, trying to collect ideas on how to make Demetrius's home more inviting. Decorating wasn't high on her priority list, but waiting around to hear about the king's will was making her antsy. Stewing on her marriage wasn't appealing, either. She needed to stay busy, even if it was with mundane things.

She wanted to call her half siblings and talk to them. They had been understandably upset at the funeral. Could she try again to connect with them under less emotionally devastating circumstances?

Thinking of the king's death, Iliana felt she had lost someone important, which was ridiculous. She hadn't known the king of Valencia. Learning of their connection a few days ago had shaken her, but had she truly lost anything?

Growing up as an only child, Iliana had wanted siblings of her own. After losing her parents, she had desperately wanted someone in that role, someone to stand next to her and to understand what she had been going through, to hold her hand and support her. Her cousins, Serena and Danae, had been there for her, but she'd been jealous of their closeness growing up and wanted a similar relationship for herself.

Iliana looked at the furniture and other items for

sale. It was too hard to choose pieces she liked because Demetrius's house didn't feel like hers.

They weren't moving in the direction of domestic bliss, and pretending otherwise made her look and feel foolish.

She left the store, aware of Demetrius's security close behind her. Would she ever grow accustomed to being followed? The only place where she had privacy was inside the house, but that was beginning to feel like a jail. She could only move around freely in one part of the house: Demetrius's private wing, where his bedroom was located. The rest was used for offices and staff members who worked closely with Demetrius.

Iliana stopped for coffee and sat, with her mug, near the back of the restaurant. Having traveled with Queen Serena, she was accustomed to people looking in her direction, although they were not usually looking at her. But one of the restaurant patrons clearly was.

The woman, who seemed familiar, approached. After she removed her hat and sunglasses, Iliana recognized her. Maria, the king's daughter.

Security stopped her, but Iliana intercepted them before they patted her down. Maria was traveling with her own bodyguards. As their security teams eyed each other with hostility, Iliana gestured to the chair across from her. "Please sit. I'm surprised to see you," Iliana said. "What brings you to Icarus?"

"Looking for you," Maria said. "I tried to see you at the president's house, but I was denied entrance."

She hadn't been told she'd had a guest. "I apologize. I will speak to my husband and his staff about our manners, especially as it relates to family." The word *family* felt awkward on her tongue but good in her chest.

Maria set her hands on the table. "I need your help. I know after the way I treated you at my father's funeral—our father's funeral—you have every right to refuse me."

She wouldn't. Her desperation for a connection to family was too great. "I was planning to call you, each of you, to reach out again. The king's funeral wasn't the place for a real discussion. Please tell me what's on your mind."

"Is there a place we can speak in private?" Maria looked around. In the busyness of the café, the four men in black trench coats and dark sunglasses drew attention. Though Iliana was open to speaking with her sister, she wanted it to be on safe ground. They didn't know who was targeting the royal family, and until they did, Iliana would exercise caution.

"We could return to the house and speak," Iliana said.

At Maria's nod, they stood. Maria slipped her sunglasses over her eyes. "I will meet you there."

Iliana arrived at the house before Maria. She now wished she had a proper place to sit with her guest. It was silly to think about, but her mother had raised her with good manners. Demetrius's place left much to be desired. She made a mental note to put some effort into her domestic and decorating skills over the next several weeks.

When Maria arrived, Iliana escorted her to the kitchen and started to fix tea. Their respective security teams waited outside the kitchen door, and Demetrius's guard appeared at the back door leading to the garden.

Demetrius's butler, Abeiron, swept into the room. He was tall and lanky, his uniform pressed and tailored, his expression neutral. He missed nothing; every detail was in his purview.

"Mrs. DeSante, please allow me." With expert precision, he took over the task, brushing her away.

Iliana sat with Maria at the wooden table. "We have privacy. Please tell me what's on your mind."

Maria took a deep breath. "Your servants can be trusted?"

Iliana started at the words *your servants*.

"The president's staff has been thoroughly vetted." If Demetrius allowed them to work in his home, Iliana had a high degree of confidence in their trustworthiness.

Maria removed her gloves and set them on the table. "I've visited with my siblings to discuss Stella."

"What about her?" No amount of discussion would turn Stella into a reasonable and kind woman. She was bent on power and being the sole heir.

"She wants to change the will. She wants everything for herself."

Stella had struck her as greedy and manipulative, so this news wasn't unexpected. "I am sure that is not a simple task. There must be provisions in place to prevent it." Her law degree was gathering dust and she hadn't practiced law in Valencia, but she presumed their inheritance laws would prevent such corruption.

"We don't know what Stella has been working on over the past couple of years while our father was sick. She could have convinced him to edit his will or write us out entirely. Who knows what Dad did when he was medicated?"

Iliana wasn't sure of her place in these matters. "While I am sorry that this situation is dissolving into a free-for-all, I don't have a strong interest in whatever inheritance the king may have left me."

Maria shot her a disbelieving look. "You stand to gain much power."

Iliana didn't know what power in Valencia would do for her. "My place is in Icarus, and my home is Acacia."

Maria's hands curled into fists on the table. "But you must feel you have a responsibility in Valencia to see that Stella doesn't take over. We need to stick together on this."

The purpose of Maria's visit was clear. She wanted an alliance with Iliana. "I don't know where my place is." She had never uttered a truer statement. "I am trying to take it day by day. I didn't have much time with the king. I didn't know him as you and your siblings did." There was no bitterness or anger in her heart, mostly just a sense of loss.

"My father was a good man. He was a fair man. At times, he could be hard and unyielding. I suppose he had that in common with your husband," Maria said.

Iliana didn't deny it. Demetrius could be unrelenting, and he didn't back down. "I'm surprised they were friends. It seems like two tenacious men would have trouble coming to terms."

"Dad liked Demetrius. I guess he saw him as a younger version of himself," Maria said. She accepted the cup of tea from Abeiron. "My father mellowed in his later years, but as a young man, he was a hothead. Always coming to blows, both verbally and physically, with the people around him."

It was a long shot, but Iliana was looking for a connection. "Did my father ever mention me?"

Maria shook her head. "My father was a difficult man to read. He would be quiet and contemplative, but it was hard to know if that was because he had political matters on his mind or if he was thinking of something personal."

Iliana was disappointed that the king hadn't said anything about her, but she'd anticipated that. He had kept her parentage a secret. "What can I do to help you?"

"Join us and stop Stella from taking everything. The courts won't believe that we are cut out of the will, especially if we stand united and don't sabotage each other."

Iliana wouldn't stab anyone in the back, but she also had no power or connections that would allow her to persuade the courts she was a rightful heir. She didn't feel like a rightful heir. She felt like an interloper. "I will have to think about it."

Maria shook her head. "That's a dismissal."

Iliana hadn't made up her mind. "No, it's as I said. I will consider it." As much as she longed for a family, she wouldn't ally herself with people who a few days ago wished she didn't exist. At this moment, fighting beside her siblings and being granted her inheritance meant nothing to her.

Demetrius entered the room and sat next to her at the table. He moved so quietly, she hadn't heard him approach. "Welcome to our home, Maria. Please tell me what brings you to Icarus and into consultation with my wife." His words were polite enough, but Iliana recognized an edge in his tone, an indication that he was close to doing something drastic.

What had him riled up now?

Demetrius could not allow Iliana to turn her back on her position within Valencia. If she didn't ally herself with her half siblings, when the will was read, they could work together to snub her or convince the courts Iliana shouldn't inherit anything.

"Maria has some concerns about the king's will," Iliana said.

"About Stella?" He could have played stupid, but he didn't like to pretend when it came to matters of grave importance.

"There are rumors flying that she convinced my father to change his will," Maria said.

"If she did, any magistrate who isn't on the take will see through her scam," Demetrius said.

Sitting behind Iliana with his chair angled toward Maria, he smelled his wife's hair. The scent was like his garden in the spring. When Maria left, he would try to talk to Iliana again. How long could they live with this rift between them? It wasn't good for either of them.

"You just said it yourself," Maria said. "If the barrister and magistrates involved aren't being bribed. Stella will make sure her friends and allies rule in her favor. She isn't above buying support."

If the king's children had spent more time with their father in the past couple of years instead of jetsetting to luxury destinations on his dime, perhaps they wouldn't be in a panic now trying to secure their positions. Despite their ages, the king's heirs hadn't taken their places as adults in the royal family, and therefore the powerful and influential still viewed them as children. "You came here to ask my wife to help you. Help you do what?"

Maria looked at her hands and then back at Demetrius. "I hoped you would use your influence, as well."

He couldn't show his hand, not to Maria. If she knew how important it was to him that Iliana inherit, she could use that against him. "I think I have better things to do with my time than fight over land and money in another country."

Maria leaned forward, setting her hands on the table. "You want something. Tell me what it is."

"What makes you think I want something from you?"

Maria narrowed her eyes. "Maybe not from me, but you have an interest in Valencia. You wouldn't have involved yourself with my father if you didn't."

Maria was more perceptive that he had believed. "Valencia is my closest neighbor to the north. My interest is in making sure we stay friendly." That was his story for why he was involved in the Mediterranean.

"Name your price," Maria said.

Manipulating the situation would take time. Iliana helping him after she became the marchioness of Agot was paramount. He looked at Iliana, as if considering her. "Iliana, what do you want?"

She looked over her shoulder at him in surprise. "I want for this to be resolved fairly for all involved."

"Then, you want your inheritance?" Demetrius asked.

He saw it in her eyes. She wanted it. Rationalizing that it should mean nothing to her didn't diminish the fact that the king had left her, his daughter, an important title, land and money. The gesture was meaningful to her. "If I am the king's daughter——"

"You are," Demetrius said. He wouldn't allow anyone to question it.

Iliana cleared her throat. "Since I am the king's daughter, I would like to be accepted by other members of my family."

The hurt in her voice struck a chord with him. He hadn't realized her family's acceptance held weight. He covered her hand with his. "Then, you will need to spend time with them."

"Perhaps we should speak of this in private," Iliana said.

Maria looked between them. "If you join us against Stella, then you will be one of us."

Iliana's body tensed at those words.

Maria seemed pleased with herself. She had found Iliana's weakness, and she wasn't above exploiting it. Demetrius would have stepped in if Iliana working with Maria hadn't been beneficial to him.

Maria stood. "I will leave you to your afternoon. I will call you later to discuss this further."

"Sure," Iliana said, sounding worried. Maria slipped on her gloves and was escorted from the room by her guards and two of Demetrius's servicemen.

Iliana turned to face him. "Tell me what you think about Maria's request. You must have been listening and heard something that bothered you."

Demetrius took her hands in his. "You should accept your inheritance and use that connection to Valencia as a springboard to become closer with your family."

Iliana bit her bottom lip. "That means spending more time in Valencia."

He wasn't wild about that idea, but he kept his goal in mind. His brother's freedom was more important than having his wife nearby at every moment. "I support that if it is your wish."

"Will you visit me there? Will I visit you here?" she asked.

That she cared either way told him she wasn't as finished with their marriage as he feared. "Both. Either."

"Would you come with me to the reading of the will?" she asked.

"Yes." He hid his enthusiasm. They had a long way to go before she was named marchioness of Agot. The squabbling between the king's children and his wives was still making headlines in Valencia, and Demetrius expected the drama to escalate before it settled and a final court decision was made. The judicial system in Valencia was supposed to be impartial, but politics found its way into everything.

His primary concern was making certain that Iliana received her inheritance without being tossed into Valencia's problems.

The flight to Valencia was short, but Iliana's nerves had been on edge since she'd woken up. Facing her siblings again was nerve-racking, and she was worried about what would happen at the reading of her father's will.

What would she say if she was named marchioness of Agot? Could she decline? Did she want to?

Demetrius seemed to believe that she could not abandon her responsibilities, even if they were unexpected and foreign to her.

Her husband had kept his word and had accompanied her to Valencia. As she watched him, she wondered if he knew how sexy he could be when he was working. He was wearing gray pants and a black sweater, a simple outfit, but when he talked on the phone with his earpiece, he used his hands in an expressive way. He almost looked like an actor. Even the syncopation of his voice was mesmerizing. People didn't argue with Demetrius. He stated his demands as irrefutable and undeniable facts.

Iliana tamped back her disappointment over the night before. She had waited for Demetrius for two hours before giving up and going to bed alone. Things between them weren't going well, a gradual downhill slide after their wedding night.

He had come to bed late, and she had been groggy. He had touched her gently, but even though she had worn her most feminine nightgown, giving him the green light, he hadn't done anything else. His disinterest could be to her benefit. But when it came to Demetrius, she couldn't stop wanting him even though she barely knew him.

Maybe if she were a political rival, he'd be more attentive. When she was the queen of Acacia's secretary they had been rivals in a sense, and he had seemed interested then. Had his interest been genuine?

She and Demetrius entered the law offices where the reading of the king's will was set to begin. A piano was playing somewhere softly; otherwise the building was as quiet as a library. Iliana approached the security desk in the lobby and introduced herself. "I'm here for the reading of the king of Valencia's will," she whispered, feeling as though using her regular voice would disrupt the tranquility of the space.

The security guard stood and shifted on his feet. "My deepest apologies, but the reading of the king's will has been postponed."

Shock tumbled through her, followed quickly by suspicion. "Postponed? Why?" Iliana was twenty minutes early, and she had heard nothing about changes to the schedule. If it had been put off to a later time, why hadn't she been notified? She checked her phone to see if she had missed messages. Nothing.

The security guard seemed uneasy. "The king's widow is too distraught to have the reading today."

Iliana resisted the urge to roll her eyes. This was a maneuver by Stella, perhaps to shut out what family she could. "It's the reading of a will. Everyone involved is distraught in some manner." Even saying the words, she knew it hadn't been the security guard's call to postpone the reading.

She felt Demetrius behind her. "What's the problem?" he asked.

She looked over her shoulder. He appeared stern and taciturn. "The reading of the will is being delayed because the king's widow is distraught."

The man at the security desk shrank away from Demetrius. The disapproval in his eyes was clear. If

Iliana didn't know Demetrius better, she may have had the same reaction.

Spiro, the king's youngest son, shoved open the glass doors to the entrance of the building and stumbled into the lobby. He collected himself and ran his hand through his hair. When he saw Iliana, he moved in her direction. "Let's get this farce over with." He barked the comment into the air.

Was he drunk?

Theodore, Spiro's older brother, was ten seconds behind him. Theodore looked at Spiro with disgust. "What's the matter with you?" Then he waved his hand in front of his nose. "Really, Spiro? It's not even noon and you're a mess. You smell like cheap booze."

Spiro threw his hands wide. "My father died. I'm entitled to a little Scotch to press through the day. It wasn't cheap Scotch—that I can assure you."

Theodore snorted with disdain. "My father is dead, too. I'm not drinking myself into a coma over it. Be a man and stop embarrassing yourself and this family. We've had enough tragedy and bad press to last a decade."

Theodore pulled his brother to the far side of the lobby. They spoke to each other in hushed tones, their body language hostile.

A few minutes later, Emmanuel, the king's oldest son, arrived with his mother, Kaliope. When Georgia, Spiro and Theodore's mother, arrived, the king's two former wives stared at each other with contempt.

When the security guard delivered the news that the reading of the will would be postponed, Emmanuel, Georgia and Kaliope started speaking at once.

Spiro and Theodore joined them, adding their questions and accusations about who had caused the delay and why.

Iliana couldn't track the conversation, but it was clear that no one in this group saw eye to eye. She felt like an outsider again, and it was a feeling she hated. Maria had implied the family would work as a team, one united front, but it didn't seem that was the case now. Money made people greedy and apparently made them forget what was important.

Demetrius was quietly watching. His eyes were surveying the group, taking in the details, and he was likely assessing alliances and weaknesses. The security guard looked overwhelmed, and the noise level in the lobby was deafening.

Iliana felt the beginnings of a headache forming at her temples. She touched her head, wishing she and Demetrius had stayed in Icarus.

"Enough." Though Demetrius didn't speak louder than normal, the lobby went silent. "This is not what any of us wished. You may have noticed that Stella and Maria are missing. Stella must be home nursing her grief." He didn't hide his sarcasm. "But where is Maria?"

Kaliope looked in her designer handbag and withdrew her phone. "My daughter was planning to attend today. I will call her and see what's keeping her." She took a few steps away to make the call.

The group stood in silence, listening to one side of Kaliope's conversation.

A few minutes later, Maria's mother dropped her phone to her side. "I have terrible news. I called

Maria's cell and a stranger answered. She was a nurse at Abele General. Maria is in the hospital. She's been poisoned."

Chapter 6

Iliana was pacing inside their bedroom suite at the hotel in Valencia. Demetrius found it distracting, and not because of the back-and-forth movement. He couldn't take his eyes off his beautiful wife. She was wearing a pair of cotton pants that were loose around the legs and low on her hips and a strappy, tight tank top.

He watched her from his position, propped up in the bed. He liked the straps. He wanted to pull them over her shoulders and see where the night led. Work was constant, but Demetrius forced himself to close his computer early. Iliana may need to talk. She was worried about Maria. So far Maria's condition was stable but critical. The doctors had not yet identified the specific poison used. But his mind wasn't on Maria. Iliana had let her hair out of the tight bun, and it was wild and loose around her shoulders.

Demetrius wanted her and he wanted her now. He tried to check his reaction, tried to be sensitive about how she was feeling. "Iliana, it will be okay."

She whirled to face him. "Stella will take everything. Everything. Including the lives of my siblings. Nicholas is dead, and who knows what will happen to Maria?"

Demetrius had the NSS gathering what information they could about Maria's poisoning. They were canvassing the area around her house, looking for someone who may have seen a stranger in the neighborhood that morning or anything else unusual. "It's premature to accuse Stella. Do you have proof she was involved?"

Iliana glared at him. "Proof? You want proof? It's called logic."

If Stella was responsible, she wasn't acting alone. "I am working on the situation."

She narrowed her eyes at him. "How? How are you working on it?"

Gathering intel. Surveillance. Information from the police force. "I have ways of obtaining evidence that others do not."

"Spying. What about the will? What if Stella takes everything?"

"I thought it didn't matter to you."

It had started to matter to Iliana when Maria had sat across from her and asked for help. Nurturing others was in Iliana's blood, and now that she was involved, she wanted to help her siblings.

She wrapped her arms around her midsection. "It matters."

"Why?"

She threw up her hands. "You want me to care about it and now you're questioning why I care?"

"I want to know how you think." The insight might help his cause.

She inclined her head. "The king left his children what he thought they deserved or needed. If I am named marchioness of Agot, I can do good. I can donate the money or give the land to an animal shelter or an organic farm."

He appreciated her originality. "You don't want to keep anything for yourself?"

"Since I don't know what I'll inherit and I don't know what's involved with the title, how can I know that?"

"You may be surprised how much more good you could do with your title."

"Who is the current marchioness?" she asked.

"No one. The title is held in reserve by the king until he decides to name someone to power."

She frowned.

The lights flickered and then the room went dark, save for Demetrius's computer screen.

Demetrius didn't like the darkness and what it could mean. He took Iliana's hand and led her to the in-room safe. "Stay with me."

Demetrius handed her his phone, and Iliana aimed the light from the screen over the safe's keypad. Demetrius opened the safe, removed his guns, checked that they were loaded and grabbed his shoulder holster from the dresser drawer. He put it on and slid both guns into it.

"What exactly are you doing?" she asked, sounding appalled.

He was protecting her, like he had promised to do. "Lights went out."

"Probably a power surge," she said.

They had rolling brownouts and blackouts in Acacia. This wasn't normal in Valencia. Iliana handed him his phone. It vibrated with a message.

Two of his servicemen were investigating the cause of the power outage. The others stayed at their post outside the door. "Let's move."

"Why? Where are we going?"

"If this is another assassination attempt, the assassin will have night-vision goggles. I do not. I am not planning to sit in our hotel room and wait for someone to kill us." It was a defensible position, except they were penned in. He had only so many bullets and could only take on a certain number of attackers while ensuring Iliana's safety.

Demetrius opened the front door. His servicemen were gone, a bad sign since their last message had communicated otherwise. Demetrius peered around the corner and looked into the hallway. It was dark and empty except for the emergency lights that lined the hallway and the shadows in between.

Keeping Iliana behind him, they walked to the stairwell. Demetrius looked inside through the narrow window on the door and listened. Silence. They entered, Demetrius listening for footsteps on the concrete.

They moved down the stairs. After the turn in the staircase, Demetrius's battle instinct roared. His serviceman was slumped against the wall, bleeding from a bullet wound in his head. He tamped down his rage and anger, knowing emotions had no place in war. Demetrius checked his pulse. "He's dead."

Killing one of his men was suicide for the murderer. Demetrius would shoot to kill anyone who came at him or Iliana.

"What should we do?" Iliana asked.

Demetrius wouldn't leave his man for long. He'd return for him when it was safe. "I'll take you somewhere I know you can't be harmed, and then I'll come back for him."

They heard footsteps on the stairs and Demetrius pointed up. He practically carried Iliana up the stairs and they entered the floor where their room was located. Two men were in the hallway, holding guns.

Pinned between two killers in the hallway and an indeterminate number of men in the stairwell, Demetrius went with the odds. He turned a hall table on its side. "Get down." He pushed Iliana on her hands and knees behind it. "Keep your head covered."

He moved down the hall, one gun in hand and unsnapped the other in case he needed it quickly. One of the intruders turned toward him and took aim. Demetrius got off the first shot. The noise had the other man swinging a gun in his direction, and a third man rushed from the room Demetrius had been sharing with his wife.

Demetrius shot them. One in the heart, one in the head. Repeat. They wouldn't get past him to hurt Iliana. Their target could be him or her or both.

Demetrius checked that the hallway was clear and hurried back to Iliana. He didn't know how many assailants there were. While he didn't want her in the middle of gunfire, he didn't want her alone, either.

He extended his hand to her. "There's another stairwell. We'll go that way."

Keeping her tucked close to him, they rushed into the stairwell. Having her close felt good, and she wasn't shrugging away from his touch. She stayed next to him, gripping his shirt. He wished she was wearing more than her thin tank top, but he couldn't stop to worry about her attire.

After descending two flights, Demetrius opened the door to the hall. After a quick visual sweep, they entered. Some of the hotel guests were milling around in their pajamas and sweatshirts, robes and slippers.

The holster on his shoulders would make others uneasy, and Demetrius tried to blend in. They followed others to the lobby, where hotel employees were offering reassurances that the power issue was being handled and they'd called maintenance. They seemed to be unaware of the shooters on the top floor or how much danger they could be in.

Demetrius led Iliana to the kitchen. The assassins could be searching the crowd for them. Behind the kitchen was the service hallway. A white light flashed, illuminating the path to the exit. Jogging, Demetrius shoved open the metal door and they hurried outside. The night air hit him, and the smell of gunpowder in his nose dissipated.

"What do we do now? Where can we go?" Iliana asked. The back entrance was near the large and now-silent HVAC systems. It provided cover from the parking lot.

"We'll stay away from the people trying to kill us."

Iliana held out her hands. "Demetrius, just stop for a second." She leaned against the brick hotel and ran a shaky hand through her hair. From nerves or the chill of the night, Demetrius wasn't sure.

"You killed those men," she said.

He had. They'd given him no choice. "You were supposed to be hiding behind the table." He hadn't wanted her to see him take another life. But with her own life at stake, it hadn't been the right time for sorting his options. Moreover, he didn't know where his servicemen were. He feared they were dead.

"Regardless of what I was supposed to be doing, I saw what you did."

"They would have killed me if I had not killed them."

"You didn't hesitate. You looked so cold."

He'd had his eyes on his targets. Whenever he used his gun, he was focused. He didn't shoot men in error. Every pull of the trigger was deliberate and purposeful. "You couldn't see my face."

Her eyes were moist. "You looked back at me once. Your face was emotionless."

If he had looked at her, it was to check for threats from behind. "I was protecting my wife. Crisis is not a time for emotion."

"But you're always in crisis."

He didn't feel that way. Responding to attacks and threats had been part of his life since he was a teenager. It was a sad truth. "When I married you, I wasn't in crisis."

"You married me to help you out of another catastrophe, the details of which you are keeping secret."

Demetrius glanced over his shoulder. Though it had to happen at some point, now was not the time to have a heartfelt discussion. They were out of the hotel but not necessarily out of danger. "We can't stand around debating my reasons or what crisis this may be. We need to move somewhere safe." He took her hand. "Let's go."

She shook him off. "I'm not going with you. I can't live my life this way."

Staying wasn't an option. "Regardless of what you want, you are who you are. Your connection to the king brought this forth."

"My connection to the king or my connection to you?"

Why did she want to discuss this now? Didn't she understand the urgency of the situation? "I won't deny that the assailants could have been gunning for me. But an assailant came to your house in Acacia before we were married. That had nothing to do with me."

Iliana started to cry. Demetrius was startled. He didn't know what to do. "Stop crying."

She looked at him through reddened eyes. "What? Stop crying?" She started crying harder.

"I don't know what to say to you when you cry."

"Are you a robot? Can't you offer comfort to another human being?"

He could. But the men under his command didn't cry. He couldn't remember the last time he had cried. He hadn't been around a crying person in decades. "Tell me what's wrong and I'll fix it. Then, you won't have a reason to cry."

She shook her head, looking miserable. That socked him in the gut. "You know what's wrong."

If he knew, he wouldn't have told her to explain it. "Is this about the king?"

She didn't reply.

"Our marriage?"

Silence.

"Maria?"

Still nothing.

"Come on, give me a clue."

"Maybe it's about all of it, Demetrius. Maybe it's that you came into my life and you've shaken everything around and now I feel lost and afraid and sad."

Demetrius understood it was a lot for her to cope with, but it bothered him more than a little to know she was distressed. When he had thought she was angry at him for withholding information about her father, her anger was an emotion he could deal with. He could argue and offer compromises or work with her. But loss, fear and sadness? How did he deal with those? "You aren't lost. You're my wife and the queen of Acacia's cousin and the future marchioness of Agot."

"Wife is a new position for me. I am not biologically related to the queen, apparently. If Stella has her way, I will inherit nothing."

"You don't need to be afraid. I won't let anyone hurt you."

"Yet I'm standing outside a hotel, cold and on the run from killers."

"Which is why I need you to come with me."

"Come with you where?" she asked.

"I will find a safe place for us." The sound of sirens filled the air. "Please, Iliana."

This time when he extended his hand, she took it.

Demetrius selected a car in the parking lot. He could have looked for his car, but that could be wired to explode. A generic older sedan was his pick. He got lucky—someone had left their door unlocked. Calling on ancient, rarely used skills, he hot-wired the car and it roared to life.

Iliana was standing on the sidewalk, her mouth agape.

"Get in!" he shouted.

Iliana looked around, hesitating. They didn't have time to debate this again.

"Please," Demetrius said, knowing a little softness could go a long way with his wife.

Iliana climbed into the passenger seat and fastened her seat belt. Demetrius's phone buzzed, and he handed it to her.

"What does it say?"

"Your guards are looking for you. They are injured but safe. They have their fallen comrade with them."

Relief and pride for his team's actions passed over him. "Ask for their password to confirm it's them." If they were dead, though their phones were secure, they could be used to track Demetrius.

She typed the question. Once their identity was confirmed, she sent them a message that she and Demetrius were safe and to meet at the airport.

Ten minutes later, they were on the highway, headed toward the designated rendezvous.

Iliana couldn't name the emotions passing through her. She felt as if she were coming apart at the seams. She needed something to ground her. During her college days, whenever she had felt confused, she had called her parents. That was no longer an option.

"I have a request," she said to Demetrius. "I don't

want to go to Icarus. I want to go to Kontos." Her biological mother had been born there.

If she visited the place where her mother was born, she may feel a connection to her. It was silly to think about it in those terms, but learning her roots might help her rebuild what she had lost.

"Your birth mother's hometown," Demetrius said. "Why? What's there?"

Couldn't he take her without question? Why didn't he understand her emotional needs? She had thought their chemistry and intensity equated to emotional intimacy, but now she saw their marriage differently. It had been a hasty, hormonal and haphazard decision, and Demetrius's ulterior motive—still a mystery to her—was behind it all. "I want to know who my mother was. More than her name, I want to know who she was as a person and what her life may have been like."

"She's dead. Going to Kontos won't change that." His voice was hard. He thought it would be a mistake to take her there.

Iliana couldn't back down, not when this meant so much to her. "Someone had to know her in her hometown."

"It was a long time ago, Iliana." This time his voice was gentler.

She wasn't ready to let it go. "There has to be information for me in Kontos. Maybe my grandmother is alive. An aunt. Someone."

Demetrius's mouth quirked to the left slightly. It was his tell.

"Tell me what you know." She had no patience for his hiding information, not regarding this matter.

Demetrius shook his head. "Don't go to Kontos."

Suspicion crept over her. Sometimes being married to the man who knew everything was annoying to the point of madness. "You could tell me what you know and save me the effort."

Demetrius pressed down harder on the gas pedal. "I would rather you hear this from someone else."

"You told me the morning after our wedding that my biological parents weren't the people who raised me, but now when I am asking you for information about my birth mother, you're close lipped."

"The timing made it essential for me to tell you about the king. I did not want to tell you the morning after our wedding. Believe it or not, I had hoped we would have some time as a honeymooning couple."

Her heart thumped a little harder at his words. "This may not matter to you, or you may feel as if we have all the time in the world and I can find out terrible things in due time, but I want to know now. It is essential to me."

Demetrius glanced at her. "Persephone Paphiti was from a broken home. She was raised by her grandmother until she died when Persephone was five. She was briefly in the foster-care system until she became a scholarship student at a boarding school, where she lived from the age of six to the age of seventeen. When she met the king, she was eighteen and working at an ice-cream store."

"That doesn't sound so bad," Iliana said.

"Just a minute." Demetrius took out his phone, flipped it to speaker and spoke to someone in French. She didn't understand French, but she understood her name.

"What was that about?" she asked.

"Someone will meet us at the airport and bring clothes and essentials."

"Does that mean we're going to Kontos?" she asked.

At his swift nod, surprise and delight rolled through her. He had agreed to her request. She had thought it would require far more persuasion. "Thank you. This means a lot to me."

"You're looking for family. You lost your parents in a terrible car accident. Serena is busy with her new family. The king died, and his family hasn't been welcoming to you. I understand what you hope to find. But I want to warn you that Kontos will not make you feel better. It won't bring you closure."

"I'm not expecting that."

"Sure you are. The heart is reckless with hope and imagines some exists in the darkest hour, even when it is impossible."

His voice was haunting. "Are you speaking from personal experience?"

"I am speaking what I know. I will help you look for family and ties and connections if that is your desire, but you'll see that I am your family, too."

His words touched her. She had been feeling adrift and he was throwing her a lifeline. "Do you mean that?" she asked.

"I do. When I spoke those two words at our wedding, I meant them then as I do now."

She reached for his hand, slid hers into it and laid her head on his shoulder. "I'm sorry I accused you of not knowing what comfort was."

"I was honest with you. I am glad the truth brings you relief."

* * *

Aboard the private jet, they were flying to Kontos. Something had shifted between them. Demetrius didn't believe she would find the answers she was looking for, but he was willing to indulge her.

Iliana was looking at him differently. She was glancing at him almost shyly. It reminded him of the way they had circled each other when she was the queen of Acacia's personal secretary and he was the pain in the queen's ass.

He wanted to move them onto that ground again. He wanted to recapture what they'd had the night he'd proposed and they'd married.

Testing a theory and fueled on hope, he shut off his computer and set it to the side. He gestured to his guards to give him privacy. They turned to look out the window. It was the best they could do within the confines of the plane.

He took Iliana's hand, pulling her into the circle of his arms. He nuzzled her neck, and she leaned into him. "Come to bed with me," he whispered.

She didn't answer with words, instead letting her body language agree. He led her into the plane's private bedroom. She arched her body into his, her hips brushing his, her fingers raking through his hair.

"You gave me my way," she said.

"In regards to your travel request, yes," he said.

"Can I have my way now?"

She lit him up so quickly, he could barely form a cohesive response. "You are my wife. I will not deny you."

"This doesn't mean everything is better," she said.

"I understand that," he said. "But it's a chance. I'll always take a chance with you."

She fisted his hair and brought his mouth to hers in a possessive and hungry kiss. Waves of emotion poured off her.

She pulled at his shirt, dragging it over his head while he kicked off his pants. Cool air rushed over his skin.

She ran her fingers over his shoulders and his chest and down his abdomen. Her skin was soft against his. Moving her hands down his arms, she set his hands on her hips. He gave them a light squeeze and positioned himself against her, lining up their bodies to create perfect friction.

She took his face in her hands and kissed him, long and hot and hard.

He slipped his arms around her waist and anchored her to him, then slid back on the bed, bringing her on top of him. She brought her knees to either side of his hips and positioned her hands on each side of his head. Iliana was a sexy, passionate woman, and he was seeing that passion in action.

He had missed this, missed touching her and kissing her.

Demetrius ran his hands up her tight thighs. He slid his hand into her pants. She removed them, tossing them on the floor. His fingers brushed the strips of fabric on her hips. Lace? Some textured material, but he didn't want it in his way.

He tugged the fabric aside, but it wouldn't stretch enough to give him the access he needed. He tore it away from her body.

She giggled. "That was efficient."

She reached between them and stroked him. Pulling him out of his boxers, she positioned him at her entrance. She wiggled, and the heat between her legs made him want to thrust in hard and deep. He kept his control, knowing this needed to be on her terms.

He didn't have to wait long to have satisfaction. She impaled herself in one smooth stroke. Then she let out a sigh and her hair fell forward over her face. He shifted to brace his feet on the floor. Then he used the leverage to move them together.

She pushed her hair away and gathered it in her hands as she rode him, rocking her hips and letting out moans of pleasure. The sight was beautiful and erotic. He reached to cup her breasts, pinching her nipples lightly and evoking more sounds of excitement from her. He was close to release and he counted backward slowly, needing for her to come first.

Then she leaned forward, setting her arm on his side. He smelled soap, spicy and sweet. He had never known a woman to smell as good as she did. She dropped a kiss on his lips. The friction and the heat between them imploded, and he held her right while she came. A few seconds later, he followed her into oblivion.

This was what he remembered about his wedding night, the passion and the chemistry, the lazy, unhurried exploration.

"You don't have to stay with me in Kontos," she said. She was spread over him, her hair across him and the pillows.

She was an interesting woman. Independent, and yet he felt like her man, as if she needed him. "You say that while I'm inside you? I'm staying with you in Kontos."

And he was staying with her as her husband.

Kontos was a small town close to the sea on the eastern shores of Valencia. The population was about a thousand people. It had once been a booming fishing town, but now most residents commuted to bigger cities for their jobs. Iliana had learned from an internet search on the flight over that the most notable and historic place in Kontos was the library. It was a beautiful building the residents had constructed from stones collected from the bottom of the sea, hauling the rocks to the center of town in wheelbarrows and wagons. Standing in its location for more than a hundred years, the library had been retrofitted with modern conveniences, water and electricity. It sounded like a place she'd love to visit.

Their plane had landed at a nearby private airport, and they were driving the remainder of the distance. They were traveling in a caravan, four cars in total. She assumed the additional cars were decoys for security.

"I have a couple leads on people who may have known your mother," Demetrius said.

Iliana couldn't hide her surprise. Her husband seemed to know everything, but he wasn't exactly an open book. "How did you find that information?"

"I have sources looking into the matter."

She ventured to guess he wouldn't be sharing those sources with her.

"Would you like help investigating the leads?" he

asked, closing the distance between them and taking her hand.

Not a good idea. "I can handle this. If you come with me, you'll scare everyone into silence." In some situations, Demetrius's strength was a huge advantage. Since she had nothing to offer in return, she had to rely on the kindness of strangers for information, and she might have more success with her own methods than his intimidating ones.

"I don't scare people," he said, sounding a little grumpy about it.

He released her hand, and she instantly missed his touch.

"Sure you do. You give someone a look and they go silent or they cower, afraid of what you may do to them," she said.

Demetrius frowned at her statement. She had heard of people speaking to Demetrius and being thrown in jail for offending him, but her experience had been different. He didn't laugh often, but he had a sense of humor. She was given the breadth to speak plainly to him without fear of recourse.

He handed her a piece of paper, and she glanced at it. Three names and three addresses. "Thank you."

"Security stays with you. No exceptions."

"Ask them to hang back, okay?" For the same reason she didn't want Demetrius along, she didn't want his security intimidating people.

"They will keep the greatest distance possible while keeping you safe," he said. "I will keep my phone close. Call if you need anything."

She kissed him on the cheek. Before she could

exit the car, he snagged her hand and kissed her full on the mouth.

"That's a proper kiss," he said.

"Wish me luck," she said. She took her handbag and phone.

Demetrius drove off, and the other car remained nearby. Following her phone's GPS, she walked to the first address on the list, aware of Demetrius's guards on foot behind her. The address led to a pharmacy with a small retail store in the front. She approached the salesclerk and tried to appear confident. "Hi. I'm looking for Azar Hondros."

The woman, who had long gray hair with pink highlights, looked at her fluorescent-yellow nails and then shook her head. "Sorry, you're out of luck. He won't be back until next week. He's on vacation with his family. Who are you, his mistress?"

Disappointment streamed through her as she tried not to be offended by the woman's assumption. "I don't know him personally. I am looking for someone who may have known my mother. Her name was Persephone Paphiti."

The woman frowned, continuing to inspect her hands. "Sorry. I've only worked here a few months. I hardly know anyone in town." She leaned forward. "But you know, you should talk to Katerina Panagopoulos. She works in Kyklades, the ice-cream store. Well, *works* is an exaggeration. She mostly hangs out there, giving unsolicited advice and yelling at people who break her rules."

Katerina Panagopoulos wasn't a name on her list. "Her rules?"

"Wearing white socks with dark shoes. Talking

loudly on your cell phone. Fashion and etiquette
rules," the salesclerk said.

Iliana could be fashionable and polite. "I will talk
to Katerina Panagopoulos. Thank you."

As Iliana walked toward Kyklades, she wondered
if her mother had ever walked this same path. Where
had her mother lived? What had she liked to do with
her leisure time? Did Iliana have anything in common with her?

Her mother had died more than thirty years ago.
Would Iliana find anyone who remembered her?
Demetrius had found three names connected to her
mother, but how close had they been to Persephone?

The businesses in town seemed to be clustered
around a few streets. Iliana arrived at the ice-cream
shop. A woman wearing a floor-length floral dress
sat outside the front windows at a small table covered
by a green-and-white umbrella. As she approached,
the woman shot her an up-and-down appraising look.
"Nice outfit."

Did that mean she passed the fashion test? Dis-
tracted by Katerina's etiquette rules, Iliana almost
forgot her manners. "Thank you. I'm Iliana DeSante.
I am looking for Katerina Panagopoulos."

"You found me," she said. She stood and picked up
a wicker hat from the table and placed it on her head.
What Iliana had thought was a dress was actually a
jumpsuit.

"You don't look familiar, and your accent is strange,"
Katerina said.

"I'm not from around here. I'm looking for information about Persephone Paphiti."

Katerina narrowed her eyes. Iliana realized she

was holding her breath. She let it out and relaxed her shoulders.

"I remember someone with that name," Katerina said.

"What do you remember about her?" Iliana asked.

"Bright girl. Long, dark red hair and big brown eyes."

That was a generic description and didn't tell Iliana anything about her mother, about who she was. "Did you know her?"

"I did. I went to school with her. She was two years younger than me. Too adventurous for her own good. She and another girl, Helena Kariolis, used to stay at the school even over winter and spring break."

Excitement thundered through her. Finally, some actual information about her mother.

Helena Kariolis was another of the names on her list. Her mother had likely stayed at the school because she had nowhere else to go. "What do you mean by too adventurous?" Iliana asked. She didn't want to uncover bad things about her mother, but she had to have tough skin about this. It dawned on her that if her mother had slept with a married man, she didn't have a perfect moral compass. Then again, who did? Love and passion had a way of scrambling logic and ethics.

"Persephone used to sneak out and visit the boys' boarding school across the lake. She missed curfew. She had flowers in her room weekly, sent by her latest admirers. She would have been expelled, but she was a fast talker. Sweet and genuinely kind to the people around her. She cared about people's feelings, and if she was asked for help, she gave it freely. It was easy to be jealous of her but hard not to like her."

Iliana smiled and felt relief. The picture Katerina was painting of her mother wasn't so bad. "You mentioned she had a friend, Helena Kariolis. What do you know about her?"

Katerina gave her a strange look. "You should talk to her yourself. Helena Kariolis has her vacation home around here. If you're lucky, she might be home if court is not in session. But she's a busy woman, being a judge and everything."

Iliana tried not to let her hopes shoot up too high. She and Katerina talked a little longer, and when the conversation circled around to the same stories about her mother, Iliana politely disengaged.

She met her security guards at the corner of the block and asked them to drive her to Helena Kariolis's home.

When she arrived at the designated address, there was no answer. Disappointed that she was striking out at her leads, she had security drive her to the last address on the list Demetrius had given her.

Ladonna Caras lived in a small white Cape Cod located across the bridge, on the side of town that seemed more run-down. The streets were empty and the area had a dismal feeling to it. A light in the front window advertised fortunes in bright red letters. Not getting out of the car yet, she called Demetrius. He picked up the phone on the second ring. "Having fun? Learn anything that I should know?"

How much had he known before sending her out to look for information? "Nothing important yet. Do you know that the last address on the paper you gave me is for a fortune-teller?"

"Yes."

"You cannot believe that a fortune-teller will see into the past."

He laughed. "I don't know what her abilities may be. But she was friendly with your mother."

"I'll see if she'll talk to me. I've struck out with the other two names on the list. One is on vacation, and the other wasn't home. But I ran into someone who knew my mother. She had nice things to say about her."

"That's great, Iliana. Don't give up. If you don't find what you need today, we'll try again."

Iliana wanted to know everything she could now. She said her goodbyes to Demetrius and stepped out of the car. She took the cracked cement stairs to the black front door. The house was in need of a sanding and paint job. The railing was rusting and the door was loose on its hinges, squeaking as she opened it.

"Hello?"

An attractive woman with jet-black hair and dramatic makeup stepped out from behind a purple paisley curtain. "Greetings." She folded her hands in front of her, the dozens of gold bangles on her wrists jingling, and said nothing else.

"I'm Iliana DeSante. Maybe you knew I was coming."

Ladonna didn't smile at Iliana's joke.

"I'm looking for information about my mother," Iliana said.

Ladonna smiled. "Please come in and sit down." She looked out the front window. "You travel with armed escorts? Are you with the police?"

"Not law enforcement. My husband works for the government." It was the simplest way to explain it.

Ladonna nodded as if she understood. "Tell me what knowledge you seek."

"I want to know any information you have about Persephone Paphiti."

Ladonna frowned. "First, I will give you a reading. Then I will tell you the rest."

Iliana reached for her wallet. She knew how this game was played. She laid some money on the table. "You'll get the other half when you tell me about Persephone Paphiti." Worried that Ladonna would try to defraud her if she knew how important the information was, she tried to stay cool.

Ladonna frowned. "Set your hands on the table, palms up."

Iliana did as she was asked.

Ladonna pointed to her wedding rings. "You are newly married. Congratulations."

"Thank you."

"Except it's not a happy marriage."

Was this a therapy session or a psychic reading? Maybe Ladonna's clients got both. Iliana didn't want to talk about Demetrius, but dancing around it would prolong this discussion. "It's had its ups and downs." A neutral enough statement.

"He is dynamite in the bedroom."

Iliana felt the blush creep over her cheeks. "Yes." How had Ladonna known that? Maybe women made hasty decisions about marrying men who were fantastic in bed.

"But he's disappointed you in other ways."

A generic statement, but true. "Yes."

Ladonna waited.

Iliana wanted to push through this part quickly. "He isn't a big fan of telling the whole truth."

"He has not cheated on you. He will not cheat on you."

Iliana didn't think he'd cheated, but she was intrigued and felt herself getting pulled in. "What makes you say that?"

"He's a powerful man." She pointed to the car. "You are a strong woman. He had his pick of women, but he picked you because of your strength, your heart and your mind. That's what will keep him coming back for more. It will always be more."

Iliana shivered. "I am not sure the marriage will last." She whispered the words. It was a fear that had crossed her mind when she thought about how different they were and how much they had to overcome.

Ladonna touched Iliana's middle fingers. "It will last. He will be faithful. Even if you leave him, he will not stray. He will pursue you for the rest of his life."

"As you said, he's a powerful man with his pick of women. After he gets what he wants from me, he'll move on." Ladonna could spout whatever pseudo-romantic notions about devotion and forever, but Iliana lived in the real world. In her world, her husband had lied to her about something important. He was using her for a purpose, and when that purpose was met, he would continue with his life with or, more likely, without her.

"What do you think he wants?" Ladonna asked, wrinkling her nose.

Iliana pulled her hands away, feeling exposed. "I don't know. But everything my husband does is for a purpose. He did not marry me because he loves me.

In fact, he hasn't said those words to me." Another truth that was hurtful and difficult to admit. What was it about Ladonna that had her spilling secrets? She had come to find information, not wear her heart on her sleeve.

"But you feel his love," Ladonna said. "In your heart, you feel his love for you."

At times she did. When they had started their relationship, before they were a couple, it had been exciting and fresh and new. Whenever she had heard that he was coming to the castle, she had felt jittery and anxious in anticipation. When she saw him, she felt overcome with desire. He had seemed mysterious and strong and wonderful. They would exchange private looks, and he would sometimes stop at her desk to whisper to her, a secret message between the two of them. "Sometimes."

Ladonna's eyes opened wide. "You need to be careful. There are people who want to hurt you."

She knew that. It was why she was traveling with security. "Can you tell me about Persephone Paphiti now?"

Ladonna blinked as if trying to clear her head. She brought her hands to her temples. "You claim to be Persephone's daughter, but that cannot be true. Her daughter died with her in childbirth."

"That was a lie told to keep me safe. How did you know my mother?"

Ladonna stood and paced the room. "She was my foster sister. Just for a few months before she was taken to boarding school. I felt bad for her. She didn't have a family. A lot of girls were jealous that she and Helena received the scholarships, but it was sad that they didn't have anything else." Ladonna folded her arms. "She just wanted a family. She told me that once."

Iliana was familiar with the sentiment. "Do you think she ever found it?"

Ladonna shrugged. "I don't know. Like I said, I only knew her those months after her grandmother died and spoke to her infrequently after that. She was pretty sad and quiet. Is that why you came to Kontos? Looking for family, too?"

Iliana supposed she had. Hers and her mother's lives ran in a strange parallel, and now Iliana felt it had come full circle. She was lonely and involved with a man who may not be able to give her the future she wanted. She coveted a family of her own.

"Did Persephone have other family?" Iliana asked.

Ladonna shook her head. "I'm sorry. I don't think so. It was why she was in foster care. No one else to take her in."

They spoke a few more minutes, but Ladonna wasn't able to share anything new.

"Let me leave you with this piece of advice. Do not be so quick to think you know the heart and thoughts of others. Some in your life wish you harm, but others are truer than you believe."

Iliana wasn't sure what to make of that statement. Was Ladonna talking about her half siblings or Demetrius? Someone else entirely?

Iliana thanked Ladonna and paid her the remainder of her fee. She had hoped to learn more, and, for the briefest second, she had hoped Ladonna would tell her that Persephone had other family.

Iliana exited the psychic's home and climbed into

the back of the car. She called Demetrius, needing to hear his voice, needing a friend. "Can you meet me for a late lunch?"

"Sure. What happened? You sound upset."

Ladonna had stirred emotions in her, and she didn't know how to settle them. "My mother didn't have a family. Ladonna said she wanted one. Maybe that's why she slept with the king. Maybe she wanted to be part of his life, his family."

"That's one theory."

Iliana wanted to believe that her mother had good intentions. "Let's meet at Kyklades, the ice-cream store on Main Street. I saw a sandwich shop across the street."

"I'll be there. See you in thirty minutes."

Iliana communicated her plans to her security. Talking to Demetrius would center her. Maybe he'd have some ideas of how to get in touch with the others from her mother's past. Maybe they would paint a more hopeful picture of her mother, someone with a happy and full life.

Driving across the narrow bridge leading into the heart of Kontos, she felt an impact from behind and the car lurched forward. Iliana twisted in her seat and saw two cars bearing down on them. The first car was moving closer to ram them again, and the second car was speeding up the left side.

"Stay in your seat!" a guard shouted.

Her driver sped up, but the car was struck a second time. Iliana grabbed for her phone. It had been thrown forward. She needed to call Demetrius for help. If she took a picture of the cars, perhaps they could find the person responsible for Nicholas's death and Maria's attack.

"Get down!" her security guard shouted at her.

Iliana covered her head and braced her arms and legs in the back of the car. Shots rang out and glass rained down on her. The car was hit again and fishtailed wildly. Would they be thrown from the bridge?

Chapter 7

The car slammed to an immediate stop. Both her guards climbed out, holding their weapons. Their bulletproof vests were visible, and Iliana prayed they would be safe.

She scrambled for her phone and couldn't find it. She heard shouting and more gunfire. Were Demetrius's guards in danger? The men were trained and skilled, but who were they up against?

She had been left alone in the car. The backseat car door opened and she looked up in surprise, half expecting to see Demetrius.

It was a stranger with a ragged scar across his lips and a tattoo encircling his neck. "Get up!"

Before she had time to react, the tattooed stranger dragged her from the car. Iliana twisted and kicked at him to break free, but his arm was around her waist, holding her tight, squeezing her hard. It was difficult to draw a full breath.

Another car pulled onto the bridge. Would she be forced into the car and taken away? She fought harder. She could disappear in Valencia and no one would find her. Without her phone she couldn't call for help.

Demetrius needed her. She needed him. She bit her attacker's arm. He swore and jerked her to the side. Her brain rattled in her head enough that she felt dizzy.

"Do that again and I'll throw you off the bridge," he said.

She could swim. Then again, surviving the fifty-foot drop onto rocks presented some problems.

Demetrius stepped out of the car. His hands were empty. Of all times to be without a gun! They had been planning to meet for lunch escorted by his security. She couldn't let her husband be harmed. "Demetrius, no! Run!"

The man holding her whirled toward Demetrius, putting her between Demetrius on one side and his guards on the other. Her assailant pushed a gun against her head. "Don't interfere or I'll kill her."

Demetrius's guards had disposed of the other men and were moving in her direction. They looked furious and bloody, as opposed to Demetrius, who appeared unmoved by the entire scene. He was wearing a crisp suit and looked as if he were about to walk into a board meeting, not into a showdown with a killer.

She knew how to read Demetrius now. His coldness, his indifferent facade, masked his plans and his emotions.

Demetrius held out his hands to stop his guards. "He has my wife. Don't provoke him."

It was so unlike Demetrius to take a defensive stance. What was his plan?

"Iliana, are you okay?" Demetrius asked.

"Yes." Except for the gun to her head.

"Let my wife go and I won't kill you," he said calmly.

The man laughed. "This isn't about you, President DeSante. Go back to Icarus and choose a new wife. I have my orders."

Demetrius continued advancing. "You have new orders. Release her."

The gun pressed harder into her temple. "If you don't kill me, the man who hired me will and then send someone else after her. You can't win this battle."

Dark shadows passed over Demetrius's face. Iliana doubted Demetrius ever accepted defeat. He fought until he won. She had never known a man with more grit and determination. "Who hired you?" he asked. Not a casual question; he was composing his hit list. Whoever had done this would pay.

The man walked backward, yanking her with him. She tried to use her shoes to slow their progress, but he was too big and strong. She was close to the edge of the bridge, the steel cables within reach. It would be a simple matter to toss her over.

"A man known as the Ghost makes the arrangements. I don't know his real name or who put the hit out on her." Her assailant was nervous, his words coming out in a stammer. He knew the odds were against him.

Who was the Ghost and where did he get his name?

From having the ability to hide behind his hired assassins? The Coward might be a more suitable name.

Demetrius cracked his knuckles. "I've heard of the Ghost. He hires exceptionally competent criminals. These attempts have been bungling at best. It's missing the hallmarks of the Ghost's work."

Demetrius had said not to provoke the assailant. Why was he criticizing the attempts on her life? The assassin's inability to succeed was why she was still alive.

She smelled sweat and fear and gunpowder. "The Warlord of Icarus is hardly a weak opponent. The Ghost knows this and has assembled many teams."

The Warlord of Icarus? Demetrius wouldn't like that title. It was the first time Iliana had heard it. Demetrius was often portrayed unfairly in international news. But he was a respectable man and had done good work for his people.

Demetrius let out a bark of sharp laughter. "Is that what I'm being called now?"

The man with the gun to her head laughed nervously. "Among other things."

Demetrius shrugged. "Let my wife go. You can die at my hands or take your chances with the Ghost. I'll kill you quickly. That's my best offer."

The assailant didn't respond, but he loosened his grip. Iliana dropped to the ground, unable to fully process what had happened when she heard the sound of gunshots. Three gunshots. She squeezed her eyes closed for a moment, then, not feeling pain, opened them and assessed her body. Had she been hit?

Demetrius was holding a gun, as were his guards. Her assailant was on the bridge, leaning against the cables, bleeding. Was he dead? Iliana stood, her legs weak, and approached him. Could she help? Was it too late?

"Iliana, stop. He is dead." Demetrius put his arms around her and turned her to him. "Come."

"We have to call the police."

"My security will handle it."

"Call for an ambulance," she said.

"Do you need one?" He held her at arm's length and looked her over.

She pointed to the assassin and Demetrius's guards. "He is bleeding. They are bleeding."

Demetrius studied her face. "You're in shock. The man is dead. My servicemen are fine. They will take care of themselves, and I will take care of you."

"Those men tried to run us off the road."

Demetrius led her toward the car he'd arrived in. "They've paid for their mistake."

Iliana tucked herself against him. "They would have killed me."

Demetrius kissed the top of her head. "I know, and I'm sorry. I should not have allowed you to be in this town alone. I should have stayed with you."

He opened the car door for her and helped her inside. She noticed the knees of her pants were torn. She touched the back of her neck and felt wetness. "I'm bleeding."

Demetrius knelt on the ground and looked. "It's not your blood. I will get you cleaned up, okay?"

She could feel it, a panicked tremor in her soul, the inability to wrap her head around what had happened today. She'd come to Kontos to learn about her mother and had instead found herself targeted again by assassins. Demetrius had come to her rescue. Without him, she didn't know where she would be. Gratitude for him swelled inside her. Her hands were shaking and then she realized her entire body was trembling. "This is not okay. Nothing about this is okay. Who is the Ghost?"

Concern was plain on his face. "I will find out."

An angry rush of emotions rose up inside her. "Why does he want me dead?"

"I doubt it's a personal agenda. He's an agent for assassins."

"Did you shoot that man?" Iliana asked.

"Yes."

"You didn't have a gun."

"I always carry protection." He slid her seat belt over her, clicked it into place and then closed the door.

He circled the car and climbed inside. As they drove in silence, Iliana went over the events of the day. Nothing made sense. Her brain felt foggy, and fear trembled through her. Her one pillar of strength and confidence was the last person she expected—her husband.

Demetrius hated seeing Iliana upset. He shouldn't have allowed her to visit Kontos without him. He had hoped his guards would keep her safe, and they had. But if he hadn't shown up, there was no telling how the situation would have played out.

Iliana was distressed about the incident. She kept repeating the same statements about the day and then looking at him as if she wanted him to elaborate on them or confirm she had it right. He wouldn't provide gruesome details that would haunt her. He offered her facts that may help her understand what had happened without terrorizing her more.

Inside their hotel room, Demetrius bolted the door and led her to the bathtub, trying to keep her from looking in the mirror. She had blood smeared on her neck and face, and the back of her clothes was spattered with it.

He helped her undress, shoving her clothes into a plastic laundry bag. He turned on the shower. When it ran hot, he escorted her inside. She stood under the spray for a long time.

Demetrius watched her, afraid she would have a breakdown. She was a strong woman and she had spirit, but this would catch up with her. It had to.

Steam billowed from the shower, filling the bathroom. He felt only concern for her in this moment. She was naked, and normally that was the starting gun for his libido, but this time the emotions he confronted were entirely different. He didn't have a name for them, but they were more complex than lust and heat.

He ran the water in the tub and dumped in some purple bubble bath from the amenity tray the hotel had provided.

"That's too much." She was watching him from inside the glass-enclosed shower.

"What is too much?" he asked. He was careful to keep his tone neutral. He was upset by what had happened today, but he didn't want her to misunderstand his anger. It was directed at the people who had tried to harm her.

"The bubble bath. You poured in half the bottle."

He'd never taken a bubble bath. "I'll buy you more.

Why don't you soak in the bath and I'll order some wine?"

"I don't want wine." Despite the heat and humidity in the bathroom, her teeth were chattering.

"Tea?"

She shook her head. "I feel sick."

"Just the bath, then. We'll see how you feel after."

He helped her from the shower and into the bath. She sank down, and he found a washcloth and soap. He washed her back, cringing at the memory of the blood that had covered her. Did she want to talk about it? What could he say to make her feel better?

When he was in battle with his men, during any war, he didn't talk about how he felt. He focused on success and winning and finding strength in the face of insurmountable odds. He rarely asked a soldier how he felt about death, injuries or violence. He helped him concentrate on the tasks leading toward his goal.

But Iliana wasn't a soldier. Her life wasn't filled with violence. "Can I do anything for you?" he asked.

"You are being very kind." She leaned her head against his hand, and he brushed her face lightly.

"Iliana, you mean a lot to me." The words felt garbled in his throat.

"Because of my inheritance."

Not just that. She had always meant more than that. Her ability to help Alexei was important to him, but when he had met her, he had been captivated by her. "That's not true. I've told you before that you are important to me."

"That's good, Demetrius, because sometimes I think I could fall in love with you. Sometimes I think I already have."

He couldn't think of a time he'd heard that expression from a woman. His mother had not shown him affection. He'd had lovers, but none of them had spoken those words. He hadn't wanted them to because he couldn't love them back. But now could he?

Parts of him were dark and twisted. He could be cold and mean and unforgiving. He worried how Iliana would react if she knew about that side of him. "I would like a wife who loved me."

Not even on the scale of what he wanted to say, but even this admission was harder to articulate than he'd thought. He spoke his mind. He was blunt. Why were words so difficult now?

"Have you ever loved someone?" Iliana asked.

His brother came to mind. Casimir, his oldest friend. People he had established relationships with, who had earned his loyalty and respect. He cared about Iliana. She was important to him. But romantic love? "I know how to love."

Iliana closed her eyes, and Demetrius leaned against the wall next to her, leaving his arm on the rim of the tub. She interlaced their fingers, her warm, wet hand heating his. She had stopped trembling.

He relaxed and stopped trying to think what to say. Words weren't needed. This was enough.

The Ghost was an urban legend who had existed for the past decade, or so Demetrius had believed. No one, not even Amon or his NSS spies, could confirm the identity of the man who offered his services under that alias. Demetrius had worked with some dark and dangerous people in his life, but to his knowledge, he hadn't crossed paths with the Ghost before today.

Demetrius could think of a dozen masterminds who had used street names to establish their reputation. They were inevitably killed or cut down by the competition. It took more than whispers on the street to maintain a lucrative business and stay alive.

With a name, Demetrius could focus his effort on finding the person hunting Iliana and her siblings. If the Ghost was taking out a hit on Iliana, that was a direct assault against him and that could not be tolerated. Demetrius had his spies spreading that message on the street. Let the Ghost think twice about coming at him. The Warlord of Icarus had his own reputation.

"Maria is awake," Iliana said from her position on the hotel room couch. He'd obtained another phone for her, and she had been using it to stay in touch with the hospital about Maria's condition.

Demetrius wasn't thrilled about staying in Valencia. He could keep Iliana safer in Icarus. Working in unknown territory made a job more complex for any assassin. Icarus would be unfamiliar, and attacking the president's wife in her homeland was far more perilous.

Demetrius would ramp up his security, and he'd err on the side of caution when it came to Iliana.

"I need to see her," Iliana said. She sounded desperate.

Demetrius looked up from his computer. "I think we should return to Icarus. You can visit with Maria when I have a better handle on the Ghost."

Iliana circled the hotel desk and pushed his rolling chair away. She sat on his lap and linked her hands around his neck. "I know what happened on the bridge was bad, but I need to see her. She might know who poisoned her. She might have more information about the Ghost. She's my sister."

Demetrius wasn't convinced that Maria was trustworthy. She and Iliana didn't know each other well, and Maria seemed quick to ask Iliana for favors. "What happened today was a well-planned attack. You don't know how long you were followed." He had spoken at length to his servicemen, and they had not noticed anyone on their tail until they'd left the psychic's.

"I would assume not long because the assassins had other opportunities to kill me and they didn't."

It was distracting to have her on his lap, her body so close. "That doesn't make me feel better."

How had the assassins known where Iliana would be? How were they tracking her movements? He'd swept the car and her belongings for bugs. The Ghost's network could be extensive, and perhaps anyone willing to pay for information could find it for sale.

"The fortune-teller says you are good in bed," Iliana said. "Does that make you feel better?"

It was a little upshot to his ego. "It's more important to me to hear what you think. Besides, how would she know that?" He would have remembered sleeping with a psychic.

"Educated guess. I didn't deny it," Iliana said.

He wasn't sure where to go with that. "Is this your way of stroking my ego so I'll agree to go to the hospital to see Maria?"

"If we go now, I promise to thank you properly tonight."

"That is an offer impossible to turn down." It was increasingly harder for him to say no to Iliana. She was sweet and smart, and he wanted her to be happy. If he agreed to take her to the hospital now, he could look forward to a night alone with his wife at home. "But then we return to Icarus."

"Thank you, Demetrius, for understanding what this means to me." She kissed him, but the gesture was unsure, tentative. He wanted to kiss her hard and fast and bend her over the desk, but he calmed himself. She had been through a trauma. He wanted to be a good man and a good husband. She didn't want him pawing her now.

This was about comfort. He slipped his arms around her waist and held her close. He rubbed his nose along her jawline and stroked her thigh softly.

"You'd tell me if you were worried."

A command, but also a question. He sensed she wasn't speaking her mind.

"You know most of the problems worrying me."

"I want to know all the problems on your mind."

"Why?"

"So I can fix them."

She shook her head. "You can't fix all my problems."

He refused to believe that. "I can try."

She stared into his eyes, searching. "If you mean that, then I want to know the truth."

She wanted him to tell her the reasons he was interested in her inheritance. He felt the words rising to his tongue. Speaking them might bring them closer. Where did he start? Did he tell her about his mother? Could he tell her about his family, his sick father and how he worried he had those same demons living inside him? "I have secrets."

She ran the back of her fingers down the side of his face. "Tell me what they are, and we'll share them."

What if he told her and she decided she couldn't live with a man like him? "I've done bad things. I've hurt people. I've been selfish."

She took his face in her hands. "You need to tell me."

He couldn't take the chance and risk her leaving. "This is not the time and place. Maria is waiting."

Iliana seemed disappointed as she stood. "Give me a few minutes and we'll leave for the hospital."

She was upset, but he didn't know how to make it right without making their marriage worse.

The drive to Abele General took forty minutes. When they arrived, he and Iliana used a back entrance to avoid the media waiting outside for news about the late king's daughter.

Demetrius was pleased to see two members of the royal guard posted outside Maria's room. He and Iliana were allowed to enter.

Emmanuel and Theodore were sitting at her bedside. Maria looked pale and fragile, but she was awake.

She smiled faintly when she saw Iliana. "I was hoping you would come." Maria looked at her brothers and Demetrius. "Could you give us a minute alone?"

Demetrius didn't like leaving Iliana, but she shot him a pleading look and he acquiesced. "I'll be right outside." He kissed Iliana's cheek and squeezed her hand before leaving her to speak with her sister.

When the men left—Demetrius reluctantly—Iliana closed the door to Maria's private suite. "How are you feeling?" she asked, sitting in Emmanuel's vacated seat.

"Stella did this."

Iliana hadn't expected her to point the finger at someone so quickly. "How do you know?"

"She killed Nicholas and she tried to kill me. I warned Emmanuel, Theodore and Spiro to be careful, but they laughed me off. You'll take me seriously, won't you?"

Iliana was taking the threats to heart. The incident on the bridge was fresh in her mind. "Of course. Can you prove it was Stella?" She didn't want to tell Maria about the Ghost. She wanted her sister to be safe, but Demetrius was looking into the man's identity, and before they knew more, they couldn't know if her assailant's dying declaration held any truth.

"Not yet. But she called me the morning of the reading of the will. She was angling for some kind of alliance between her and me, as if I would side with that lunatic over my brothers and my mother."

"What makes you think she poisoned you?" And how would she have gotten inside Maria's house to do so?

"She was furious when I told her that my father's will should stand and I wouldn't manipulate anyone to take more than my share. I took a shower and when I came down for breakfast, I had the weirdest sensation of being watched."

Iliana listened intently.

"The poison was in my morning coffee," Maria said. "The doctors confirmed it. Stella knows I drink coffee. Then she didn't show up to the reading of the will and she delayed it."

If Stella was responsible, was their lead on the Ghost false? Or was there a connection between the

Ghost and Stella? "It doesn't look good for your step-mother, but I don't know how we can prove it was her."

Maria let her head fall back on the stack of pillows. "She's making a play for the crown, and she wants our support."

Stella was taking a long shot. To convince the king's legitimate heirs to walk away from the will, she'd need to offer them something in return. Unless she picked them off one by one. "She won't win me over."

Maria seemed pleased by that. "Me, either. But my brothers, I mean our brothers, I don't know. They aren't immune to a woman's charms. Stella flirts with everyone. She lies and she makes promises she can't keep—or has no intention of keeping. I think she could persuade my brothers."

"Flirt with their stepmother?" The idea left Iliana feeling queasy.

"She'll offer whatever she can to get what she wants. Money, land, future goodwill after she is queen. I don't trust her."

"I am sure Emmanuel, Theodore and Spiro are smart enough to see through whatever she offers."

Maria frowned. "I don't know. They underestimate Stella, and that's exactly how she'll win."

Iliana squeezed her sister's hand. "You need to rest and get better. Demetrius is looking into this. He'll find the truth. If Stella is involved, she'll pay."

Maria pursed her lips in thought. "Demetrius cares for you."

"He's my husband."

"What's that like? To have a powerful man on your side?"

Secure and comforting, especially in difficult times like these. "You had our father on your side. How did that feel?"

Maria sighed. "Our father was busy. He took a distant interest in our lives. When I wanted to learn to play the violin, he hired a teacher for me. When I wanted to learn to paint, he had a well-known artist work with me. But I'm not sure that's the same as what you have with Demetrius. He's always right there." She gestured to Iliana's side.

Hearing about how the king had raised his children, Iliana was grateful for the man she had called dad. He hadn't just signed her up for piano lessons. He had sat in the room while she'd attended them. He had listened to her practice. He had hung her artwork, as messy and imperfect as it was, in his office. Her parents had recorded her dance recitals and her games. They had showed the recordings to family members at her birthday parties. They had been proud and supportive.

Iliana felt overcome with emotion. A sob escaped her, and soon she couldn't stifle her grief.

Demetrius burst into the room. "What happened?"

Maria patted Iliana's hand. "She's just upset. This is a lot for us to deal with."

Demetrius put his arms around her. He didn't say anything further. He just hugged her until she pulled herself together.

"I think you should talk to a psychiatrist," Demetrius said as they prepared for bed. They had returned to Icarus. Iliana was glad to be somewhere familiar and safe.

Iliana was taken aback by her husband's comment.

She'd cried today, but that was hardly cause for needing a therapist.

She had slipped into pajamas that were less for sleeping and more for enticing. She'd been thinking about Demetrius and how he had protected her, and it had turned her on. Her emotional release in Maria's hospital room had been therapeutic, and she was feeling better since the incident on the bridge.

But Demetrius's statement was a cold, wet blanket over her libido. She wished she hadn't spent the past forty minutes in the bathroom preparing for bed.

"A psychiatrist. Why?" She didn't hide the defensiveness in her voice.

"You've been under a lot of stress. I've seen it happen to the best men in the field. You need a release."

She needed a release. But not a verbal one. After her good cry, she wanted to sleep with her husband. "I cried, Demetrius. Deal with it. It will happen sometimes. Usually when I have my period. I have my friends if I want to talk. But right now I don't want to talk. I want what only my husband can give me."

She walked across the room, hoping her saunter was seductive. But it was hard to strut in five-inch heels. Bedroom shoes, shoes that wouldn't see the light of day. She crawled into the bed, and Demetrius set his tablet on the nightstand. His eyes went from her face to her chest and hovered there for an extra moment before continuing down her body. "You don't have to do this. You've had a hard day."

What was his problem tonight? She was offering herself up on a silver platter and he was turning her away? What gave? "Are you telling me you don't feel like it?"

"I'm not a jerk. I'm trying to be sensitive to your feelings."

Why couldn't she and Demetrius get on the same page emotionally? "My feelings right now are sexual." She leaned forward.

He set his hands on her shoulders, keeping her from coming closer. "Serena called me and told me to take it down a level. I can only assume that the message is being filtered through her from you."

Iliana rolled her eyes. "She called me, too, because she saw the incident on the bridge on the news. She worries. She's about to be a mother, and that makes her worry more."

"Iliana, I'm trying to be a good husband, but you're wiggling around in barely anything and I'm only a man."

She'd have her way. Iliana lunged at him. She was cold and her feet hurt. Forgetting the day was her first priority, and sex with Demetrius had a mind-erasing effect to it. She kissed him insistently and let out a sigh when he kissed her back. Her little noise seemed to be the starting gun for him. It was all-systems-go time.

She straddled him and shoved his shoulders down, forcing him to lie flat on the mattress. She rolled her hips and he lifted his, the hardness of his body exciting her. Iliana peeled his T-shirt over his head and tossed it to the ground. She tugged his pants down his hips, hooking her fingers in his boxers and taking them down, too.

Demetrius liked to be in charge. He made it obvious with every decision. But in their bedroom, they were equals. Since being married, they had experienced more drama than most couples did in an entire year. He had remained at her side and he had protected her and cared for her. Now she would take care of him.

She kissed his bare chest, letting her fingers scrape across his skin. Making love could be about almost anything. Tonight, it was about feeling close to him, about feeling gratitude and a connection and wanting to indulge in it.

He flicked the straps of her nightie over her shoulders, and she let the thin fabric fall around her waist.

He grew harder between her legs. "Are you screwing with me?"

She shook her head. "Nope. I plan to screw you, though."

He reached for her breasts and palmed them. Sensations rippled over her. He massaged slowly, squeezing, lightly pinching the peaks. Her hips swiveled, and her shoe fell off and hit the ground with a thump.

She rested her hands on his hips. His impressive length grew. Following her desires, she moved to lay vertical to him, her head near his hip. She took him in her hand and licked his tip. He fisted the sheets and she knew he wanted to grab the back of her head. She licked and sucked and kissed along his length. Then she took his hand and brought it to her hair. He threaded his fingers into her long strands and set the pace he liked. She took him deep, opening her throat, hollowing her cheeks.

His toes were curled and a sweat had broken out on his forehead. The great and mighty Demetrius DeSante was rattled by some caresses from her hands and mouth. The power was intoxicating.

She blew across the tip and he shivered.

She loosened her jaw, to relax and do what brought him pleasure. With Demetrius, it was never enough. She bobbed up and down and he fisted her hair in his hand, no longer moving her head, just holding on to her.

She lifted her gaze to make eye contact. It may have been the connection or her hand, but he lost control.

He pulled out of her mouth with a pop and rolled her onto her stomach. She heard the crinkle of a condom wrapper. Seconds later, he was lifting her hips and pushing inside her.

He rode her hard and fast. She pushed back against him, loving this uninhibited side. She wanted to tell him to say words of forever, words that made her precious to him. Words such as *love, my only* and *eternity*.

He wouldn't speak the words.

His pace frantic, he reached to massage her in the right places, bringing her with him, higher and hotter until they both saw stars.

Chapter 8

Iliana's first formal invitation as Demetrius's wife arrived the next day, tied with a purple satin ribbon and closed with a wax seal with an *A* stamped into it.

Abeiron stood next to her after delivering it, staring at the wall. He did that whenever they were alone, staring at nothing, as if afraid to look at her.

"Whose seal is this?" she asked.

"The baron of Aetos in Valencia."

Iliana broke the seal and unrolled the silky paper. The details were written in precise calligraphy.

Abeiron cleared his throat. "A courier brought it this morning."

Abeiron was dressed as he always was, wearing formalwear before 8:00 a.m. Iliana wondered if he slept fully clothed and changed only to keep his garments looking neat and pressed and smelling fresh.

Iliana took a sip of her orange juice and swallowed her multivitamin. "Who is the baron of Aetos?"

Abeiron sniffed. "He is the most well-known baron in Valencia. Some fear him because of his eccentricities."

"Eccentricities?" Iliana asked. That could mean anything. She wanted details before she agreed to meet with him.

"He keeps to himself in personal matters, but inserts himself into political matters. The side he takes is usually the side that wins. He has allies and enemies, but his enemies often go silent and find themselves at his mercy."

He sounded…creepy. "Why does he want to see me?"

"Tradition. You are new to Valencia. He wants to welcome you, as is the custom. The baron of Aetos serves as the country's official welcome ambassador."

"I should meet with him, then," Iliana said. Perhaps the baron could share his thoughts on the situation with the king's will. She would be careful to ask vague questions, as to not pit him against her by inadvertently appearing to take sides or to have already made up her mind.

Maria had warned her that Stella was sly. She could already have formed an alliance with the baron of Aetos.

"That is your decision. I've heard that the baron makes life easier for those who he calls friends."

She could use allies in Valencia, especially if she was pitted against Stella, who'd had years to gather supporters.

"I suggest you speak to the president about it," Abeiron said.

Iliana would do that. Demetrius knew everyone and he would likely tell her about the baron of Aetos. Excited, she ran to Demetrius's office. When she entered the office, he was on the phone and switched to another language.

One day she would study the languages he spoke and then he wouldn't be able to shut her out of conversations. When he hung up, she circled the desk to show him the invitation. "Guess what came today?"

She had received many similar invitations for the queen of Acacia. She hadn't before been the intended recipient, except when invited as the queen's guest.

"I'm guessing it's good news."

"An invitation to dinner in Valencia from the baron of Aetos."

If she had added, "which includes a postdinner orgy," it would have garnered the same response from Demetrius. His face was cold and hard, the same expression he possessed when he had a gun in his hand and planned to use it.

"You aren't going," he said.

He liked to throw down edicts. She wasn't his to command. If he wanted her to decline the invitation and set a precedent that she was reclusive and rude, she needed a compelling reason. "I know you are concerned about security—"

"My objection is not about security. Iliana, please for once in our marriage, will you do what I ask of you without question?"

It didn't seem fair. Why was he getting upset about

this? "I can't just do as you ask. You need to give me a reason. If I decline, it will look discourteous."

He snatched the invitation from her hand. He swore in another language, and she knew from his tone he was furious.

"Is it because he's a man?" she asked, but she sensed this wasn't pointless jealousy. "You need to tell me what is going on." She hated when Demetrius kept secrets.

"Iliana, you cannot attend. Please be reasonable."

What did Demetrius know about this man to garner such a negative response? "Are you worried he'll tell me something about the king that will hurt me?"

"This isn't about your father."

Somehow this conversation hurt worse on the heels of the night they had spent together. He had held her and made love with her so passionately, and now he was treating her as though secrets between them were again required. "Tell me why." If she let him call the shots and not give any reasons, then they wouldn't grow closer. Demetrius's secret keeping had almost destroyed her ability to trust him. Why couldn't he see how important the truth was to her?

"This is not a conversation I can have with you. Do not go to the baron's house."

When he said *the baron* his voice shook with anger. "Do you know him?"

"I know everyone of importance."

"Aren't you full of yourself," she said.

"I am not full of anything except concern for my wife. You aren't going, and that's final."

"I'm not going, and that's final? You're acting as if I'm your subordinate, but I am not. I am your wife."

Did he hear how unfair he was being? "Unless you give me a good reason right now why I shouldn't get involved in Valencia, I'm going."

"He is not someone you want to associate yourself with."

"Why? What will having dinner with him do?"

Demetrius locked his sights on her. She didn't avert her gaze. This conversation was about more than an invitation. It was about him seeing her as an equal and trusting her with information. "It will make me furious."

"Well, you're making me furious right now!" Iliana felt tears welling in her eyes. Another tap on the door and three of his advisers were standing in the doorway looking uncomfortable. She would not cry in front of them. She stood, snatched the invitation from his hand and hurried from the room, pushing past the men. She mumbled, "Excuse me," but could only manage the words in a whisper.

Iliana would gladly stay away from politics involving Icarus, but she could make a mark for herself in Valencia.

She was going to meet with the baron of Aetos. She would find out what secret Demetrius was keeping.

Chapter 9

The baron of Aetos lived on a spread of land about fifty miles from the capital city of Abele. The sky was dark and overcast, and she had a heavy feeling in her stomach, but Iliana didn't want to consider the possibility she was making a mistake.

She had left Icarus and flown to Valencia without Demetrius's approval. He hadn't wanted to discuss the matter further. She had tried to talk to him. He had been busy, in meetings and on phone calls. When she'd brought it up, he'd looked at her, told her she couldn't go and left the room.

Iliana had Demetrius's security with her. They were likely keeping the president informed of her whereabouts and she supposed they would have stopped her if this was a mistake.

Maria had thought she should go. Maria had met

the baron. She'd described him as a crotchety old man but said he wielded power and influence over politics in Valencia. If the king's children wanted him on their side, Iliana had to win him over. Anything to keep him from joining Stella's camp.

The baron's steward escorted her to her host's dining room. Expecting a dark and somber place, she was surprised to see it was well decorated, bright and inviting. The baron was blind and his guard dog was at his side.

After a brief exchange of pleasantries, Iliana sat and sipped the wine that was offered to her.

"Thank you for meeting with me. As the official in charge of welcoming you to our country, I am pleased you agreed to meet me, especially on such short notice. I meet with numerous barons and duchesses throughout the year to take a pulse point. I thought it was important that we speak, especially since it seems you will be the first marchioness in my lifetime."

Welcoming her and other titled royals to the country meant inserting himself into the thoughts and plans of the movers and shakers. It was a smart play, and Iliana would be careful not to be taken advantage of.

"Thank you for your hospitality," she said. The key was neutrality. She sensed they were circling each other, but she wouldn't let this escalate into a fight.

"I'd like you to see me as a friendly adviser, someone who would love to hear your thoughts and offer council."

He was a stranger with an unknown agenda, and he wanted her to confide in him. That was bold. She would proceed with caution.

"Thank you. You've been the first to reach out to me in an official capacity." She was intentionally avoiding answering his question.

"And your husband? Could he not join us tonight?"

Had this dinner been an effort to meet Demetrius? What had happened between the two men in the past? She wouldn't tell the baron how angry Demetrius had become at the idea of her coming here. "Demetrius was busy with state matters." Did the baron sense the lie? Demetrius was busy, but he should be with her tonight.

"There are some in the country who are worried your husband will use your position to make a play for the crown."

Iliana laughed softly, not to insult the man but to convey how ludicrous she found the comment. "I can assure you that my husband has plans for Icarus, but none of them include expanding the borders. He is eager to stay friendly with his neighbors."

The baron nodded. "That's good to hear. What about you, Iliana? What are your plans?"

She felt as if she were on a job interview and had none of the correct answers. "I don't have plans at the moment."

"Would you like some advice?"

"Of course." She sat forward in her chair and waited.

"It has been over a hundred years since someone had held the title of marchioness of Agot. When the last one passed away with no heirs, the reigning king decided those powers were too great for a nonmonarch to wield. I am surprised the late king decided to pass those powers to you. My understanding is that he did not know you well."

She and the king, aside from the biological connection, had been strangers. "What powers are you
concerned about?" Was that the heart of the matter
and the reason she'd been invited here tonight?

"They are numerous. The land you inherit has worth.
You will have influence in politics. Your vote in state
matters is important. Many who are inexperienced
choose not to vote, concerned their immaturity will
lead them astray."

"I will not vote on matters I do not understand, but
I will make it my responsibility to understand matters
of importance," she said.

He nodded and smiled slightly. "I asked my steward to describe you. He said you were beautiful, and
I have no doubt that is true. You have confidence and
strength I would not have expected from someone in
your position."

Was that a criticism? "What position is that?" She
kept her voice calm and tried to edge out the sweet-
ness that bordered on sarcasm.

"You are the queen of Acacia's distant relative and
former assistant. You had no position or authority.
Within a matter of days, you were married to a powerful warlord of one country and the heiress to a great
fortune in another."

"Demetrius is not a warlord." She felt herself growing defensive over Demetrius. Was the baron needling
her to see where her weaknesses lay? She gathered
herself and tried to remain calm.

"My apologies. He is president, of course."

"You are forgiven this time. Please do not insult
me or my country again."

"Then, Icarus is your country? What about Valencia? Acacia?"

He was digging around into matters she had not yet come to terms with. "I have loyalty to all three."

He scoffed. "That is not possible. In a war, who will you side with?"

"Why would there be war? I would use my influence in all three countries to avoid it," she said.

He smirked at her. "You should decide, when the time comes, who will have your loyalty. I am antagonizing you to see how much fight you have. I like your spirit. Not everyone speaks as honestly to me."

"I have no reason to lie to you," Iliana said. "I have questions of my own. Do you know my husband? You seem more interested in him and Icarus than in me."

The baron paused for a long moment. "I do not know him, but I have known men like him. He is not to be underestimated."

His words led her to believe the baron had some beef with Demetrius. She would ferret out what it was.

"As the marchioness, you will find many knocking down your door, asking for favors, for pardons and similar. Every criminal will swear he is innocent. Every beggar will be a man down on his luck that needs a helping hand. You must have a firm heart about these matters."

"I had not considered that," she said. "I am a fair and honest woman, and I am not easily fooled." Except as she spoke the words, she wondered if the baron was laughing at them. She had been fooled by Demetrius and her parents. Was she blind to the truth when it might hurt her?

"Let me tell you how I make decisions about convicts. I am fair and ethical and follow strict standards. Every prisoner must work for their food. I don't grant luxuries like access to medical care or time to be outside. It's every man for himself."

Iliana's stomach turned. She made a noise of noncommitment, but his words nagged at her. Why was he so angry at prisoners? And what did he mean by working for their food? This was the twenty-first century, not medieval times. "It sounds as if that's a personal cause for you."

His eyebrows twitched together. That was his emotional tell. He was hiding something or outright lying.

"I take it personally when someone breaks the law. People should pay for their crimes and be held accountable for their actions."

"You don't believe in second chances?" she asked.

He made a face of disgust. He had to be aware of his facial expression, even if he could not see hers. "I believe that some people are beyond redemption."

"No one is beyond redemption," she said.

"Then, you've lived a sheltered life. There is a prison three miles from here filled with men not worth saving." He sounded angry.

"I'd like to meet some of these men. I'd like to talk to them."

"Why?" he asked. Hostility was plain in his voice.

This conversation was becoming adversarial, and she hadn't intended it to turn this way. "Let's say I'm open to what you're suggesting, but I'd like to see for myself." Clearly they didn't see eye to eye on the subject, but his calling this meeting and then steering the conversation in this direction had her curious.

"I'd be happy to arrange a tour for you. After dinner?"

Was he calling her bluff? Seeing if she was serious about visiting? Demetrius would be furious with her, but this was her new world to explore. "That would be very educational."

The rest of the meal, the baron of Aetos lectured her. It took everything Iliana had not to be rude to him. He treated her like a simpleminded child incapable of understanding complexities.

She had to wonder what she was missing in the baron's intentions. He wasn't spending the evening with her for enjoyment. He wanted something from her, and Iliana wasn't sure what it was.

Arrangements had been made for Iliana and her guards to visit Blackstone Prison. As they drove the winding country road that would take them there, she wondered what she would be allowed to see when they arrived. When she was marchioness, she could make demands. However, now she was subject to whatever rules the baron had communicated to the warden.

"Mrs. DeSante, I have informed the president of this visit and he forbids it," one of her servicemen said.

Iliana didn't heed him. Demetrius was angry she had come to Valencia to meet with the baron when he had asked her not to. "I won't get you into trouble with the president. You may drop me off if you wish, and I will make arrangements to return home."

The guards exchanged looks. "We have instructions not to leave you alone."

"I'm going into this prison with or without you," Iliana said.

The prison beckoned her, and yet she couldn't explain why. Perhaps it was such a place of sadness, she wanted to know if she could do anything to make it better.

Past the gate, inside the prison grounds, they drove through two security checkpoints. Their car was searched and they were scanned for metal objects. Once cleared, she and her guards entered the building. It was a depressing place. Cinderblock walls, barbed wire and metal, the smell of sweat and grime. Her stomach quivered with nerves and her heart slammed against her ribs. She hadn't been inside a prison before.

Was this a test? She wouldn't be allowed inside the prison unless it was safe. If the baron was trying to rattle her to see what she was made of, he would find she was strong and capable.

The warden met her in a small room that smelled of urine and sweat. He didn't smile. He stoically extended his hand. "It is not common for a woman to be inside the prison."

"I am sure the baron explained the purpose of my visit over the phone. I would like to see the facilities and talk to a few prisoners."

The warden shook his head. "You may observe prisoners at a safe distance. I can't allow you to come into contact with the general population. I can't ensure your safety."

Iliana frowned and lifted her chin, hoping she conveyed confidence. "My security will not allow anyone to harm me. Show me what you can."

Reluctantly, the warden introduced her to the five prison guards who would be escorting her and her security through the building. They were armed to the teeth. As they walked, the floor alternated between slick and slippery and sticky. She gagged at the putrid smells. It seemed every surface was covered in slime, refuse or bodily fluids.

When they reached the inmates' cells, she noticed it was darker. "Are the lights broken?"

"No, ma'am. We find the dark is more calming," said one of the prison guards.

More calming? "Where are the inmates?"

"In their cells."

No one was moving around the area. "Do they spend every moment in their cells?"

"With good behavior, some are permitted twenty minutes in the yard per week."

Her stomach tightened. She felt silly speaking when she knew almost nothing about how to care for prisoners, but it seemed these men were housed like animals, poorly treated ones at that. "How many inmates earn that privilege?" She braced for the answer, knowing the figure would be low.

"Three percent."

She shivered. The men spent their days in dark cells. How did they not go crazy? "Let me closer."

"That's not safe," the prison guard said.

"I will be fine. Let me inside."

The prison guard stepped back, muttering about

it being her funeral and allowed her inside the area. On TV and in movies, she often saw inmates swarm to their cell doors, reaching out, calling and banging at visitors. Nothing like that happened here. It was silent. She walked to the first cell, then the second. The situation was the same for each prisoner.

The inmates seemed broken and frail. They didn't acknowledge her. They said nothing to her or the guards. They wore filthy clothes and stared at the floor or their bare cell walls.

Her nerves were rattled, and she wished she had been better prepared to see this.

How many men incarcerated were mentally disturbed and in need of health services, not jail? How many had gone insane from being locked away, starved and beaten?

She could change it. She didn't care if the baron of Aetos was angry at her for interfering. Her husband was Demetrius DeSante and he would kill anyone who crossed her. She wouldn't give away how she felt now, though her anger at the injustice around her shook her to her soul.

She was wise enough to know that being critical and mouthing off now, when she had seen only a few minutes of the routine here, would not be well received. Waiting and planning and then making her move when no one expected it would be smarter.

As she walked past several doors with only small windows, she pointed to them. "Who lives there?" She wanted to be told they were maintenance closets, but she knew better.

The prison guards exchanged looks. Her servicemen moved closer to her.

As she peered inside, her core shook and slammed around inside her. Had the king of Valencia known about this? Did her siblings?

At the end of the row, she rose on tiptoes to look through the tiny window into a gloomy cell.

What she saw struck terror into her. "Open this door!" The words escaped her mouth as a shriek. Though she had been working to maintain some outward appearance of calm, hysteria overtook her.

Inside the cell, Demetrius was slumped on the ground against the wall.

She banged her fist on the door. "Open the door now!" How had this happened? Was the baron's invitation a ruse to get her away from Demetrius so he could be captured and brought here?

"We cannot. He is our most dangerous prisoner."

"Open it or I will see you thrown inside this cell."

After a brief conversation between the prison guards, the door was opened and Iliana entered. The man looked up from his position on the floor. He was half starved, dirty and lethargic. He looked so much like Demetrius, a thinner, bruised Demetrius. It was not her husband, but the eyes were hauntingly similar. His face was covered with a beard, unkempt and gnarled.

She knelt on the floor. Her guards moved closer, and she held up her hand to stop them. This man wouldn't hurt her. How could he hurt anyone? He was barely moving.

"What is your name?" she asked. If he was the most dangerous prisoner, what had been done to him to make him this still and vacant?

The man said nothing.

"Please, what is your name?" she asked again.

His head lolled to the side, turning away from her. "Eight three two four one."

It took her a minute to understand him. "Not your prisoner number. Your name."

He looked at her with Demetrius's eyes, and she saw flashes of a spirit, wounded but strong. A strange sensation crept over her and took hold. She lowered her voice so no one could hear her. "My name is Iliana. I am married to Demetrius DeSante."

At the mention of her husband, the man's eyes flickered with recognition. She didn't understand why or how, but this man was the reason Demetrius wanted her to be marchioness. He was the reason Demetrius hadn't wanted her to see the baron. She didn't have all the information, but as she struggled to piece things together, she felt sad and sick.

The man closed his eyes. For a moment, she thought he was dead. His rib cage extended from under his shirt, and the slight up and down of his stomach indicated he was breathing.

"I will come back for you. I will rescue you. Do you hear me? I won't allow you to live this way."

Scared her overinterest in this man would alarm the guards or subject him to more brutal treatment, she allowed them to escort her from the cell. She struggled to provide a plausible reason for her reaction. "That man is dying. I thought he was dead."

If her guards had recognized him and his similarities to Demetrius, they said nothing. She would reward them for their loyalty.

"He will be dead soon," the prison guard said with such indifference, it lit her fury hotter.

Soon? Such callousness over a man's life was unspeakable. "Where I come from, prisoners are not treated this way."

The prison guard sniffed. "We have rules. I follow them. I don't always agree with them."

Iliana wanted to weep, but she held it together until she was alone on the plane to Icarus.

She felt as if she were a ship smashing against the rocks, pieces splintering in all directions and slowly sinking beneath the water. She needed to speak with Demetrius immediately, but in person, not over the phone. The words were coming together in her head, but they were a jumble of questions and fears.

For the safety of the man in prison, she would speak to no one about what she had witnessed until she had discussed it with Demetrius. He would know what to do.

When she arrived at the house, she swept inside and raced to their bedroom. She turned on the lights, and Demetrius sat up in bed and stared at her. He looked angry.

Before he could launch an accusation at her, she lobbed the most critical one at him. "How could you not tell me about your brother?"

Fury and alarm mixed inside Demetrius, forming a volatile cocktail.

Iliana was screaming about his brother. She had gone to see the baron of Aetos. Had he told her about him and Alexei? Did the baron know that his son was the president of Icarus?

"What have you done?" Demetrius asked. As he considered a way to fix this, ways to protect Alexei, he needed every detail from her.

If the baron of Aetos had told her about Alexei, was Alexei dead?

"What have I done? I've done nothing. I went to Blackstone Prison and saw your brother or someone who looks like your twin rotting in a prison cell."

"Alexei is alive?"

"Barely. Who is Alexei? Are you admitting he's your brother?"

"My twin. My identical twin." If she had recognized him, could others? Alexei had been beaten and starved and it had been years since they were together.

Iliana stared at him, openmouthed. "You didn't think you needed to tell me about this?"

Timing was everything. He hadn't anticipated this latest twist in his plans. "I need to protect Alexei. Does the baron know that I am Alexei's brother?"

Iliana touched her temples. "I don't know what he knows. He's proud that he's the psychotic prison ruler or some ridiculous thing. I went to see for myself because the baron is deranged and he seemed to want me to see Blackstone Prison. Maybe he wanted to intimidate me or prove that I couldn't handle being marchioness and defer to him on all matters."

"I asked you not to see the baron." She should have listened to him.

"Is that what's most important now? You could have given me a reason. You could have brought me on board with your plans. When I saw Alexei, I thought it was you. I demanded they open the door."

Demetrius wanted to howl in frustration. His brother was alive, but his wife's actions may have sentenced him to death. "What did he say to you? How is he?"

"He said nothing except reciting his prisoner number." She sat on the bed and folded her arms around her midsection. "He wasn't well, Demetrius. He was starving and so lifeless and bruised."

Demetrius had anticipated this, but hearing it confirmed, rage pummeled him. He wanted to declare war on Valencia and strike, hard and relentlessly, to free his brother from that prison cell. Iliana had been so close. She had inadvertently accomplished what he had been trying to do for years. "I will kill the baron for this."

"I am sure you will."

"The baron will want to know why you showed interest in that particular prisoner."

"I told the prison guards I thought he was dead. Maybe they think I'm some Dorothea Dix on a mission."

"If they know he's my brother, they will use him and hurt him."

"They don't know he's your brother. I saw the eyes. His eyes are the same as yours. The rest is…not similar. Alexei is what this whole thing has been about, isn't it? You want me to use my title to free your brother."

No point in lying. "Yes."

"Tell me what he did."

Alexei had done nothing. "Is it enough for you that I tell you he is innocent?"

Given her fixation on the truth and finding information, he didn't expect her to relent. She touched his knee. "Yes, it's enough."

That was surprising. "Will you help me?"

"I will help all of them."

"All of them?"

"Every prisoner in that place."

That was taking on more than she may be able to handle. "How?"

"I haven't figured that part out yet. Is this why you didn't want me to see the baron?"

In part. The baron was a sadistic, crazy man. "Yes."

"You didn't want me to know about the prisons."

He hedged. Could he tell her the truth? She had uncovered most of it on her own. But the truth was harsh and twisted. "Don't you see the family resemblance?"

"I told you I did. You and Alexei have the same eyes."

It was grueling for him to reveal this information to her. "Not Alexei and me. The resemblance between me and the baron."

Iliana's eyes grew wide, and she brought her hands over her mouth. "He's your father."

Demetrius nodded.

Iliana brought her hands to her temples. "He put his son in prison?"

"He's a sick man."

Iliana shook her head and looked at him, her eyes deep pools of sadness and hurt. "You should have told me sooner."

"You couldn't have done anything about it. I needed to know I could trust you. That you will tell no one. That you will discuss matters relating to Valencia with me for this very reason."

Her hands were in fists on her lap. "Can you trust me? Are you convinced that I'm worthy? Look at me,

Demetrius. Do you see that I am hurting for you and your brother? That I wish I could have taken Alexei from that place?"

Demetrius looked at her, at the emotion reflected in her eyes. "Yes, I think I can." It wasn't easy for him to trust anyone. He was used to being stabbed in the back.

She looked at him intently. "You can trust me to do the right thing."

Demetrius didn't know what the right thing was to her. But he would have to trust her. "Can I tell you what happened?"

Iliana nodded. "Please. I want to know."

Demetrius had told this story to two people: his mother before she had died and Amon. Talking about it reminded him he was a failure. He shouldn't have been so foolish. He should have planned more carefully. What had happened to Alexei was the reason he took each step carefully, thinking through every possible outcome. "My mother ran away from my father with Alexei and me when we were children. Our childhood was filled with poverty and struggles and never an explanation as to why my mother felt she had to flee and hide. Nineteen years ago, my brother, Alexei, and I approached our father, the baron. Our mother had told us disturbing stories about him, and we were consumed with anger and the need for revenge." He had been hasty, believing they could strong-arm the baron for answers.

"Our mother had warned us to stay away from the baron, but she was dying of cancer and we wanted to give her answers. We wanted to see for ourselves if he was a monster and find out if he had regrets about the past and his actions."

Iliana said nothing, but she reached and took his hand in hers.

Demetrius had wanted to look into the face of the man who had hurt their mother and rejected them as children, to know if he had remorse. "We reached Valencia in the evening. We didn't call first or announce our arrival. We knocked, and when the baron's steward opened the door, we stormed inside and found the baron sipping Scotch by the fire.

"He wasn't blind yet, but his sight was failing. He recognized us." Demetrius had seen only cold, hard bitterness inside the baron. He was an angry man, and being forced to face the past had only angered him more. "He refused to answer our questions. He refused to speak to us, and instead he called the police and claimed we were thieves and would-be murderers. He used his connections to the prison and to friends in the legal system to deprive us of a trial and have us thrown in jail. He chose Blackstone for us, the prison reserved for repeat offenders and the most dangerous and violent criminals.

"We were given life sentences. Being inside the prison for a day, we knew if we didn't escape, we wouldn't survive. Hunger and torture and mind games are the warden's specialties. He broke prisoners and he was proud of it. Because the baron took an interest in us, the warden was bent on tormenting us to win the baron's favor."

The worst days of his life had been inside that prison. Hopelessness, fear and pain had dogged him every second.

"I plotted our escape. Alexei and I were young and ill equipped to protect ourselves. I learned to barter.

After taking a few beatings, I started giving them out and establishing myself as someone not to be messed with. It took me six months to establish my dominance in the prison hierarchy. I used that power to protect Alexei, as well." His rage and need for revenge against his father had driven him hard.

"I tripped the electricity in the main hallway and shorted it out in the bathroom. When the jail contacted an electrician to come make the repairs, I grabbed him and used his electrical tester and tools to open my jail cell. I took his clothes and left him locked in my cell.

"I broke Alexei out in much the same manner. My brother and I ran for freedom. When we hit the yard, the prison was on full lockdown." Snipers had shot at them. The dogs had been turned loose. "Using a pair of wire cutters, we cut the gate and ran. The only way to escape the dogs was to hit the swamps, swim and pray that whatever lurked in the swamps didn't eat us." He and Alexei had stood on the shoreline, listening to the dogs' barking. Alexei had turned to him, huffing with exhaustion.

"Something had gone wrong. Alexei was hit in the calf. He was bleeding, and the fact that he was still standing was a testament to how strong he was and how much we thirsted for freedom."

Iliana's eyes filled with tears, and she wiped at them.

"Alexei told me to go. But I couldn't. Not without him." Alexei had warned him that the dogs were close and they would be caught. "I grabbed Alexei and forced him into the water. I swam with him, trying to get to land." His lungs had burned, his muscles had screamed and he'd felt things brushing his legs. He had been hunted, aware they had miles to go.

"Then I heard the helicopters overhead." The thought of leaving his brother behind had been unbearable. But if they had been recaptured, beatings or death would have been waiting for them. With Demetrius free, if he could start his life over, he could return and save Alexei.

"I knew we couldn't make it with Alexei's injury. I swore to Alexei I would come back for him."

Emotion choked him. He had gone over that moment a million times, wondering if he could have survived with Alexei. "I hid him beneath some logs and leaves and I ran. I ran like a coward."

Iliana shook her head. "No, Demetrius. You did what you could."

For four days, he had waded through swamp water, eating whatever he could find, half starved and dehydrated. When he had managed to sleep, terrible nightmares haunted him, nightmares of Alexei's death and the beatings and the hell that was Blackstone Prison. He had thought he could hear his brother's screams echoing through the marsh.

"A boy found me curled up in a small, shallow cave." Demetrius had thought he had died. The boy had appeared so clean and innocent and happy, like sunshine after a hurricane. "He asked if I was the criminal from Blackstone. I tried to lie to him, but he told me that he knew the truth, but he would protect me."

The boy had run away and returned with provisions. For two days, the boy had come faithfully, even bringing a small blanket and a book for him to read, *The Red Badge of Courage* by American author Stephen Crane. He hadn't read the book until years later and wondered if the boy had known how fitting it was to his situation. Demetrius had been a coward. He had left Alexei behind.

The boy had given him food and water and hidden him in a cave he had used for play. "The boy was true to his word. He took care of me, and when I was strong enough, I ran. Being close made me a danger to him and his mother."

Demetrius had kept tabs on the boy as well, manipulating his situation and putting him in a position that would allow Demetrius to one day return the favor. That man was now the king of Rizari.

Demetrius hadn't told his old friend that story. What had happened with Alexei was a source of deep shame for him. "I've tried, Iliana. Many times I've tried to get my brother. Political maneuvering, black ops missions, bribery. Anything and everything except war."

Iliana hugged Demetrius. "You have nothing to be ashamed of. You did what you could. You are still doing what you can. But now you have a partner. You don't have to do this alone. You have me, and I promise you, Demetrius, I will help you and Alexei."

Some of the crushing weight lifted from his shoulders, and for the first time in years, he had real hope of rescuing Alexei.

Iliana's phone rang early the next morning. Maria's number was on the display. It took Iliana a few seconds to clear her head. She had been dreaming and thinking of Demetrius and Alexei since Demetrius had confided in her the night before. The emotions were too hard to shake off, but she tried to inject some warmth into her voice. "How are you feeling?"

"Pissed off," Maria said.

"Oh, no. What happened?" Iliana asked, walking out into the garden. This was a private conversation, and while Demetrius's guards had their eyes on her and nowhere in her home was truly private, she wanted to talk freely.

"Stella has been visiting with the dukes, duchesses, barons and other high-ranking officials to win them over. She's been giving away gifts and treasures from the royal vault in return for their support."

"She's bribing people?" Iliana asked.

"Not being secretive about it, either. When I asked her about it, she told me it wasn't too late for me to join her side."

The woman had no scruples. "What did you tell her?"

"To screw off. I don't care if she bribes her way into being queen of Valencia. I won't stab my family in the back. More than that, why does she want to be queen so much?"

"Money. Power. Influence," Iliana said.

Maria made a sound of disgust. "How did it go with the baron of Aetos?"

"He's an interesting character," Iliana said. She checked every word to be careful that she wasn't giving anything away about Demetrius or Blackstone.

"Yes, he is. When I met him the first time, he sniffed me as if I was a dog. He said he remembered people by their scent. If I remember him by his scent, I would call it eau de wet dog and sweaty crotch."

Iliana laughed. "You're hilarious."

"Just being honest. But what are you doing about the Stella problem? I tried to talk to Emmanuel and Theodore about it. Emmanuel told me to have faith in the law, which is crap. Theodore said he was looking into the matter."

"I could talk to Demetrius about it." Now that she knew the reason behind his interest in her inheritance and how important it was, she knew he'd move mountains to ensure she inherited the title of marchioness of Agot. Iliana guessed Demetrius had safeguards in place to make it so.

"Do you think he has time to trifle with this?"

Demetrius would make time. She wouldn't let Maria know how much it mattered to Demetrius. "I'll ask him about it. He's my husband and he supports me."

After chatting for a few more minutes, she hung up with Maria and went in search of Demetrius.

She found him in his library. He had a dozen books open in front of him, and his hair was mussed as if he'd been plowing his hands through it.

"What are those?" she asked.

He looked up from the books. "Legal texts from Valencia."

"Anything of use?"

"I've scoured these books before. Your title is the key. Stella could sway the courts to authenticate another will if she had the right documentation to prove it was written by the king when he was of sound mind."

"Maria says that Stella is gathering support in her fight to be named queen."

Demetrius leaned back in his chair. "I've heard."

"Any chance of stopping her?"

"You mean counterbribing? In some cases, it's possible. But it wouldn't be a sure thing with Stella involved. She has more connections and has had more time to plan her coup."

He seemed tired, as evidenced by the dark circles under his eyes. "Can I make you some tea?" she asked.

He shook his head. "I'm fine."

Iliana rubbed a hand across his shoulders. He wasn't fine. She could feel his stress and tension. "You know that I have a law degree. I didn't pass the bar, but I could take a look at these and see if anything pops."

"Why didn't you take the test to become a lawyer?"

"I did take it. Three times."

"Take it again."

She shivered. "One day. Maybe I'll study for the bar in Icarus, too. I went to law school because I loved this stuff. Let me help."

He slid a few books toward her. "Please. I welcome your thoughts. Maybe you'll see this in a way I haven't considered. I feel as though I'm running out of time. If Alexei dies in prison, I won't forgive myself."

"You've done everything you can to help him," she said.

"That's not true. I must be able to do more. But I know you didn't come here to talk about my brother. What can I do for you?"

"I came to tell you about Maria's suspicions about Stella."

"I don't trust Stella," Demetrius said. "But I don't know how big of a threat she is yet."

"Have you found anything else on the Ghost?"

He nodded. "Some. Whispers. Rumors. Nothing concrete."

"Will you tell me what you've heard?"

"Those matters don't concern you."

She took offense. "How do they not concern me? The Ghost was hired to assassinate me."

"Iliana, I can't share state secrets with you."

"I am not asking for state secrets. I am asking you to talk to me about a situation that directly involves me."

Demetrius rose to his feet so suddenly, she jumped. "Stop asking me to be someone I am not." His voice was cold and angry.

He was on edge because of Alexei, but why couldn't he see that in this matter, she was on his side? She wanted to help him. How could she prove it to him?

"You talk to your secret spies and your advisers all day. Why can't you talk to me, your wife?"

"Because you are my wife. That's the circular answer. I am supposed to protect you. Not shove you out in the middle of a mess. I already feel terrible for putting the burden of Alexei's imprisonment on your shoulders."

"You didn't put anything on my shoulders. I want to help you."

He said nothing and stared at her, his expression unreadable. "I will not change because you demand it. I need to protect you. I didn't protect Alexei, and look what happened."

"Nothing bad will happen to me."

"You can't know that!" he shouted.

Was this their life? Demetrius pushing her away and then pulling her close when the situation called for it? Demetrius deciding what she knew and what she was allowed to be involved in and keeping secrets from her? She wanted to be equals. "I swear to you that I will free Alexei as soon as I am able. But I want something in return."

She wondered if she had the courage to throw down the gauntlet. To give herself the freedom to start over if she chose to.

"What do you want in return?" His voice was icy.

"You must grant me a divorce."

Demetrius went still. He blinked at her. Iliana felt the words to retract her statement bubble up in her chest.

Demetrius turned sharply and left the room. He closed the door behind him.

Iliana gathered the books in her hands. She would read them, and she would help Demetrius. He would see that he had married a strong and capable woman, and maybe then he would finally respect her as an equal.

His wife wanted to divorce him. His wife of less than a month wanted out. Demetrius couldn't blame her, except he had convinced himself that she cared for him and that despite some initial problems, they would find the right footing and remain married. She had said she would at least give him until the reading of the will, but now she was finished.

Demetrius had everything: money and power. He had his way more often than not. Except the most important and crucial parts of his life—those intangibles were out of reach.

His mother had died a broken and bitter woman.

His brother was in jail.

His father was a monster.

His wife wanted to leave him.

Night had fallen, but Demetrius couldn't go to bed. Not when he knew Iliana was upstairs. If she was in his bed, it was laughable that she would pretend now that she wanted to sleep beside him, after she had clarified her intentions. If she had moved to the guest bedroom, he wasn't ready to face that, either.

He had confided in her about Alexei. Maybe she had thought on the matter and had decided that he was a coward. Maybe his actions disgusted her. God knew he was disgusted with himself.

Needing to burn off energy, Demetrius changed into jogging pants and a T-shirt and pulled on his running shoes. He didn't often run outside, and when he did, he was accompanied by his servicemen. Tonight, he wanted the darkness and solitude to clear his thoughts. He needed quiet. He needed to be alone.

He started out on his run, following a familiar route to the sea. He didn't like to run on the sand, but Icarus had beautiful jogging paths that ran parallel to the water. Music wasn't needed. Tonight his thoughts ran through his head on repeat.

He wasn't keeping track of the time or how far he had run. He decreased his pace, letting his breathing turn even and calm.

Love of country and loyalty to family were the most important values to him. Iliana didn't share either, at least not when it came to Icarus or him. How could he have thought she was right for him?

The answer came immediately. She was right for him because she was. When he was with her, he could stop thinking about state matters and problems and revel in being with her. She was warm and welcoming; she was sweet and a little innocent. She made him feel like a man. Not a president or a warlord or a leader, just a man.

Sex with her was mind-blowing. He knew the difference between going through the motions and passion. He and Iliana had passion in spades.

A noise behind him had him turning. Another jogger. In the moonlight he caught a glimpse of an item in the jogger's hand. A gun? A music player?

Demetrius reached for his ankle gun, but the man was already on top of him, throwing a punch.

Demetrius avoided the first strike and grappled for the weapon in the man's hand. A knife, long and serrated.

It had been a long time since Demetrius had lost a fistfight. He wouldn't lose to a common pickpocket. Then four more men appeared.

Demetrius had control of the knife, but it wasn't enough. The other men had guns.

"The Ghost says to back off."

The message would be delivered with a painful warning. Demetrius flinched when the first bullet hit him. He fell to the ground and reached for his phone.

He didn't want to die in the street, but if this was

his fate, he needed to tell Iliana something important. He needed his wife to know that in the ways that mattered, she would always be in his heart.

Chapter 10

Abeiron appeared in their bedroom doorway. Considering it was so unlike him to invade their private space, Iliana knew something was wrong.

Was she being escorted out of the country? Taken to live elsewhere away from Demetrius? He hadn't spoken to her since that terrible conversation in the library. She regretted what she had said to him, knowing that trying to force Demetrius to do anything was pointless. She should have won him over, not tried to batter him into doing what she wanted with ultimatums and the threat of divorce. "What's wrong?"

Abeiron would not look at her. "You need to come with me. The president has been shot."

Panic tore through her. She grabbed the first clothes she could find and hurried after Abeiron.

On the drive to the hospital, Iliana prayed. Demetrius could not die. He was the toughest man she knew. He was practically bulletproof. She asked Abeiron questions he didn't have the answers to. They were nonsensical, and she was repeating herself. She was a wreck.

How had he been shot? Where was he? What had happened?

When she arrived at the hospital, Demetrius was in surgery, and a hospital administrator met her in a private lounge. "I want to be in there with him."

"I'm sorry, Mrs. DeSante. You cannot. I will take you to a comfortable place to rest."

"Rest? Do you think I'll rest now? While my husband is in surgery?"

Iliana had a flashback to when her parents had died in the car accident. It had been terrible, clinging to the hope that the doctors and nurses could help, when she had known they could not. She had prayed it had been a case of mistaken identity and her parents were still alive.

This could not be happening again. Someone she cared for was slipping away, and she couldn't do anything to stop it.

"I want to be close to him. Take me where I can be close to him."

They allowed her to sit outside the operating room on the floor. Her guards remained with her. As a nurse passed, she knelt next to Iliana. "We are praying for your husband. Do you know that I'm a nurse because of him?"

Iliana didn't follow. "What do you mean?"

"The president set up a program to help single parents get an affordable education. Instead of working two jobs and barely making ends meet, now I make good money here." She patted Iliana's shoulder. "He'll be okay."

Another nurse stopped and handed Iliana a rosary. "This was my grandmother's. I want you to have it. Say prayers for your husband and the Blessed Virgin will hear them. The president is a good man."

As more people stopped to console her, Iliana realized that his countrymen had seen the same side of him that she had in private. He was harsh and direct but honorable, too. He wanted to help his countrymen and women.

Iliana kept to her post outside the operating room. Eight hours later, the surgeon came to speak to her. She rose to her feet, knowing if she had anything in her stomach, she would have been sick.

"Your husband has lost a lot of blood. The Good Samaritan who called us saved his life. Any longer without medical care, and the president would have bled out."

She wanted to cry from stress and worry and exhaustion. "What was he doing alone?"

"I can't answer that," the doctor said. "Hopefully, tomorrow morning, you can ask him that yourself."

A few hours later, Iliana was curled on a bench underneath a window in his hospital room. Demetrius was hooked to machines that beeped all night. The sound was comforting. It meant her husband was alive.

When Demetrius woke, he remembered what had happened. If he hadn't, the aching in his shoulder that pulsed through his arm and across his chest was a painful reminder. The jog in the park and his insistence that he run alone. Stupid, considering the Ghost was targeting his wife, and since Demetrius had made no secret of his mission to uncover the Ghost's identity, he was a target.

His behavior disgusted him for myriad reasons. He knew better. He didn't go into battle alone. He didn't run from his problems. He'd needed a release. Iliana got under his skin and into his head and confused him.

No other woman had ever made him feel this way.

His shoulder and arm felt heavy and sore, but at least his arm was still attached. Wiggling his fingers, he was relieved they moved. He must be drugged, which he didn't like. Making decisions quickly required a clear head.

What time was it? No clock in his room. How long had he been unconscious?

A dozen pressing issues sprang to mind. He had meetings to attend and decisions to make. He didn't have time for this! He struggled to sit up, ignoring the pulling from the various cords taped to his body.

His eyes fell on his wife, who was sitting, or rather sleeping, on the couch under the window on the far side of the room. She was curled up with her legs tucked close and her head resting on her elbows.

Surprise washed over him. "Iliana."

She opened her eyes, and she smiled at him. After the sleep cleared from them, her smile faltered. Was she remembering their argument? Concerned about him? Was his condition more dire than he thought? He felt okay. He was breathing on his own and no tubes were shoved down his throat.

"How are you feeling?" she asked, crossing to his bedside. She was wearing a green dress that flowed to her ankles, and it swayed with her feminine stride.

His throat was dry. He swallowed. "How long was I asleep?"

"Twelve hours," she said. She reached to his bedside table and handed him a cup with a straw.

With a nod of thanks, he took the cup from her hand. No way was she helping him drink. He wasn't that weak. He took a sip. "Twelve hours is long enough. I need my phone."

Worry darted across her face. "You need to rest."

"I will rest. While I work."

Iliana set her hand over his arm. "I don't think you understand what happened."

"I understand it." He didn't want to go over what a fool he had been. He knew. Most of the country probably knew.

He pressed the call button for the nurse. Perhaps his wife would not obey him and deliver his phone, but others would. A nurse appeared in moments, wringing her hands. "Yes, Mr. President?"

"My phone. I need my phone."

"Yes, sir." She hurried from the room, hopefully to find it or someone who could give him a new one.

"Demetrius, you need to take a break. You were shot twice."

He pressed the button to move the bed into a sitting position. Pain shot across his chest. He ignored it. "I know I was shot, Iliana. I'm pissed this happened. I never go running without my servicemen."

She set her hand on his forearm. "Why did you last night?"

He had wanted to blend in and disappear. Demetrius was smart enough to know that he was recognizable. He was a target, and his position dictated he needed protection. His hubris had allowed him to believe he could defend himself. Being alone without quick access to his weapon, he'd been an easy mark. But running with his gun strapped to his chest hadn't been an option.

Yesterday, he had wished he wasn't president. People surrounded him all the time. More than two hundred people worked in his private residence. Seventy members of his government either advised him or reported to him on a weekly basis. He was the president, but he also wanted to be himself. In recent years, he wasn't sure who that was anymore.

As the leader of a great nation, he'd always known that he'd sacrifice his personal life for the good of the country. He hadn't cared about that until he had met Iliana. Now he wanted a small piece of himself just for her. "I wanted to be alone."

Iliana bit her lower lip, and it drew his attention to her mouth. Her luscious, kissable mouth. "Did you want to be alone to think about our fight?" She whispered the question, her voice strained.

The fight had upset him. Many things upset him. Most of the time, he shoved "upset" and related emotions into a deep, dark unvisited corner of his mind and focused his attention on critical situations. Using that technique to solve his problems with his wife didn't work as well. "In part."

Her eyes filled with tears. "I'm sorry, Demetrius."

He couldn't interpret the tears. He reached to wipe

one that fell down her cheek. "Are you sorry that I was shot or sorry that you plan to divorce me?"

His words hit their mark, and she winced. "Both." She wiped at her tears and reached for a tissue from the box mounted to the wall.

He didn't want to talk about his failings as a president or his failings as a man. His personal life was a mess. Not having an example of a satisfying, healthy relationship, he didn't know that he'd ever find one, or if he did, what it would look like. He'd thought Iliana could be that for him, but she didn't want him. That knowledge didn't make him angry. It made him sad.

He didn't like dealing with sad.

In desperate times, he turned to what he knew, which were facts. Dealing in battle plans and countermeasures made sense. Navigating love and marriage blew his mind. "The attack was orchestrated by the Ghost. It was a message for me to back off."

She inhaled sharply. "The Ghost? How do you know? Never mind, you know everything. You could have been killed."

"Dying would have saved you the trouble of divorcing me," he said. A half joke, but in some ways on point.

She flinched. "Don't say things like that. You're lucky to be alive. I was scared for you, Demetrius. I was scared we would have these unspoken things between us."

Unspoken things? He didn't think adding more marital problems to the conversation would make it better, and he didn't need for things to be worse now. "I talked you into marrying me. I talked you into giving us a chance after you learned about your father.

I can't keep convincing you to stay with me." Pride kept him from telling her that she'd turned his head around and that she meant a lot to him. If she turned away after he threw those emotions on the table, he couldn't handle it.

He wouldn't press her to stay, even if losing her meant losing the happiest part of his day. "I won't force you to live a life you hate." His father had done that to his mother for too many years before she had escaped. His mother hadn't spoken of how she had managed to leave, only that friends had helped her run away with her children and that she had started over from nothing.

He wouldn't subject another person to that.

"You think in black and white, right and wrong. I will free Alexei, and that is a vow I will hold in my heart. But with us, I don't know what to think."

"Not knowing what to think is different than wanting a divorce." If she would be clear with him, he'd give her anything she asked for, even if it killed him.

"I deeply regret the last words we spoke to each other."

Regretted them out of guilt? "If the words you spoke were the truth, why regret them?"

"You could have died."

"No," Demetrius said, touching his shoulder. "I would not have."

"Stop being so difficult! According to your doctors, you almost died. The media was reporting grim news and people were sending flowers to your house and making a memorial out of the location where you were attacked. Strangers stopped me in the hospital to offer their sympathies, as if you were already dead. I only held it together because I knew that you were alive. But how do you think I would feel if you had died?"

He didn't understand her. She wanted to end their marriage and yet she would have mourned his death? "Tell me what you would have regretted. Say what you need to say now, while I'm strapped to these monitors and can't leave." He reached to turn off the pain medication dripping into his IV. He didn't want his senses to be dulled to the physical pain, and no medication would help the hurt he'd feel when Iliana walked out on him. It was a depressing and sobering thought and he didn't want to look too deeply into it. Because she was his wife and he cared for her? Loved her?

She shook her head. "You're an impossible man."

"I've made no secret of that."

She folded her arms, closing herself off. "You're controlling and domineering and secretive."

"That's also true. I didn't lie to you about that or pretend otherwise."

"Before we were married, you were sweet and considerate."

"I am still considerate of your feelings when the situation allows," he said.

She shook her head in disbelief. "I feel as if I'm talking and you're not listening. Do you wonder why this marriage frustrates me? It's because I need to be with someone who trusts me and values me enough to share his innermost secrets and who treats me like an equal. You know things, things that could affect me, and you hide them from me because you think I'm weak."

Demetrius blinked at her. She had told him yesterday she planned to leave him. Today she wanted inside his private life. He wanted to let her in. He wanted to trust her. Could he? "I see."

"Demetrius—" She stopped short when his doctor walked into the room.

Demetrius was grateful for the interruption. His feelings for Iliana were unclear. He wanted her as his wife, but he wouldn't force her to remain his. He wanted her in his bed, but he didn't know if he could trust her to sleep beside him. She wanted to be closer to him; at the same time she wanted to leave him.

What was he supposed to make of that?

Demetrius exited the hospital, holding Iliana's hand. Cameras flashed and reporters called out questions. Iliana and Demetrius were wearing bulletproof vests. His had been put on over his bandages, which were well hidden below his suit. His movements betrayed no indication of the pain she knew he was feeling. Demetrius had refused to take pain medication and waved off the doctor who had offered him prescriptions. Iliana had taken the pill bottles and slipped them into her handbag when Demetrius was signing his discharge papers.

He was a hardheaded man. The pain would catch up to him and she would be ready to help him when it did. If she had to grind up the pills into his food as if he were a child, then fine.

She giggled at the idea.

"What's funny?" he asked her, leaning close to her ear.

Cameras snapped around them. Must have been a good photo op. Or she looked deranged laughing on the heels of her husband being hospitalized. She blamed stress and lack of sleep.

"I was thinking if I have to medicate you, I will."

He gave her a sideways look. "Are you talking about drugging me?" His tone had a teasing sound to it.

"Only if you leave me no options."

He smiled at her, a huge smile she knew was covering pain and hurt. He was acting as if the incident had been as minor as twisting his ankle and that their marriage was rock solid.

Iliana waved and smiled to the crowd. She had seen her cousin do this a hundred times, hiding her anxiety and stress and fear beneath a facade of calm.

They climbed into the waiting SUV. Demetrius released her hand immediately and moved to the farthest side of the bench. The media couldn't see into the tinted windows. The walk from the hospital had been a show. Her heart fell, and she wished again that she knew how to pretend she didn't care.

His aid turned around in the front seat and handed Demetrius his tablet. Within seconds, he was engrossed in the computer.

For the time being, she was a ploy to make his presidency appear stronger. They needed to give the impression they were newlyweds in love, that nothing was wrong and they had a deep and meaningful connection.

"You two will need to attend a function tonight," the aide said.

Demetrius was typing on his tablet. "What and why?"

"General Ambrosia is retiring. We'd previously

sent your regrets, but we want you to look strong by appearing in public."

Demetrius made a noise of acknowledgment. "I can manage that. Iliana, is that okay?"

She didn't want to attend a social function, but she understood the importance of presenting a united front. She was surprised he had asked for her approval. "Yes, that's fine."

"Don't sound so excited," Demetrius said drily. He finally turned his attention from his tablet and looked at her, really looked at her with that scrutinizing gaze.

Given their recent arguments and her current stress level, expecting her to pretend to be happy and relaxed was asking too much. But she held her tongue. "I was up all night worried about you, sweet husband. I was hoping to have time alone with you tonight, not to entertain guests at a stranger's house."

Demetrius shot her a look of amusement. "Maybe you can drug me and we can both have some fun tonight."

She shook her head. Demetrius was difficult, but then he looked at her a certain way, touched her, teased her, and she found herself falling for him all over again.

When they arrived home, she strode directly to their bedroom, expecting Demetrius would walk straight to his office. She wanted to be alone and sleep for a few hours. Sleep would help her wrangle her emotions under control. A sob rose in her throat. She couldn't hold back the tears for a moment longer.

The bedroom door slammed shut and she whirled. Demetrius had followed her. "I understand that you want this marriage to end, but if you can't pull it together, then you can stay here tonight. It was considerate of you to be at the hospital because your position called for it. As for the retirement celebration, I will tell the general you are tired and need rest."

Iliana didn't want out of their marriage. She just needed it to change. "I'm not crying because I want this to end. I'm crying because you almost died and it was upsetting and traumatic. Are you so cold that you can't understand that?"

He seemed shocked by her words. "I understand it. But it dawns on me that asking you to act like my wife in public may be too much."

"I am your wife. There's not a lot of acting involved. Then again, acting as though I like you is difficult at times. Do you really think I was at the hospital because it was appropriate for my position?"

He stared at her as if he didn't know the answer.

"I was at the hospital because you are my husband and I was worried about you. I didn't even consider how it would look, nor did I care."

He looked away from her. "I don't know what you expect from me."

To show emotion. To let her inside. "I was scared when they told me you were shot."

"I'm sorry you were frightened. It was not my intention."

Her emotions twisted around her heart, making her feel strangled. "I will be the woman you need tonight at the general's. I know the importance of country. But I need you to think for a few minutes about how I felt. Please, will you lie down with me for an hour, just one hour, and let me hold you?"

He recoiled. "Iliana, I have twelve hours of missed time to catch up on."

She threw her hands in the air. "Fine, Demetrius. Do what you must. I will do the same."

She turned from him and went into their bathroom, closing and locking the door. After she had calmed down, she opened it, half expecting he would be standing on the other side waiting or lying in their bed.

The room was empty. The bed was unoccupied. She was alone.

On the drive to the general's house, Iliana was unusually quiet. She didn't play with her phone or make idle conversation. She either stared straight ahead, refusing to make eye contact with him, or looked out the window.

She wouldn't speak to him, but Demetrius sensed Iliana had a lot to say.

His shoulder was throbbing. Though his doctor had looked at it before he had left the house, Demetrius had refused to take the proffered pain medications. He would be meeting with important people tonight, and he needed to appear strong and in control.

The Ghost had targeted him once, and it could happen again. Demetrius wouldn't stop hunting his pursuer, but he would be more discreet about it. He'd lure the Ghost into believing he had given up his search. Maybe the man would make a mistake and reveal himself.

"Are you sure you're feeling up for this?" Demetrius asked.

Iliana looked at him. She had fixed her hair a certain way that was both elegant and sexy. Her dress was perfect, molding around her body, and her shoes were high, the heels thin and pointed. She looked so good, he hungered for her. But touching her was out of bounds. He knew it from her attitude. Was she torturing him on purpose?

"I can handle it," she said.

They pulled to the front of the general's brightly lit and well-designed custom-built house. Women in gowns and men in tuxedos were entering the premises, laughing and smiling. Could he and Iliana be one of those couples?

Demetrius waited for the door to open. When it did, he stepped out and his servicemen closed around him. He extended his hand and helped Iliana from the car. Her expression had changed from distant to happy. It pained him to know it was a front.

She smiled up at him and then turned that hundred-watt smile on the crowd around them. For security reasons, they didn't stop to speak with anyone, but moved quickly into the general's house.

Demetrius was armed, but he wasn't checked for a weapon. Even if he had been, he wouldn't have given it up for the occasion.

After introductions, which Iliana handled well, especially given the interest in her, they took their seats in the general's dining room, a beautiful space lit by crystal chandeliers and accented in gold. The tables were set immaculately and the waitstaff dressed formally, their uniforms crisp and clean. Demetrius had heard that the general's wife liked to shop and was a stickler for details. This celebration was a testament to that.

Demetrius had introduced Iliana many times as his wife, and the words rolled naturally off his tongue.

He squeezed Iliana's hand. "What do you think of this room?" he asked, after exchanging small talk with the tenth person of the night.

"Big," Iliana said. She took a sip of her wine.

"That's it? Big?"

Iliana smiled, but he saw something more in her eyes: hurt and anger. "I'm still mad, Demetrius. You don't listen to me."

He'd heard what she'd said to him. "You mean I don't do what you want."

Her face flickered with annoyance. "Why is it so hard for you to compromise?"

He didn't compromise. Being in a position of weakness was a place he refused to revisit. "Could we discuss this later?"

Iliana's eyes shot daggers. "Of course."

They were seated at a table near the front of the room. The general's dining room easily sat four hundred.

As appetizers were served, Iliana spoke with everyone at the table, putting them instantly at ease. She conducted pleasant conversation without awkward silences or boredom. This was part of his job Demetrius dreaded, but Iliana was a natural. Life was easier with her.

He needed her, and it made him uncomfortable to realize that. He was stronger with her. She was providing a good cover for his shoulder injury. While he was struggling to focus on the conversations and ignore the pain, she was smiling and laughing and engaging the table. She was skirting around questions related to the attack without sounding dodgy. She was skillfully handling what amounted to a PR problem with grace.

Needing her was a strange feeling. Demetrius worked hard not to need anyone.

He could sense her anger but he didn't know how to defuse it. Demetrius wouldn't throw himself at her and beg her to forgive him.

He wished he could turn back the clock to the night of their wedding. He'd tell her about her father before they were married and trust that she would still marry him and help him free Alexei. She was a good woman with a warm and caring heart, and he believed she would have done both.

Iliana leaned close to him. "You're staring at me and it's weird."

"It's not weird for a husband to look adoringly at his wife. You look beautiful tonight." She had her red hair up in a twist. He wanted to pull the pins from her hair, watch it tumble across her shoulders and then splay those red strands across his pillow.

He grew excited at the idea, and then his shoulder pulled, reminding him he was injured.

"Thank you. You look handsome," she said.

Was she acting, knowing people were listening, or did she mean that? He set his hand on her thigh and squeezed lightly. Her eyes grew almost imperceptibly wider. He moved his hand higher. Her gown was soft and silky, and he imagined lifting it up her thighs, gathering it around her waist and then pushing inside her.

"Do you want to dance?" he asked.

She might not want to sleep with him, but dancing meant she would be in his arms.

"That might not be a good idea," she said, her gaze darting to his shoulder.

It sounded like a challenge. "Once around the dance floor. Everyone will see us, and then we can leave."

"Isn't that rude? We haven't eaten dinner."

"I don't stay at these events for long. The rest of the room can see you, and they know we're newlyweds. They know why I would want to have you alone."

He stood and she took his right hand. He led her onto the dance floor. Grasping her hand in his, he rested his left hand on her hip as he swept her across the floor.

She was light on her feet, and she seemed to sense how to move with him, keeping their bodies close, dancing gracefully and smoothly.

It was the same in bed. They instinctively understood each other's needs and wants. Their chemistry and passion were undeniable, and they worked on so many levels. Could he seduce her tonight? He knew she would shut him down if he didn't open up to her. He couldn't reveal everything, but could he tell her some truths? His truths? She seemed to want him to lay his emotions bare. He had told her about his cowardice in regard to Alexei. Didn't that mean something to her? "Being with you is simultaneously the hardest and best part of my day. You challenge me to be a better man."

She stumbled on her feet. He was getting to her and he liked that. It meant that, despite her anger and her proclamations about wanting a divorce, she wasn't immune to his charms. It gave him something to work with.

"I didn't grow up in a loving, open household. I envy that you did. But that means I don't instinctively know what you need. I try to make you happy and when I fail, I don't give up. I just hope that I'll have another day with you to try again."

Her eyes misted.

"Iliana, my wife for as long as you'll allow me the pleasure, I can tell you the truth. I've told you secrets I haven't told another human being. But I haven't mastered when to tell the truth and when to hold back to protect you."

Iliana drew herself closer and rested her head on his good shoulder. His arm was aching, but he couldn't let her go. It felt as if everything they had together stood on shaky ground and would fall away with the slightest wind.

Iliana heard the shower running. She was waiting in their bedroom in case Demetrius fell or called for help. He was pushing his body too hard. His physician had stopped to speak with her before they had gone out for the evening, emphasizing the need for Demetrius to take his prescribed antibiotics and pain pills. He needed sleep and not to toss and turn all night.

The water shut off. Concerned, she tapped on the bathroom door. "Everything okay?"

"I'm changing my bandages. I'm fine." He sounded decidedly not fine.

Iliana sighed and opened the bathroom door. "I can help you. Why didn't you tell me that's what you were doing?" She gasped when she saw the wound.

She wasn't sure what a fresh gunshot wound looked like and she understood it would take time to heal, but this did not look right.

"We need to call your doctor," she said. He was sweating. She reached for a hand towel and dabbed his forehead and his skin. "Do you have a fever? You could have an infection."

"I don't have a fever. I took a hot shower, and applying this bandage is difficult. I didn't want to put you under further stress," he said.

Put her under further stress? Like the stress of sitting in the hospital for hours, unsure if he would live? Providing basic wound care was a cakewalk compared with that.

She took the scissors from his hand. She cut the bandages as the hospital had instructed her. "The doctor will return tomorrow morning to check the wound. Let me do this so I don't look like a negligent wife."

"Is that the only reason you're doing it?" he asked.

No, but she didn't think Demetrius would relinquish control that easily, and she needed a reason for him to acquiesce to her help. "I'm taking care of you because I want to. The doctor said not to get this wet." The wound was seeping. Was that bad? Or was it a sign of healing?

"How can I shower without getting it wet?"

"I could have helped you. We have plastic bandages."

"You would have showered with me?" he asked.

"If that's what was needed, yes."

"If I had known that was an option, I might have taken you up on it."

She rolled her eyes and kept dressing the wound.

The makeup he had worn to hide his facial injuries had been washed away, revealing cuts and bruises. She took his face, his handsome, strong face, in her hands. "Please let me put ointment on your cuts."

He nodded, and she sensed the concession had been difficult for him. Using a clean cotton swab, she applied ointment to the injuries on his face and hands. He closed his eyes and she took the opportunity to scrutinize his wounds.

How was he walking? Her threshold for pain was practically nil, and if she had been shot, cut and bruised, she'd be in bed, begging for pain pills. The pain pills she had in her handbag. "Do you want medicine for the pain?"

He shook his head. "The pain means it's healing. I just need my bed and my wife."

She could give him both.

She helped him put on a pair of cotton pants, and he got into bed. She pulled only his sheet over him, concerned about how hot his skin felt.

"Now I feel like a child," he said.

"Just a man who is sick," she said. "Give me a minute. I'll be back." She wanted to put some ice on his bruises.

She returned with cloth-wrapped packs of ice and laid them over the worst of the bruises. She hurried to clean up in the bathroom and get ready for bed.

When she climbed into bed, Demetrius was asleep. She was glad he was resting. She had considered sleeping on the floor, but it felt silly with so much space in their king-size bed.

"I can feel you watching me," he said, his eyes closed.

"You said at the general's house that you'd share more secrets. Tell me one."

"I have plenty of secrets. Which ones in particular interest you?"

She didn't need state secrets. She didn't care about government intel. "Tell me something about you that no one else knows."

He took a deep, shuddering breath. "I realized tonight that I need you."

She hadn't expected that. She had expected a story from his childhood or a tale about his first kiss. "What made you think that?"

"You complement me. You're soft and warm and kind. You make me want to be better."

"Really?"

"You asked for a secret. I gave you one."

"Thank you, Demetrius. That means a lot to me."

"Will you sleep close to me?" he asked.

After his confession, how could she not? She removed the ice from his bruises, careful not to touch his shoulder. As she lay next to her husband in their bed, she prayed he would heal and that tonight would be the start of something good and honest between them.

Chapter 11

Stella could not delay the reading of the late king's will any further.

The king's barristers had arranged the reading to take place in their private offices in Abele. The entire family was gathered at a large conference table. With the king's ex-wives, late wife, children and their lawyers in attendance, it was standing room only. The room was hot even though the ventilation system was blowing cool air and several windows were cracked open.

The barrister handling the king's official will of record began to read. The first ten minutes of his monologue made Iliana's eyes glaze over. It was legal jargon, outlining definitions of words contained in the will. Iliana listened and watched the faces of her siblings and their mothers.

Maria seemed to be listening intently, her hair pulled into a tight bun and her dark clothes somber. Theodore and Spiro appeared bored, leaning back in their chairs and looking at the barrister with blank expressions. Emmanuel seemed focused, his hands clasped on the table as if in school. Georgia and Kaliope appeared nervous.

Stella looked smug. She was wearing a wide-brimmed hat with a small black veil across the front. Her mourning clothes were appropriate, but Iliana found the ensemble too dramatic for the occasion. If she was grieving deeply, perhaps she shouldn't be smiling. Iliana wished she could wipe the expression off Stella's face.

Demetrius was seated beside her, and he had refused to wear a bandage or sling, claiming he'd appear weak to his enemies. Demetrius needed to take better care of himself. He was sleeping less than five hours a night, and it was fitful sleep, at best. She didn't know if it was worry or his pain keeping him awake.

He had increased his security, and Iliana took care to ensure he was being watched. She had previously left those matters to Demetrius, but she needed to take responsibility for their safety, too. She wanted him to view her as his equal and confidante. She couldn't be his other half if she didn't take an active role in decision making and their lives.

The barrister began reading the items that were part of the king's personal estate. Those items belonging to the crown went to the heir to the throne, who had not been named. The laws of succession dictated that the crown should pass to Emmanuel, but in some cases, another person was named. The tension in the room was palpable. The king's first wife, Kaliope, was bequeathed the land they had expected her to receive. After conferring in whispers, she and her lawyer seemed pleased with the outcome. The king's second wife, Georgia, received a similar parcel of land. She glanced at Kaliope, perhaps feeling as if she had been cheated, but Kaliope wasn't making eye contact.

"The king's land and holdings in Santari are left to his loving wife, Stella Floros. The king's land in Carfu is left to his loving wife, Stella Floros."

Maria's face turned ashen. The land in Carfu was to have been hers, along with the title of baroness.

"The king's land in Kaphalonia is left to his loving wife, Stella Floros."

Theodore's expression switched from disinterested to furious. He spoke to his lawyers, and the conversation grew louder. The barrister continued reading. Every remaining item in the will was left to Stella. As if that weren't enough, the king's will stated there would be an election among the Assembly to determine his successor.

Stella's frequent visits to titled royals made sense now. She had known the will stipulated those terms of succession, and she was preparing to win the vote. Had she been clued into the contents of the will because the king had given her a copy or because she had doctored it?

"She changed the will! I call fraud!" Spiro said, coming to his feet and pointing his finger at Stella.

Stella stood and smoothed her black designer skirt. "I'm sorry if you are disappointed, but we will honor the king's wishes."

The room erupted in outrage. Accusations were flung, and the lawyers had to intercede to protect Stella from Maria. The lawyers were arguing but in a more civilized manner, without swearing and shoving.

Only she and Demetrius were quiet. Iliana leaned close to her husband's ear, not only for privacy but because there was no way he could hear her over the roar in the room.

"What are you thinking?" she asked.

"I anticipated this."

Iliana considered her options. "I'll lodge a complaint and follow the procedures to have the king's will reviewed." She was comfortable with legalese and a lot was at stake. This experience, as taxing as it was, inspired her to want to take the bar again.

Demetrius nodded in approval. "We can request that another lab validate the will's authenticity."

"What about the other matter?" Alexei was still in prison. Iliana needed to be titled to release him. If the will held up in court, she had nothing to help Demetrius or Alexei.

"We won't talk here. Let's go. No progress will be made in this room."

They left the room. Their security had been waiting outside the doors and immediately surrounded them. Exiting the building, they pushed through the crowd gathered outside. Questions were flung at them about the king's will and who had inherited what. Demetrius ignored them, and Iliana followed his lead. They strode directly to their waiting car.

When they were inside with the door closed, Demetrius fell back against the seat as if exhausted.

Worry consumed her. Why didn't Demetrius listen to his doctors? Why didn't he listen to her?

"You're in pain, aren't you." It wasn't a question.

"I'm fine. I've been shot before," he said, rubbing his shoulder and chest with his right hand.

True as that may be, he hadn't taken enough time to rest. "You were shot twice and you aren't wearing your sling or following your doctor's orders. You're putting too much pressure on your healing shoulder."

He closed his eyes, breathing hard. "I can't look weak."

"Instead, you want to look stupid?"

He opened his eyes and let out a bark of laughter. "Only you can speak to me that way and get away with it."

Their relationship was strained, but Iliana knew that Demetrius wouldn't harm her. She longed for the days before she'd known she was the king's heir, when they had a comfortable rapport. "Please, let's go home where you can wear your sling and take some medication and rest."

"No pain pills. Cloudy thoughts lead to bad decisions."

Iliana wasn't willing to let it go so easily. "Extrastrength acetaminophen won't cloud your thinking."

He grunted, but Iliana knew she had won.

Back home, Demetrius invited her into his office. After locating his sling with Abeiron's help, she helped Demetrius put it on, careful not to jostle his shoulder. A couple of pills and a glass of water later, Demetrius was decidedly less grumpy.

"Open my safe?" he asked. He pointed to the one mounted to the wall.

He hadn't asked her to do that before. "I don't know the combination," she said.

"Run your finger over the reader and stand in front of it." Iliana did as he asked, and the safe popped open.

"How did you get my fingerprints and retina scan?" she asked.

"Fingerprints from a drinking glass. Retina scan from your last optometrist's visit."

She decided not to make a fuss about the invasion of privacy. He had given her access to his safe. It was a small step in the direction she wanted them to move.

She opened it, surprised how far it extended.

"There's an orange folder inside. Please retrieve it." She did as he asked.

He opened it and pointed to the documents. "Copies of the king's will from the past ten years. The king had a bad habit of changing his will often. When he was upset with his children, he cut them out. Then he'd add them back around the holidays and their birthdays. A cyclical pattern for a man who was more sentimental than he'd have admitted. Until the past couple of years, after he fell sick, each of his children was written into his will, and what they were to inherit was similar in terms of land size and dollar amounts. What's notable is that you are the only child to be named a marquis or marchioness."

"Why do you think that is?" she asked. In previous versions of the will, her siblings were given titles and enough money and land to live out the rest of their lives in luxury. She could have been given the same. Why treat her, the daughter he didn't know, differently?

"Perhaps he felt you could handle it."

The king had thought she could handle a position she knew nothing about in a country that was unknown to her? "That's impossible. He didn't know me."

From his position on his black leather couch, Demetrius watched her with those dark, expressive eyes. He had more information.

"Tell me," she said.

"Your father kept tabs on you when he could. He wanted to be involved in your life, and he knew that he'd given up his chance and may have made an irreversible and unrecoverable mistake."

Dark thoughts crossed her mind. "Did he send you to spy on me? Is that why you inserted yourself into my life?"

"He didn't send me to spy. I mentioned in passing that I had a meeting with the queen of Acacia and her personal secretary. After that, the king asked me a lot of question about you and Serena, pretending he was interested in the politics of the region."

"Did you tell him how you felt about me?"

"Yes. Before I married you."

"Did he approve?" She wasn't sure why that would have mattered. She didn't think her father, the man who had raised her, would think much of her marrying Demetrius. Her father hadn't liked the men she dated. In his mind, no one was good enough for her.

"I think he did. He knew he didn't have a lot of input after he had given you up for adoption. I'm a man of means and power, who is capable of protecting you."

Iliana sat on Demetrius's desk chair. It was his

space and it looked like him; it smelled like him. She wondered what it would be like to be him. Closed off, secretive and always plotting. Could he ever relax? Did he know the meaning of the word? Even when he slept, he was restless and spoke. His phone rang at all hours of the night. But he wasn't all hardness and political maneuvering. Demetrius was thoughtful and smart and sweet when he wanted to be. "My father, my real father, wouldn't have cared about your money or power."

Demetrius leaned against his desk. "Tell me what he would have cared about."

"Happiness. That you made me laugh. That you made me feel wanted and special. That he could trust you not to break my heart."

"Is that your way of telling me that I would have been a disappointment to him?"

She hadn't been trying to start another argument with him. "I just meant that there's more to being a husband than power. It takes a strong man to be tender and kind and loving."

"You don't think I'm a kind man?"

She had seen kindness and other times only coldness. "You can be anything you want. I've seen you be warm and generous and considerate. When you were in the hospital, people kept telling me how you had changed their lives for the better. They kept telling me what a good man you were and how they were praying for you. I was happy someone else got to see the softer side of you."

Demetrius seemed embarrassed by the praise. "That is nice to hear."

"I thought you would wake up and be a changed

man." After a near-death experience, didn't people re-evaluate their lives and want to be warmer and more affectionate?

"Did you expect me to lie in bed for weeks and thank the Lord for a second chance? For me, this wasn't a second chance. It was a tenth chance. I've been to war. I've been injured, and I've had nights where I wasn't sure I would wake in the morning."

"I don't expect you to spend your days sleeping and praying in bed, but you haven't said you're happy to be alive."

He appeared incredulous. "Where do you come up with this stuff? I am happy to have survived. Alexei is counting on me."

What about her? Did she factor in? "Have you thought about me?" About how she had felt when he was injured or about how she might feel if he died?

"I think of you all the time, Iliana, but you have to be more grounded. It's as if you have this idea about marriage, that it's rainbows and flowers and sunshine."

More grounded? He could stand to be a little more romantic. "Marriage is supposed to be happy. Especially for newlyweds."

"The beginning is the hardest part," he said.

"I married you because I wanted this to work."

"You're the one who pulled the ejector seat and wants out."

That wasn't fair. He had trapped her, and she had been trying to find a way to breathe. She wanted to stay in a marriage because it worked, not because she'd been trapped. "It would be easier to be married to you if it was a choice."

"It was your choice."

"To marry you, yes, but now you behave as if it's my obligation."

His phone rang. "Excuse me."

He answered. She didn't stand from his desk chair. He brought his free hand over his face. "I see."

Something bad had happened. She could read it in his posture. The tension and stress weren't good for him, especially now when he needed to heal. When he disconnected, he stood.

"Everything okay?" she asked.

"Stella has launched her campaign to become queen. She has appearances scheduled, and some of her wealthy allies have arranged fund-raising and campaign events for her."

"She works fast," Iliana said.

"She's likely been preparing since before the king died."

"If she becomes queen, we'll never free Alexei."

"That's not an option, Iliana. We'll counter her campaign and present our own candidate for king. I will use everything in my power to make sure that woman doesn't destroy my plans."

The king's children initiated their political campaign with Emmanuel as their front-runner for king. Though their father had been well connected, they were not, and loyalty to the king did not automatically transfer to Emmanuel. This would be an uphill battle for them.

Iliana had not given her public support to anyone. Demetrius was still contemplating the best course of action.

Though she and Demetrius were being carefully neutral, the family was gathering at Kaliope's home. The official reason was that Emmanuel planned to announce his intentions to be king and hoped that checkbooks would open up in his support. The unofficial reason was for the family to discuss how to handle Stella. She was proving herself to be a formidable adversary.

"My presence could make Emmanuel more enemies than supporters," Demetrius said. He was wearing a black suit and wearing it well. Looking at him made Iliana's heart skip a beat. She thought of the night they'd married, and a rush of emotion brought tears to her eyes. She had been so hopeful that night, believing they would be happy and together forever. Too much had changed, and she didn't know how to get them back to that place.

"What did I say? What's wrong?" He handed her a handkerchief from his inside breast pocket.

"I was thinking about the night we were married."

His eyes lit with concern. "Were those sentimental tears or sad tears?"

"Neither. I was happy that night. You made me feel special. I thought we would have that every day."

Demetrius rubbed his jaw. "Do you want to attend this party alone? I can wait for you outside."

"Don't be ridiculous. We're here now." He was quick to pull away, and she couldn't blame him. She felt the same. They had hurt each other, and they didn't know how to make it right. Except in bed. They connected well there. But it seemed tension underscored every other interaction.

After being checked by security, they entered the

house. Kaliope's love of blues and grays was obvious. A double stairwell made of gray wood was the focal point of the grand foyer. The floor was covered in shiny silver tiles, complementing the misty-blue walls of the vaulted ceiling. Silver furniture and the abstract art in shades of gray and navy completed the look.

Party guests were spread across the main floor and waitstaff circulated with food and drinks on black trays. A string quartet played in the lobby, and the music floated into the rooms.

Demetrius mumbled under his breath.

"What's wrong? I don't understand French," she said.

"That wasn't French. It was Dutch. I see some individuals I know."

It didn't sound as if those individuals were friends or that he was looking forward to a happy reunion. "Are you on bad terms with them?"

He had an indecipherable look on his face. "Not bad terms. They're men, and one woman, who I've worked with. They're assassins."

Fear jolted her. "What are they doing here?" Her family was being targeted by the Ghost. Would he have sent assassins into Kaliope's home? Presumably any opportunity to strike would be exploited.

"Maybe they are working, but they could be here to support Emmanuel. Their work is heavily invested in politics."

"Could you find out?" she asked.

Demetrius seemed unsure. "I will see if they are on the guest list under their real names. Then I'll strike up a conversation."

Iliana prayed they were not in Kaliope's house to

conduct business. Kaliope had hired extra security for the occasion, but the Ghost had proved to be smart and capable. Positioning a threat in plain sight could be his next tactic.

The assassins Demetrius knew were not attending the party under their real names or any of the aliases they'd used for jobs he'd been aware of. That didn't bode well. Why were they here? Three assassins, two men and one particularly vicious woman, gathered in the same place. The murder-for-hire community was small. They would have some familiarity with each other, though they'd have no reason to interact socially.

Demetrius approached Rahl. He was a ruthless killer. Demetrius's intel had revealed he was an American, former special operations, who had turned in his red, white and blue flag for a big fat green paycheck. The last Demetrius knew, he was living in South America. What brought him to Valencia?

Demetrius didn't shake his hand. He stood beside him. "Rahl."

"Demetrius."

The two men didn't look at each other directly. "I'm surprised to see you here. I didn't think public functions were your gig." Rahl lived off the grid.

"I had to come out. I have a stake in this mess."

"What stake is that?"

Rahl shot him a sideways look. "I can't talk about that."

He could talk about it. He just wouldn't. Demetrius needed to get the information another way. "You here for a job?"

"Relax. I'm not gunning for your wife. Or you."

The assassin community would know that Demetrius and his wife had been targets and that Demetrius was out for revenge. "That's great to know. Want to do me a favor and tell me where the Ghost is?"

Rahl looked around. "Don't let anyone hear you talk about that."

"He's not Bloody Mary. He won't appear if we chant his name too many times. The Ghost openly came at me. He expects backlash. Might even be disappointed if I do nothing in response."

Rahl rocked back on his heels. "I heard you took a few bullets. Do you want to take a few more?"

"Threats are below you."

Rahl sniffed. "Not a threat. That's not how I work. But I was hit a few months back. Stomach. Bullet through and through. I missed a month of work. I'm pissed."

"The Ghost was responsible." Educated guess.

Rahl gave one swift nod, and anger lit hot in his eyes. "The Ghost is making the rounds."

"Making the rounds and doing what?"

"Leaving bodies."

"Why?" Demetrius asked. Assassins killed for money. What was the Ghost trying to accomplish?

"Power play. Wants to be the only game in town. Work for him or don't work at all."

Rahl wasn't a team player. "What are you planning to do about it?" Demetrius asked.

"Put someone I can trust in power in Valencia. I've heard the Ghost works out of this area. Then go on the offensive."

"Dangerous game."

Rahl smirked. "High risk, high reward."

"Do you know who he is?" Demetrius asked.

Rahl shook his head. Demetrius believed him. If he did, he wouldn't be standing around rubbing shoulders with Valencian royalty. He'd be plotting his attack.

"We have a common enemy," Demetrius said. "Call on me and I'll help." It wouldn't be the first time he'd worked beside Rahl, and he knew that while the trained killer had loyalty to no one and nothing, he was a good man to have around when guns were needed.

High-pitched shrieks from outside the house had Demetrius racing in the direction of the commotion. He kept an eye out for the assassins at the party. A diversion like a screaming woman was a great time to make a hit.

Worry torpedoed him when he spotted Iliana. She was outside with Maria. They were holding hands and looking out into the garden, terror written on their faces.

Reaching her quickly, Demetrius put his arms around his wife, needing to feel her close and shield her with his body. "What's wrong?" Before she could answer, he followed her gaze up, up to the second story balcony overlooking the garden.

Spiro was swinging from the terrace with a rope around his neck.

"Cut him down!" Iliana shouted, grabbing Demetrius's suit jacket.

Spiro was dead. Though it was horrible to see the man swaying in the wind, the smarter play was to leave the scene untouched and allow the police to gather evidence.

Had the Ghost struck again?

"One of the assassins must have done this," Iliana said, her voice quiet, but Demetrius could hear the hysteria shaking in it.

"Could be."

If this was a professional hit, the assassin would have covered his—or her—tracks well.

"He won't stop until he kills us all," Iliana said.

Demetrius tightened his arm around her. "Not you. I won't let him harm you."

Iliana felt as if a fog had settled over her brain. In the three days following Spiro's death, speculation ran rampant. Kaliope was a mess, devastated her security had failed her. Maria suspected it was an inside job, someone close to the family who was striking out at each heir.

Spiro had followed his father's precedent for a burial at sea, and Kaliope was hosting a reception at her home in Abele following the service. According to Maria, Kaliope had been unable to return home since the incident. It was tearing her up. It was destroying all of them.

Iliana went in search of Maria and found her drinking wine in the drawing room, away from the grieving family and friends who'd come to pay their respects.

When Iliana had lost her parents in that disastrous car accident, the funeral and the weeks following it were a blur. She'd taken poor care of herself, eating comfort food and forgetting entirely about her health. She'd gained fifteen pounds in the year after their deaths.

The downward spiral had ended when she had attended a royal event wearing an empire waist dress and someone had asked if she was pregnant. That night she had looked at herself in the mirror and had seen eyes that were deep wells of sadness, and grief etched into her face. That had jolted her out of her unhealthy behavior. With Serena and Danae's help, she had clawed out of her anguish.

Iliana sat next to Maria. "You holding up okay?"

Maria took a sip of her wine and then swirled it in the glass. "I'm dealing. Spiro could be a real pain in my butt, but he was a good guy. He loved his family, and aside from the squabbling over the past several weeks, he was fun to have around."

"I'm sorry for your loss."

Maria finished her wine and reached for the bottle tucked behind her chair. She poured more into her glass. "I should stay in Valencia and throw my support behind Emmanuel, but I can't. I'm going to stay with a friend overseas."

Getting out of the spotlight might keep her alive. "That might be wise," Iliana said.

"Keep that between us. I don't want the assassins tracking me. Let them think I'm hanging out in Valencia."

"I won't say anything. If you need me, call. I'll do what I can to help you."

Maria leaned across and hugged her. "Thank you, Iliana. I was angry when I'd heard my father had another daughter. First, because the timing meant he was still having affairs and second, because I figured you'd be gold digging for anything you could get your hands on. But you're not what I expected. I've been pleasantly surprised."

She was glad to have had the chance to prove she wasn't trying to put the screws to anyone. "I didn't have plans to make a grab for money or power. I was looking for family."

"You have Demetrius."

Maria had confided in her. Could Iliana admit to her sister that all was not what it seemed with her husband? "We're newlyweds. We're working through some issues."

"In the bedroom?" Maria asked.

Iliana laughed. "No. That's the one place where everything is good."

"My mother told me when I wanted to have my way from my future husband, I should put him in a good mood, and then ask. I assume putting him in a good mood means getting him into bed."

"I don't think Demetrius would fall for that."

"I think you'd be surprised. I've seen him making moony eyes at you."

"Really?" Mostly he looked indifferent. Demetrius internalized everything.

"He's into you. No doubt."

"Hard to tell sometimes."

"That's macho-guy stuff. Like pretending he's strong and doesn't need you when he obviously does."

Iliana couldn't see Demetrius needing anyone. "Maybe. He wants to provide for me and keep me safe." Yet he hadn't spoken the word *love* to her.

"Does he have a brother? 'Cause Demetrius is hot and I could get in on that action. It's old-fashioned, but I like a little chest-thumping, protect-your-woman stuff."

Iliana laughed and avoided the question about Demetrius's brother. At the moment, neither of them had the power to free Alexei. But if Emmanuel were named king, would Maria convince Emmanuel to free Alexei as a favor to Iliana? A shift in power would cause upheaval in the region, and freeing one prisoner wouldn't be out of the question. Perhaps Emmanuel could work for prison reform.

Theodore joined them in the drawing room and closed the doors behind him. "So this is where everyone is hiding out. Mind if I sit with you for a while? I can't be polite to strangers for another minute."

"Sit," Maria said, and produced another wineglass from somewhere. She poured Theodore a glass and handed it to him.

He sniffed it but didn't sip. "I found interesting documents in my mother's safe. Old copies of Dad's will. For years, he left us everything. I'm not buying that at the end he decided that harpy Stella should get it all. They were married for a minute and a half."

"Anything recent to support that theory?" Maria asked.

Theodore shook his head. "Not in the past five years. But I'm not giving up. That black-hearted shrew killed Nicholas and Spiro. Her days are numbered."

Iliana heard the deep grief and the sharp anger in his voice. Would Theodore take matters into his own hands and attack Stella? "Let's not do anything rash." A warning to keep heads cool.

"Like change the king's will and pay off people to lie about it?" Maria asked.

Kaliope came to the door. "Maria, could I talk to you for a minute?"

Her usually polished appearance was decidedly rough.

Maria stood. "Excuse me."

Theodore sat in her vacated chair. "How is she? Maria, I mean."

She was stressed and afraid, planning to run away to protect herself. "She's sad. Grieving."

Theodore snorted. "She hated Spiro. She's probably drinking toasts to the man who killed him."

He sounded sure about that, but Iliana didn't believe him. Maria seemed genuinely upset. "That's not true. She was just saying that Spiro annoyed her at times, but that she missed him."

Theodore lifted a brow. "She's working you. Trying to make you think she's a nice person who wants what's best for the family. That's what this family does. Plays people and manipulates them to take sides. We might not have spent much time with our father, but we learned some things. We learned how to win people over. My siblings are experts at that."

"Aren't you, as well?" Iliana asked, trying to keep her voice gentle.

"No."

"No? You don't try to work people?"

Theodore sighed. "Perhaps you've noticed that I'm not close with my siblings. There's a good reason for that."

"As an outsider, I'm hardly in a place to judge your family. I didn't have brothers or sisters growing up. I don't know much about the dynamic. My cousins used to fight when we were young, but if anyone so much as looked at either of them funny, the other was right there, ready to defend her sister." It had made Iliana envious. Even if Serena and Danae had included her in their games, she hadn't been inside that relationship or as close as the sisters had been.

Theodore snorted. "That is not the relationship we have. My mother dealt with our father's affairs by ignoring them until she couldn't take it anymore. We didn't know you existed. My mother and Kaliope used us as pawns and raised us to hate each other."

"I'm sorry. No one told me you were involved in your parents' problems."

"That's a nice way to say it," Theodore said. "But I guess being married to Demetrius, you're the master of diplomacy."

Iliana wasn't sure about that. She wished when it came to her husband she was able to influence him without every disagreement escalating to a fight.

Maria entered the drawing room, still carrying her wineglass, red liquid splashing out of the cup. "Emmanuel is gone."

Iliana came to her feet. She reached for her phone to call Demetrius. "What do you mean, gone?" She needed every detail. Demetrius was somewhere in the house. Was he aware of this?

"I mean gone. He left the funeral, and no one has seen him since. He disappeared between there and here. His car is missing. He isn't answering his phone."

Iliana looked at the grandfather clock on the other side of the room. It had been a couple of hours since the funeral. "Try to stay calm. Maybe he went somewhere to be alone." Not everyone grieved in public.

"Or he's been kidnapped," Maria said.

"Or killed," Theodore said.

"Let's not jump to those conclusions," Iliana said, but a bad feeling settled in the pit of her stomach.

"His security detail is missing, too. No one is answering their phones."

Demetrius messaged her that he was on his way to the drawing room. He was calm and collected in these situations, and he would know what to do. He had spies everywhere—they would help. She rushed to meet him.

Demetrius caught her on the stairs. "Are you all right?"

"I'm fine. Emmanuel is missing," Iliana said.

"I know. Everyone is panicked."

Everyone except Demetrius.

"What can you do to help?" Iliana asked.

"This is a matter for the police."

A scream of anguish echoed from the first floor. Demetrius and Iliana took the stairs to find Kaliope on her knees on the ground, sobbing. "Not my boy. My beloved boy. Someone has taken him. We have to find him."

She looked around the room, and when her eyes landed on Demetrius she rose to her feet. Her eyes were red rimmed. "You. You know every dirty deed that goes down in this part of the world. Tell me where my son is."

Demetrius inclined his head. "I do not know."

Demetrius's mouth quirked to the left. It was so slight and if she didn't know him so well, she would have missed it. He knew something. He might not know where Emmanuel was, but he wasn't clueless. Maybe he had spoken to someone and they had confided in him or perhaps he had heard rumors.

"I don't believe you. My son could be anywhere, dying, begging for his life, and you're standing here calm and unconcerned. Your wife is part of this family, and her brother is missing. Do something!" She was shrieking, and the entire room was looking in their direction.

"I will do what I can to keep your son safe."

Maria rushed to her mother and put her arms around her. Maria whispered in her mother's ear, and the two women walked away.

Iliana whirled on Demetrius. "Can you help? What do you know?"

Demetrius regarded her and she knew he was checking his words. Further evidence, at least in her mind, that he wasn't clueless about Emmanuel's disappearance. He took her hand. "We should go. I will help Emmanuel."

He led her outside.

"Tell me. Now," she said.

Demetrius glanced back at the house. Two of his servicemen had followed him outside, but they were otherwise alone. "I think Kaliope's reaction is curious."

"She was acting like a grieving, terrified mother," Iliana said.

"She didn't behave that way when Maria was poisoned," Demetrius said.

"She was upset."

"She was upset. But just now, she was hysterical."

Maybe Kaliope favored her son over her daughter, or perhaps she had known that Maria was alive and under the care of doctors. "She doesn't know where Emmanuel is or how he is."

"Perhaps her fear is genuine. It's too soon to jump to the conclusion that Emmanuel will meet the same fate as Nicholas and Spiro."

Iliana didn't understand how he could be unruffled, but the entire situation was deeply upsetting for her. She folded herself into Demetrius's arms.

A sob escaped her, and he rubbed her back consolingly. "It's okay, Iliana."

She looked up at him. "How can you know that?"

He took her face in his hands. "Listen to me. It will be fine. I promise you that everything will be fine."

Chapter 12

A few hours later, Emmanuel's home, his office and his favorite hangouts had been searched. His security team was still missing. His car's GPS tracker had been found in a trash can in a shady neighborhood.

The family was devastated.

Demetrius inserted himself into matters everywhere in the Mediterranean. He knew people, assassins apparently, among others. When Iliana asked him about Emmanuel, he repeated the line that everything would be okay, yet as the hours ticked past with no sign of Emmanuel, Iliana didn't know what to believe.

She wanted to have faith in Emmanuel's safe return, but it would be so much easier with proof that her half brother was alive. She walked into her husband's office. He looked up as she entered.

"You look upset," he said.

"You keep saying that Emmanuel will be fine. If that is true, I want you to find him."

Demetrius blinked at her. "You want me to find Emmanuel?"

She had asked him a dozen times about Emmanuel. Why was he acting so dense? "What if I were missing? Wouldn't you try to find me?"

"I would find you if you were missing, but no one would be stupid enough to take my wife."

She sighed. She wasn't in the mood for a macho act. She needed reassurance. "This is important to me. Nicholas is dead. Spiro is dead. Someone tried to kill Maria. Emmanuel is missing. If the Ghost has instructions to pick us off one by one, who do you think is his next target?"

"I'll keep you safe."

She tried another angle. "Have you found the Ghost? Any leads? Do your spies know anything?"

Given the circumstances, she didn't understand how he could be so composed. "I have not found him, but he's working hard to piss off some well-known assassins. I'm not the only one gunning for him. If he's lucky, someone else will kill him. If I get to him first, I might not let death be easy."

"You have leads?"

"Yes."

"Are you planning to share them with me?" She expected him to remain silent and she contemplated how to react. They could fight. Again. Or she could walk away and make it clear shutting her out wasn't acceptable.

"I learned how the Ghost hires his assassins and

how he contacts them. I thought perhaps he moved around. A source tells me he operates out of Valencia."

Demetrius went to his safe and opened it again. He pushed a button and the safe rotated, the contents shifting to the right. He withdrew a folder and brought it to her. "This is the file I have on the Ghost. You are welcome to read it, but it can't leave this room."

Iliana accepted the folder and started reading.

"I will warn you that it gets graphic on page seven. Skip over the details of what he does to his targets. You'll have nightmares."

That he trusted her to read confidential documents was progress. As she read, she found it so normal to be with Demetrius in his office. He was working. She was reading and watching him. It was comfortable between them.

He was trying. It was a good sign and one she desperately needed.

Demetrius was working from the capitol building in Daedalus when Stella strolled into his office without knocking. She sat across from him. She was still wearing black, though she had given up the ridiculous wide-brimmed hat and veil that covered her face. Demetrius liked being able to see her face. It was easier to read her lies that way.

He'd been alerted by security that she wanted to see him, and he had allowed her to come up. He said nothing, waiting for her to give him a reason not to kick her out of the building and out of his country.

She crossed her legs and set her clasped hands on top of her knee. "You're challenging the king's will and claiming it's a fake."

A fact he wouldn't deny. "It is a fake."

She narrowed her eyes at him. If she was in his office, she was worried because his protest had teeth. He was gathering more evidence. Amon was looking for proof and following the paper trail. Demetrius had his lawyers file an amendment to his protest with every shred Amon found. It gave Demetrius satisfaction to know that everything he collected meant he was closer to freeing Alexei.

"My husband wanted me to run the country," Stella said.

"We both know that's not true." While he and the king had not been each other's closest confidants, Demetrius was certain that the king would not have wanted Stella running Valencia. She was inexperienced and impulsive, and the king's decision to marry her had been based on lust, not his desire to partner with a strong and capable leader.

"Let me put it to you another way. Withdraw your objection or I will have your brother killed."

Demetrius controlled his reaction even as white-hot anger sliced through him. Was Stella fishing for information or had she figured out that his brother was rotting in a prison cell in Valencia?

"You should know that I'm not as stupid as you seem to believe. Your wife visited Blackstone, and a prison guard reported that she took an interest in a prisoner. Imagine my surprise when I saw a picture of said prisoner. He looks exactly like you, less fifty pounds and much more broken and bruised. Either it's a wild coincidence, or this prisoner is the reason you're worried about what happens in Valencia."

When he said nothing, she continued. "It was

strange to me that you cared so much about Iliana and her inheritance. Because it's not like you need the money or the land. This has been about your brother all along."

He debated killing her right then. Threats against his brother burned him to the core. "If you hurt my brother, you'll be starting a war you can't win."

"You'd go to war over one man's death?"

Demetrius had worked hard to put Icarus on the path to prosperity and success. A war would derail his efforts and rob his country of resources they needed. He wouldn't make the decision lightly, and he had been holding back his military force from barreling into Valencia and rescuing Alexei for that reason. "If we war, I will win." A simple and true statement.

Stella thinned her lips. "We'll see about that. You should consider your next move carefully."

"You came here to threaten me. You're in my capitol building. You could disappear and not a single person would speak out against me."

Stella laughed. "You think you're much stronger than you are. That will be your downfall. You have liabilities. Your brother. Your wife."

"If you hurt my family, I will kill you."

"I'm happy to know you think of Iliana as family. I was worried your marriage to her was a sham." Her tone was mocking.

Iliana was his wife. He cared about her, and he would protect her. He wouldn't take Stella's bait. "Tread carefully."

Stella smirked at him. "You don't know what I'm capable of. I've studied you for years. That gives me the advantage. You need to understand that I will do anything to get what I want."

She sounded like a spoiled child. He, too, had been studying her. She was driven by her desire for power. Even more than money, she wanted to be respected and revered. She also had a ruthless side. "I've been warned."

"More than a warning. It's a promise. If you prevent me from inheriting what I deserve, then you'll suffer for it. I'll go after your wife, your brother and even your best friend, Casimir."

Who did Stella have working for her to give her this much confidence that she could take out his wife and Casimir, the king of a nation? Alexei was an easy mark, and knowing that cut deep. He would warn Casimir of the threat, though he doubted Stella would trifle with the king of Rizari, since that would also mean his wife, the queen of Acacia, would be involved. Then Valencia would be forced to face off against three nations. The odds of winning that battle were not in Stella's favor.

Could Stella be working with the Ghost? He'd considered it before but as yet couldn't make a connection between her and the well-known assassin. "Casimir and his wife won't be easy targets. To start a war with three countries united against you, that's a battle you won't win."

Stella stood. "You've been warned, Demetrius. If you value your wife, you'll withdraw your protest."

And leave Stella as queen of Valencia. It was a prospect Demetrius did not enjoy. If she were in power, she couldn't be trusted. "If I back away and you become queen, you'll release Alexei?"

Stella smiled. "Yes. Withdraw your complaint. Tell

your wife to keep out of Valencia's business, and I'll release your brother."

The deal was tempting. Iliana didn't need the money or land the king's will had left her. Demetrius provided for her. If Stella kept her word, Alexei could be in Icarus soon. Could he trust Stella to do as she claimed? "I will consider your offer."

"Please do."

Iliana appeared in the doorway, holding a picnic basket. She looked between Demetrius and Stella, the confusion on her face evident.

"How charming. A picnic," Stella said, brushing past Iliana, hitting her shoulder rather forcefully.

Demetrius kept his temper. He was relieved to see Iliana. She was the sounding board he needed. What Stella was asking involved her, too. "Please, come in. Close the door."

Iliana stepped inside, setting the picnic basket on the chair next to her. "What did Stella want?"

"To threaten Alexei."

Iliana gasped. "She knows about Alexei?"

Demetrius nodded. "If I back off and let her have Valencia, she'll free Alexei."

Iliana sat heavily in a chair. She folded her arms over her chest. "Maybe that's your only option."

"If I withdraw my protest, then Stella will be queen."

Iliana blew out her breath. "But Alexei would be free. Isn't that what you want?"

It was his heart's greatest wish. "I could send in another team to try to free him."

"How many teams have you sent?" Iliana asked.

"Twelve."

She winced. "I'm sorry, Demetrius. I feel as if our whole world has been shaken."

He felt the same way. The one good and right thing in his life was Iliana, and she wanted a divorce. Knowing that, his chest tightened. He had made a mess of their relationship. It had started so promisingly. He had wanted to be a good man and a great husband. He had failed on both counts.

He didn't know how to make it right. "Is that lunch for us?"

"I know it's hard to get away, but I thought you could take a break."

It was what he needed. Iliana in his life. If only he could figure a way to keep her there.

It had been a week with no word on Emmanuel. No body had been found, and no one had seen him.

Maria was incommunicado as well, but at least she had explained to Iliana that she would be disappearing to protect herself.

And then Iliana heard that Georgia had been hospitalized with a stress-induced illness. The family Iliana had only just discovered was falling apart. It broke her heart.

Her phone rang. Demetrius's number appeared on the display.

"Did you hear the news about Stella?" Demetrius asked.

What had she done now? "I don't think I can handle more bad news," Iliana said.

"I don't know if you'll consider this bad news, but she was arrested this morning under suspicion of being involved in Nicholas's and Spiro's deaths."

The room spun. "What about Emmanuel?"

A long pause. "She has not been charged with his disappearance."

"What do you think?" Iliana asked.

"About what?"

"About Stella being arrested."

"I don't think she's directly responsible."

But she was likely involved. "You think she hired the Ghost."

"Not sure about that, either. I've been looking into the matter, and I've gotten some information that doesn't jibe with her initiating the attacks. She may have doctored the will to cut out the king's children, but why go through the trouble of killing the heirs?"

"Because she wasn't sure the will would hold up in court?"

"If that was her end goal, why not go after the heirs when the king was alive?"

"Because the king would be suspicious. Someone tried to kill me before the king died," Iliana said.

"I will get to the bottom of this."

"Is that a promise?" Iliana asked.

"Yes."

Demetrius had made several promises he hadn't fulfilled yet. Could she trust him? Too much was at stake for him to fail, but success seemed impossible.

Reading autopsy reports and police files weren't Demetrius's favorite way to spend the afternoon. Amon had acquired copies of the police reports, interviews with witnesses and the medical examiner's findings related to the deaths of Nicholas and Spiro

Floros, the attempted murder of Maria Floros and the disappearance of Emmanuel Floros.

The facts didn't add up in Nicholas's autopsy. Demetrius searched the internet, interpreting the medical jargon. A science website confirmed his suspicion about Nicholas.

Given Nicholas's blood type, he was not Kaliope's biological son. She had to know. Fathers could be lied to or told they were the father. Mothers knew. No way around it.

Demetrius considered the possibility that Nicholas had been switched at birth but dismissed it. Nicholas took after his father—the strong jawline, the high cheekbones. Why was Kaliope pretending that Nicholas was her son?

He could be her nephew or another blood relative whom the king and queen had agreed to raise as their own to spare embarrassment for an unwed mother or a child resulting from an affair. But Demetrius had a darker, more twisted suspicion. King Emmanuel Floros had had an affair that resulted in Nicholas's birth, and he had forced Kaliope to raise Nicholas as theirs.

Demetrius searched for an explanation to piece together the timeline. In pictures, Kaliope appeared to be pregnant around that time, but that could have been faked.

He needed to question Kaliope about Nicholas. If she was keeping the king's secret, she could come clean now. Maybe it wouldn't answer the question of who was targeting the heirs, but it might shed light on the truth.

People could live with the truth. Lies only begat more lies.

* * *

Iliana met Kaliope at her home in Daedalus. This was their first private meeting, and while Demetrius had insisted she arrange it and that he come along to keep her safe, he couldn't protect her from Kaliope's anger or harsh words. Kaliope hadn't embraced her since learning of her existence. She had instead been distantly polite. Since Kaliope had dealt with the king's affairs and Iliana was a reminder of that, she understood the other woman's resentment.

"I wanted to meet with you to clear the air about a few things," Iliana said.

Kaliope appeared serene. Her dark hair was brushed away from her face, hanging loose around her shoulders. Her clothing was immaculate and tailored as if made for her. Perhaps it was. "Do you mind if we walk outside in the hanging gardens? My dianthuses are blooming, and it's absolutely gorgeous. Sadness lingers in me, but fresh air lifts the ache."

Iliana agreed and followed Kaliope into the garden.

"What things do you want to address with me? Has Demetrius found anything about Emmanuel?" Kaliope asked.

"Demetrius hasn't given up. He will call you the moment he has information. The reason I wanted to talk with you was more personal. I am a result of the king's affair, one of them, and you may find that upsetting."

Kaliope drew to a stop. "If we're being honest, and I see no reason not to be, then, yes, hearing that the king fathered a child with another woman was upsetting. I knew he'd had an affair with your mother, but I thought it was a brief fling that ended after one night." She didn't mention Nicholas. Could Demetrius have been off base with his theory?

Iliana had harbored the idea that her mother and the king had had a love affair. That idea seemed to be supported by what she had found out in Kontos. "Why do you think the king felt he needed to hide me by placing me in the care of friends?"

Kaliope continued walking, her fingertips absently brushing the leaves of her plants as she walked. "I can't begin to know what my ex-husband was thinking. He was an impulsive man in his personal life. Your mother wasn't his only lover. I turned a blind eye when I could, but eventually it became too much for me. His incessant affairs are what ended our marriage."

Kaliope's words cheapened Iliana's vision of the relationship between her mother and the king. Had Persephone only been significant because a child had resulted from the affair? Had her mother meant anything to the king? The age difference had been enormous. Could her mother have been an opportunist? Looking for someone to take care of her? "I'm sorry to hear that. I was under the impression that the king was worried for my well-being, and that was part of his reason for hiding me."

Kaliope's eyes narrowed. "If you are implying that I was a danger to you, I resent that."

"I wasn't implying anything. I wanted you to know that I feel badly about what's happened to Nicholas and Maria. I'm praying that Emmanuel returns home."

At the mention of her children, Kaliope's hands shook. "I've spoken to Maria, and I believe she is safe. But my Emmanuel…I am terrified for his life."

She'd said nothing of Nicholas. Had Kaliope grown to care for him? What had their relationship been like? If the king had had two children out of wedlock, why force Nicholas into their home but turn her away? Perhaps raising two bastards would have been too much for Kaliope.

Kaliope glanced to where Demetrius was standing close to the entryway, talking on his phone. "Do you trust him?"

"Of course," Iliana said, hearing and feeling confidence in her words she hadn't expected.

"I am afraid that he's involved with Emmanuel's disappearance."

Iliana was startled. "Why would you think that?"

"He's called the Chess Master in certain circles. It's one of the nicer names for him. If Stella's claim to the throne is overturned, that means Emmanuel is the king's first heir. If Demetrius has him locked away, that makes Maria the first heir."

"How does Demetrius gain anything from Maria being crowned over Emmanuel?"

"You've been friendly with my daughter. I love Maria and I admire her, but she is much more easily swayed. Emmanuel will make a good king. He is strong and fair and smart. Maria can be indecisive. She has her father's impulsiveness in certain matters."

"I'm sorry you feel that way. Do you think Nicholas would have made a good king?" Iliana asked, poking harder at the spot. She didn't want to twist a knife into a grieving mother's heart, but she was starting to think that Kaliope didn't have affection for Nicholas. Demetrius had the science to prove it, and Kaliope's behavior wasn't helping matters.

Kaliope's eyes turned hard and flat. "Nicholas was an alcoholic and a drug abuser. He would not have made a good leader. He was barely a decent man. He spent his weekends whoring and snorting whatever he could find to get high. It was embarrassing, and his death was a merciful end to a destructive life."

A harsh statement to make about her son, but anger was a stage of grieving. Demetrius would dig until he found answers, and Iliana hoped this conversation with Kaliope would help.

Demetrius opened the door to Kaliope's bedroom. The room was decorated in dark purples and whites, and the smell of lavender was heavy in the air. He slid on his leather gloves. He wouldn't leave any evidence behind.

No prescription bottles on the dresser. The room was neat and tidy, the bed made, and no sign of laundry, dust or debris. No contraceptives in the bedside table, although she did keep massage oil and candles there.

She likely didn't have a diary proclaiming why she had raised Nicholas as her own. He found a few pictures in her jewelry case of her and Maria and her and Emmanuel. None of Nicholas. Not proof, but more evidence pointing in the direction of Nicholas's questionable parentage and Kaliope's resentment at raising him.

He checked the walk-in closet. Dozens of pairs of shoes and handbags and clothing were hung neatly in order by color. Demetrius checked the drawers, knocking softly on each one, looking for a false bottom. He checked the walls, listening for a hollow sound.

Then he noticed a shoe box. Every other pair of shoes was displayed on a shelf behind a glass door. He grabbed the silver shoe box and opened it.

In the box were mementos, ticket stubs and dried rose petals. At the bottom was a picture of Kaliope and his father with his father's dog between them. Shock jolting him, Demetrius dropped the box. He bent to gather the items that had fluttered to the ground and looked again at the picture.

Kaliope had her arms affectionately around Octavius Drakos and his dog. It was hard to tell how old the photograph was, but she looked decades younger, and the baron seemed happier and more youthful, too.

Demetrius took out his phone and snapped a shot of the photo. He wasn't sure what to make of it. How did they know each other? Kaliope had taken care to hide the picture. If it was taken at an official event, why hide it? What was Kaliope's relationship with his father?

Demetrius put the shoe box back on the shelf. He checked the rest of the closet and snapped pictures in case he was missing something. Seeing the picture of the baron of Aetos and Kaliope had rattled him. He didn't have much longer to search. Kaliope and Iliana were walking through the gardens and he had pretended to slip away to take a private phone call. If he was caught in the closet, he would look guilty of being a pervert in the best case, a spy in the worst.

Hearing noise in the hallway outside Kaliope's room, he slipped away and returned to his spot on the portico. He sat on a metal bench and waited for his wife. It took everything he had not to charge into the hanging gardens, find Iliana and Kaliope and demand answers.

It was early, and Iliana was still in bed when her phone rang. Demetrius was already at work. Iliana cleared her throat and tried to sound alert as she answered.

"Iliana DeSante? This is Helena Kariolis. I was a friend of your mother's."

The words were like sunshine on her soul. Iliana had so many questions, she didn't know where to start. "Thank you for calling me. How did you get my number?"

"Your husband reached out to me."

This was a surprise to her, but she was delighted that he had. "I have so much I want to talk to you about."

"Could you meet me at the Museum of Armament in Abele?"

Iliana would have met her almost anywhere. Helena may know something to dissipate the cloud of shame that hung over Iliana after learning about the king and Persephone's relationship from Kaliope's perspective. "It will take me a few hours. I'm at home." It was the first time she had thought of Demetrius's house as home, and it felt good to say the words.

"Let's meet around one, after lunch. Would that work?"

After finalizing their plans, Iliana leaped out of bed, excited about the day.

She was early for her meeting with Helena. The

museum was closed from noon until two each day, but Iliana and Demetrius were allowed inside to wait for Helena.

Her birth mother's old friend arrived on time. She was a no-nonsense-looking woman, dressed in a practical business suit and black flats. She wore little jewelry, and her brown hair was short and stylish. Though most aspects of her appearance were unremarkable, she projected an air of power and authority that must work well when presiding over court cases. Iliana liked her immediately. She introduced herself and then addressed Demetrius.

"Would it be okay if your wife and I discussed some matters in private?" Helena asked.

At Demetrius's nod, she and Helena walked out of the lobby, both their security teams trailing at a distance.

"Thank you for getting in touch with me. I visited Kontos a few weeks ago, trying to find people who knew my mother," Iliana said.

Helena smiled. "I heard."

Iliana felt a blush creep over her cheeks. "I want closure. I want to know more about my mother. I only recently learned I was adopted, and it's been difficult to process."

They walked the long halls of the museum. On either side of them, guns in display cases adorned the walls. "This is an interesting place to meet," Iliana said.

"It's secure and private. The curator is a friend of mine. I'm glad to speak with you about your mother, but my primary and professional reason for asking you here is to speak with you about the late king."

"What about him?" Iliana asked.

"Though I've disclosed my connection to you through your mother, I am assigned to the court reviewing this matter, including your husband's challenging the authenticity of the will."

As a judge, Helena must be familiar with the matter of the king's will. Iliana hadn't realized Helena was directly involved.

"We have many different wills on file and the law is to uphold the last written will, as long as it was written in a sound frame of mind."

Iliana wished she could testify about the will and the king's final days. "I only spoke to my father once. I am not sure how lucid he was. He was reasonably able to talk with me, but I don't know if he was capable of making important legal decisions. I could see someone taking advantage of him."

"We have evidence that Stella Floros manufactured the will. Her detractors claim she not only falsified documents but that she's been working on a campaign to win over the titled royals in the country to support her claim to the throne. The descent and distribution terms in the will are unclear. That makes the line of succession blurry, leaving the door open for Stella's claim."

"I've heard similar statements from my siblings," Iliana said. *Siblings*, another word that rolled easily off her tongue now.

"Stella has been giving away items from the royal treasury in return for support. They are not hers to give," Helena said.

"Why are you telling me this?" Iliana asked.

"Professionally, my colleagues agreed I should

reach out and speak with you about the matter off the record. Personally, your mother was a good friend to me. I miss her. When I read about you in the news, I wondered if you were like her."

Iliana realized she was holding her breath. She wanted the answer to be yes, that she and her biological mother had something in common. She felt simultaneously hopeful and guilty. Her mother, the woman who had raised her, had been wonderful, and they had shared many special memories. "Am I like her?"

Helena stopped in a room containing weapons used in the early 1900s. "I don't know you well, but you have a spirit like your mother's. Nothing brought her down. No matter what happened, she believed that her dreams would come true. When she met the king, she was swept off her feet. I warned her that she would get hurt. He was married, and I didn't see a future for them. But Persephone didn't give up. She refused to end the relationship. When she became pregnant, she thought she would have the family she had dreamed of with the king."

Iliana felt a pang in her stomach. Her mother's greatest wish hadn't been fulfilled. It was sad to think about, sadder still that Iliana understood the sentiment. "It didn't work out for her."

"I don't know what would have happened. I was in the delivery room when you were born, as was the king. It was a big deal, very secret. I remember thinking when the nurses handed you to him that he might make good on the promises he'd made your mother and leave his wife. He seemed to love you and care for your mother deeply."

"Why wouldn't he keep me? Couldn't he have found a way to protect me?" Iliana asked.

"I suppose he thought there was no other way. Every person in the delivery room was sworn to secrecy, and the next day you were taken from the hospital. You disappeared, and I didn't know where you had gone. I thought of you often. I hoped you had been placed in a loving and warm home."

Iliana heard the heartache in Helena's voice and wanted to reassure her. "The people who adopted me were wonderful parents. I couldn't have had a happier childhood. They died a few years ago in a car accident and I miss them terribly, but they left me with beautiful memories."

Helena brought her hand over her chest. "I'm glad to hear that. I'd hoped the king would ensure you were safe and happy."

At the end of the exhibit, they sat on a bench and talked. Helena told Iliana stories about her mother, stories that brought her mother to life. It was a gift Iliana treasured.

Demetrius appeared in the doorway. "I don't mean to interrupt. I wanted to check that you were both okay."

"We're fine. Great, actually," Iliana said.

Demetrius pointed in the other direction. "I'll be waiting."

When he left, Helena took her hands and squeezed them. "You're happy now?" Helena asked her, catching her eye after Iliana stole another look at Demetrius's retreating back.

She wasn't sure. At times, she felt closer to Demetrius than she had felt to another human being in a long time. Other times, she wondered if she had made a mistake marrying him. "Demetrius and I have had ups and downs. We've only been married a short time, and it's been stressful."

"He cares for you."

Iliana shifted. Could she tell Helena about Alexei? "I don't know about that."

Helena's eyes darkened with concern. "When I was younger, I presided over family court. I saw many young people give up on their marriages. I saw hurt because there was still love, but it was buried under stress and problems and fighting. You have forever to get divorced, but you have now to make your marriage work."

"I want a family," Iliana said. Those were the truest words she knew.

"He could be your family. I could be your family. The king's children could be your family. It's up to you to decide who you want to let inside. Only you get to choose who you want in your life and what will make you happy."

Chapter 13

Demetrius had arranged for him and Iliana to stay in one of his presidential vacation homes in Icarus. Secluded and quiet, it was located on the water. His guards were posted outside, but he had asked for privacy with his wife. They had traveled often since being married, and Demetrius was aware of the strain on Iliana. She seemed happier after speaking to Judge Kariolis. While she hadn't revealed what the two had talked about, Demetrius was glad to see her smiling.

Demetrius entered the master bedroom—the space smelled of fresh linens and lemon—where he was arranging a surprise for his wife. He'd asked Abeiron to fill the room with candles and his butler had obliged—after mumbling something about a fire hazard. As he lit the pillars, one by one, Iliana entered the room, her gaze moving from the candles to Demetrius's face. "What's this about?"

"You need a break. You need to relax."

Iliana strolled toward him. She flipped her red hair over her shoulder. "Are you planning to seduce me?"

It had crossed his mind. "This isn't about sex. This is about relaxing and having fun with my wife."

He sensed she was giving him another chance, at least for tonight. He wouldn't think about divorce or her ultimatum. He'd give himself a break from work and problems and focus on the fun part of their relationship.

Iliana flopped onto the bed and kicked off her shoes. "I think you want to ply me for information."

Demetrius lay next to her. "Anything you want to talk about, I'm happy to listen."

"Helena didn't tell me directly, but I got the sense that the Valencian courts will uphold a previous version of the king's will. That means I'll be marchioness of Agot soon."

Demetrius had told her he would listen, but he didn't want to talk about those problems. He wanted his brother freed, but when Iliana talked about Valencia and the situation with her family, it amped up her stress. "That's good. We don't have to talk about politics, though. We can talk about anything you'd like."

Iliana leaned her head up on her hand. "What did you have in mind?"

"Tell me about your plans for our house."

Iliana frowned. "I don't have plans for the house."

"Tell me your plans for our future." He had meant to keep this night lighthearted and fun, but that question plagued him.

Iliana regarded him with eyes that were wells of pain. It hit him in the gut to know she was unhappy with their relationship, and he didn't know how to fix it. He wanted to be the right man for her, to ride to her rescue and be the man of her dreams.

"Do you love me?" she asked.

A blunt and direct question. He cared about her. He wanted to be married to her. Wasn't that enough? Love would come with time. "You need love from me?"

She sat up. "Is that a serious question? You're my husband. Of course I need you to love me."

"I will provide for you. I will help you with your problems. I will give you anything you ask for." Weren't those things that women wanted?

"Except love."

He hadn't spoken about love this openly before. "Love grows and builds with time." Discomfort hit him in waves. But if he changed the subject, she would be angry. If he left the room or made an excuse, he'd do more damage.

"If we have a baby, will you love him or her?" Iliana asked.

Another direct question, and he was unsure how to answer. "Iliana, you know that my father and my mother had a terrible relationship. Neither showed affection well. I can't recall them being affectionate with Alexei or me. What you and I have is new territory for me." He was navigating it the best he could.

Iliana rose on her knees and took his shirt collar in her hand. "Tell me what you feel now."

He checked his words, feeling as if he was walking into a trap. Could he admit he was turned on? That he wanted to make love to her, to bury himself inside her and forget about the world for a while? When he was with her, his demons were quiet. When she was in his arms, his world felt good and right.

"Don't think. Just feel. Tell me what you feel right now."

She wanted the word *love*, but he wouldn't lie to her. "Desire."

Iliana brought her mouth down on his and kissed him hot and hard. "And now?"

He couldn't figure out what she wanted from him. She knew that he wanted her. "Lust and the strongest urge to tear your clothes off. From the first time I saw you, I wanted you. So many times, I've stopped myself from kissing you, from reaching for you."

"Why? Why do you stop yourself?"

"You're my wife, but I feel you slipping away. Like holding water in my palms, the tighter I squeeze, the more I will lose."

Her eyes softened, and she pressed a kiss to his lips. "Then, do that, Demetrius. We've had the right chemistry from the start." She reclined on the bed.

He wouldn't give her time to reconsider. When she was naked, he covered her with his body. He started behind her ear and kissed a trail down her neck, across her collarbone and down between her breasts.

"You have a magnificent body," he said. He cupped her breasts and she arched under his touch.

"How do you feel?" she asked.

"Hot," he said.

She pulled at his shirt, tugging it over his shoulders. He freed his arms while she went to work on his belt buckle. He removed his shirt and kicked off his pants. Stripped from his clothes, he brought their bodies together.

"Now?" she asked.

It was hard to form words with the sensation that passed over him. "Desire. Obsession. I want you. I need you."

She parted her legs, and he positioned himself at her opening. As he surged inside her, he felt as though he was coming home. She was every bit as passionate as he was, meeting him stroke for stroke, lifting her hips and taking him deep.

Her fingernails scored his shoulders, and, with a twist of her body, she was on top of him. She rode him hard, rocking and swiveling her hips, moaning.

Reaching between her legs, he caressed her in the place she liked, gentle, rhythmic caresses, until she shattered. A moment later, the insane tightness of her body gripping him, he followed her into ecstasy.

"Now? Tell me how you feel now," she said, slightly out of breath.

He melted into the mattress, feeling hot and relaxed. "Sated."

She pulled the blankets around them and curled close. "And what about now?"

She was tucked in the crook of his arm, her head and hand on his chest, her hair tickling his forearm. She was looking for some emotional display, and he wasn't certain he was capable of giving it to her. "My actions should say everything you need to know."

Iliana's breath was searing his skin. "I need the words."

So much was hanging on the ability to tell her he loved her. Why couldn't he say the words? Iliana had given him chance after chance, turning away and then coming back to him, back to his bed. He had to give her what she needed.

The words wouldn't form. "I care for you, Iliana."

"And?"

"And you're my wife. You're my one and my only. You're the woman I dream of. You're everything to me."

She pushed up on his chest. "I need a shower." She didn't seem angry. She seemed sad, and that was harder to deal with.

She fled the bed for the bathroom. Demetrius was aware he had bungled this, and he couldn't understand why speaking that word was so hard for him.

Iliana was waiting for Demetrius outside his office in Daedalus. She was wearing a navy dress and a white cardigan. Her hands were folded in front of her. She had barely spoken a word to him since the night in the villa by the sea, and Demetrius was surprised to see her.

"Have you been waiting long? I wasn't notified you were here," Demetrius said.

He had been involved in discussions about the Ghost and the baron of Aetos with Amon and several of his most trusted spies. Unable to track rumors and his father's schedule precisely over the past twenty years, he couldn't place both the Ghost and his father in the same location at the same time. Demetrius wondered if his father or Kaliope knew the Ghost. She was hiding the fact that Nicholas was not her biological son. What else could she be hiding?

"You should have called or knocked," he said, trying to feel Iliana out. Her shoulders were tight and she seemed upset. Upset about the night they'd spent together, the last night he had touched her or new problems?

"I was told you were in a meeting and could not be disturbed. I don't mind waiting. I needed to tell you that Judge Helena Kariolis called me this morning. Stella is being held in jail awaiting trial. I will be named marchioness this afternoon."

Alexei would be freed. Joy shook him. "That's great news." Understatement of his life. While he knew that the legal process could twist and turn, this afternoon was so soon, and he could taste victory.

Iliana frowned. "Perhaps. Maria will not return to Valencia to be given her title. She is too afraid. Emmanuel is still missing."

Demetrius didn't want to have this conversation out in the open. They were in the capitol building, but the hallway was not secure. "I'd like to discuss this in private."

If news of Iliana being named marchioness became public, the Ghost would want her dead immediately. Demetrius anticipated more attacks.

Demetrius placed his hand on her lower back, surprised she allowed the gesture, and led her to the top secret space he used when he needed to be briefed on delicate matters.

Iliana sat on the edge of a leather chair. "What is this place?"

"It's the blackout room. It's secure. Information comes in. Nothing goes out. No taps in here. No chance of someone overhearing."

Iliana looked around. "Interesting concept. Why did you bring me here?"

"I have a lead on the Ghost."

Iliana sat up and leaned toward him.

"I told you I found the picture of Kaliope and my father in her closet. I think their relationship is personal but also professional. I think they may know who the Ghost is."

Iliana's jaw slackened. "What makes you think that?"

"You were attacked. If I had not interceded, you'd be dead. Nicholas was the first to die. He was not Kaliope's biological son, and she didn't seem to care much about him. She must have harbored a grudge against him and not wanted him to inherit. Spiro was killed."

"What about Maria? She was poisoned."

He had considered that. "She lived. I think Kaliope had the Ghost poison her but not enough to kill her, to throw off anyone looking into suspects who had a motive to target the heirs."

Iliana shook her head. "Why would she want to kill the heirs?"

"To ensure her children were given everything."

"Can you prove any of this?"

"I've been working on that. I have detailed information about the crimes against the heirs, and I'm looking for witnesses and a way to tie the murders and attacks to Kaliope."

"The police believe that Stella hired someone to kill the heirs."

"I don't like Stella, but I think she's been framed. I think Kaliope wields more influence in the government than she lets on, and she's using every connection she has to pin the murders on Stella and throw support behind Emmanuel."

Iliana rubbed her temples. "What are we going to do about this?"

"We'll use the findings to nail her to the wall."

"What about Emmanuel? If the Ghost took him, and she's the Ghost, why would she be panicked?"

"The Ghost didn't take Emmanuel," Demetrius said.

"How do you know that?" Iliana asked.

She would be furious if she knew, and he couldn't risk her flying into a rage and perhaps deciding not to help him with Alexei. It was a long shot, but he would tell her after Alexei was free. "It doesn't make sense for her to have kidnapped him. Or if she did, then she's a great actress and she knows her son is somewhere safe."

"This is a lot to take in. I only came by to tell you I would make good on my promise to you once I am marchioness and release Alexei."

There was a finality to her words, as if she was planning on leaving, and that panicked him. "I need to come with you."

"I thought you may want to see Alexei when he's released. I can call you to meet him at the prison," Iliana said.

Demetrius's mind whirled with details. Too much could go wrong, and he couldn't be in multiple places at once. He wanted to see his brother more than anything, but he also needed to ensure that the baron of Aetos didn't come after Iliana. The baron would be furious when Alexei was released. He would lash out at someone—and who better than the woman who'd foiled his plans? With his ties to Kaliope and therefore the Ghost and a team of assassins, Iliana would be in danger. "Who else knows you'll be named marchioness today?"

"For security reasons, only those involved in the ceremony," Iliana said.

That was too many people. The heirs knew, and so did Kaliope. It would leak back to the baron, and he would want to ensure that he had control of the situation. He wouldn't want to lose power to a newcomer. Demetrius weighed his options. "I'll stay with you to ensure your safety."

Iliana nodded once and stood. "Okay."

"Does this mean after you free Alexei you're returning to Acacia?" He wasn't prepared for her to say yes, but he needed to know where they stood. He had let her down and he had upset her. She had forgiven him far too many times, and he couldn't ask for another chance.

"I don't know, Demetrius. I don't know what comes next for me."

Iliana's hands shook as she signed her name on the document naming her marchioness of Agot.

No other heirs had attended the ceremony. Presumably they feared attacks from the Ghost and were lying low.

Judge Kariolis presided over the ceremony. She hugged Iliana and whispered in her ear, "Make your mothers proud. Both of them."

Though Iliana hadn't known her biological mother, her adopted mom had been a fantastic person with a warm heart. She had taught Iliana to be generous of spirit and to love openly. What would her mother advise her about Demetrius? To have endless forgiveness for a man who didn't love her? Could Iliana win his love? It seemed long past the time for trying to win him. What had started as a bright future for them had clouded over and seemed tentative, at best.

She looked at Demetrius. He was standing near the doorway, his arms at his sides, appearing strong and handsome. He had looked the same way at their wedding. As the memories flooded her, emotion accompanied them.

She knew in that instant she didn't want to leave Demetrius. She wanted him to love her. She wanted to put it all out there, to tell him how she felt, that she loved him and she needed his love in return. Though he seemed to doubt himself, he had the capacity to love and she would prove it to him.

Demetrius hugged her when she reached him. She hadn't realized she had been walking toward him until she felt the warmth of his embrace. "Are you ready to go?"

"Yes." She had read the documents describing the process of freeing Alexei. Though there was no formal process for petitioning a prisoner's release on the basis of an unfair sentence, her title gave her the authority almost without question.

She had the paperwork and the phone numbers in her handbag to deal with the matter directly.

"Let's go to Blackstone Prison," she said to Demetrius.

He and their servicemen escorted her from the building. Shots rang out. Security closed around her and Demetrius, practically dragging her to the car.

Demetrius? Was he okay? In the chaos, she couldn't see him. "Demetrius?"

She was pushed inside the car, and a man climbed in after her. She was pinned between two strangers.

"Where's Demetrius?" she asked.

The driver turned around. She didn't recognize him, either. "Sorry, Marchioness. We have other plans today."

She reached for the door, but the men held her arms against the seat.

"Let me out. My husband will kill you for this." The car was already weaving through traffic, traveling at high speeds.

If this man was one of the Ghost's assassins, she would already be dead. Small comfort. "What is it that you want from me?" she asked.

"My job is to bring you in for questioning," he said darkly.

Questioning by whom? "I don't know anything."

"Sure you do. You're married to the president of Icarus. He has spies everywhere. I'm sure you've had interesting pillow talk with him about many matters that don't concern you but that are of grave importance to others."

Demetrius told her no state secrets. He had not brought her into his confidence on most matters. He couldn't even tell her how he felt about her. Revealing the truth would make her useless to her kidnappers. Silence may keep her alive.

As they drove, Iliana formulated a plan. Her phone was in her handbag, but surely these men would stop her if she reached for it. Could she pretend she had to use the bathroom? Force a chaotic situation that would buy her time to call Demetrius?

Demetrius would be looking for her. No matter

the circumstances of how they had been separated, he wouldn't stop searching for her.

The surroundings were familiar and it took Iliana a few moments to realize she was being taken to the baron of Aetos's house.

Had the baron figured out that Demetrius was his son? A cold sweat broke out across her body. She wasn't as skilled as Demetrius at negotiating and reading people's intentions. The baron might detect a hitch in her voice, some strain to give away she knew more than she'd reveal. She would keep Demetrius's and Alexei's secrets the best she could, but would it be enough?

Demetrius believed that the baron had ties to the Ghost. If that was true, what horrors would she face inside his home?

The car pulled into an underground parking garage that smelled damp and musty. The walls were green with mold. She was pulled from the car and dragged into an elevator smelling of bleach. It rocked unsteadily as it rose, squeaking and grinding.

When the elevator reached its destination, the doors opened. She was escorted to a large room, where the baron of Aetos was sitting with his dog and lazily stroking his fur. She looked around the space, expecting assassins to leap from the shadows. She hadn't been in a physical altercation before, and she didn't think she would stand up well to torture.

"Sit," the baron said.

Since she had no choice, Iliana sat by the fireplace in a chair across from the baron. The blaze from the flames was intense, and the heat stung her face. Her kidnappers were waiting at the door. No chance for her to turn and run. Did the room have another exit? Could she use the fire as a weapon?

When they had met earlier, the atmosphere had been tense, but this time she smelled her own fear. Considering her options, she knew convincing the baron to call Demetrius was the key to her survival. The baron of Aetos wouldn't kill the president of Icarus. He wouldn't be so bold.

"Now that you're marchioness of Agot, you have more power than me. I don't like that." He laughed, and she found it utterly disconcerting.

"You brought me here to talk about my position?"

"I brought you here to make you understand that you have power and money all your own. My spies tell me that your marriage to the president isn't what you'd like people to believe."

Iliana gained nothing from being contrary. What did it matter to agree with the baron now? "Marriage is not what I thought it would be."

"If you're smart, you'll join me. My friends know the special treatment they receive when they ally themselves with me, and my enemies know the pain and disappointment of upsetting me."

Iliana pretended to consider it. How should she play the baron and his huge ego? "What is it that you want me to do?"

"Tell me what you know about Emmanuel," the baron said.

Iliana's stomach tightened. "I don't know much of anything. He's missing, and we're praying for his safe return."

Perhaps he heard truth in her words. "Call your husband. Tell him if he wants to see you alive and well, he'll bring information about Emmanuel to me today."

"Your guards took my phone."

Her phone was handed to her. She dialed Demetrius, her hands shaking, and he answered on the first ring.

"I'm okay," she said. "I'm with the baron of Aetos. He wants information on Emmanuel."

"I will kill him for this," Demetrius said.

She wouldn't relay that message, since the baron could do the same to her. "If you don't bring information about Emmanuel, he will kill me." She had trouble speaking the words without her voice cracking. She didn't want to die at the hands of an evil, twisted man. She didn't want to die at all.

"Can you escape, and do you have a weapon?" Demetrius asked.

"No. Please come immediately. Time is of the essence."

The sound of car engines meant Demetrius was already on his way. She had to stall long enough for him to arrive. He would rescue her.

Then she would tell her husband that she loved him.

Demetrius arrived at the baron's home thirty minutes later. The look of the place sickened him. He remembered the night that he and Alexei had come here to confront their father. It had been foolish to do so in the manner they had chosen. He had been young and stupid and thought he could get answers or avenge their mother's honor.

Their mother had described a man who was brutal

and cold. Demetrius had thought himself more brutal and colder. But he had been wrong.

Demetrius entered the baron's home unarmed and without his servicemen at his back. As he had anticipated, he was checked at the entryway and any weapons would have been taken from him. He had been unarmed in situations before and had survived. His guards were close but out of sight. They would not easily breach the perimeter, but his military was on alert. What happened in the next twenty minutes could cause a war between Icarus and Valencia.

Demetrius was led to a dark room lit only by a fire in the hearth. Iliana was seated across from the baron. Her head was tilted up, and she was silent. She appeared uninjured. He was proud of his wife for not weeping or begging. Even in her current position, she was maintaining her composure.

Would the baron recognize him? Would his father know his own son, the man he had condemned to die in Blackstone Prison?

"Iliana, are you safe?" Demetrius asked. He strode to his wife's side and drew her against him.

"I'm fine." She squeezed his fingers.

Searching for a weapon, Demetrius saw several options. One element that eluded him was how to kill the baron and spirit Iliana from the room before the baron's guards reacted.

Octavius Drakos's eyes didn't move from the fire. "Give us the information or you both die."

Us? Before Demetrius could voice the question, Kaliope entered the room. She walked to the baron, kissed the top of his head and then patted his dog.

Kaliope narrowed her eyes at Demetrius. "Tell me what you did with my son."

Demetrius saw an opening and would play this game to his satisfaction. Kaliope would reveal herself as the criminal she was. "The media is reporting he was kidnapped by the Ghost, the same man who attacked Iliana, drowned Nicholas, poisoned Maria and hanged Spiro. The police believe Stella hired the Ghost to take care of her dirty work."

Kaliope shook her head. "You were involved with my son's disappearance. Tell me or your wife dies. If her death doesn't yield the information I want, then you die, too."

Demetrius called her bluff. Too many people knew he was here with Iliana. No chance of Kaliope getting away with murder. If she believed Demetrius was responsible for Emmanuel's disappearance, she wouldn't kill him and destroy that link. Kaliope's worry for her son was clouding her judgment.

The doors to the room burst open and Emmanuel stalked inside. "What is going on? I demand answers immediately."

Kaliope ran to her son, throwing her arms around his neck. "Emmanuel! You're safe."

Emmanuel pulled his mother's arms off him. He straightened and looked around the room, confusion clear on his face. "Thanks to Demetrius. He helped me stay off the grid for a while. I asked for his help, and he obliged."

Kaliope turned to Demetrius, bewilderment plain on her face. "You knew where he was and didn't tell me?"

"I asked him not to," Emmanuel said. "I needed to know who was hunting our family."

Demetrius watched his father's expression morph from content to angry. He didn't like knowing that Emmanuel, the most likely to inherit the throne in Valencia, was allied with Demetrius. Demetrius still didn't know if his father recognized him as his son. It had been years, and the man was blind. But his hearing was good.

"Your mother was concerned. She knew the Ghost hadn't taken you, because she is the Ghost," Demetrius said. "Or rather she's one half of the Ghost. The baron is the other half. It's been hard to trace the evidence to a single murderer because the methods vary. Your siblings' killers are different assassins working at the command of the Ghost."

Emmanuel's gaze swung to his mother. "Tell me he's lying."

Kaliope clasped her hands in front of her and took a step toward the baron. "Of course he's lying. He's a dictator and a warlord. He rose to power by killing people around him."

The baron's eyebrows twitched together.

Emmanuel shook his head. "Don't spin history. Tell me the truth, Mother. I've heard some disturbing things while I was in hiding."

"I didn't lie to you," Kaliope said.

"Was Nicholas my brother?"

Kaliope brought her hands to her face and let out a dramatic sob. "He was your half brother. Your father ran around on me. He had a baby with his mistress and he asked me to raise it as ours."

"Why would you agree to that?" Emmanuel asked.

"I was young and stupid. If I didn't agree, what would have happened to me? He could have kicked me out and kept you. I stayed for you. But his affairs continued. I couldn't handle it."

"You should have told me," Emmanuel said.

"By the time you were old enough to understand, Nicholas was a lost cause. I thought he would kill himself the way he was boozing and screwing around with women."

"When he didn't kill himself, you helped him along, ensuring you and your children inherited more of the king's assets," Demetrius said.

Emmanuel looked disgusted. "You had Nicholas killed? You tried to kill Maria?"

Kaliope looked at the baron, then Iliana, then Emmanuel. "This is a family matter. Let's talk about this in private."

Emmanuel shook his head. "We are among family. We will talk about it now."

"How dare you talk to your mother that way," Kaliope said.

Emmanuel sighed. "This afternoon, the court upheld one of Dad's old wills clarifying the line of succession. I was crowned the king of Valencia. As your king, I demand the truth."

Kaliope fell to her knees. "Everything I did was for you and Maria."

"You poisoned her!" Emmanuel hollered.

"I was assured she would survive."

"She almost didn't," Emmanuel said. He pointed to one of the baron's guards. "Arrest her."

When the guards didn't move, Emmanuel shouted, "Guards!"

This time, the king's guards entered the room. They stood, awaiting his command. "Take my mother into custody under suspicion of conspiracy to commit murder."

Kaliope was handcuffed. She sobbed and pleaded with her son to change his mind, but he seemed indifferent to her hysteria.

Before she was taken from the room, Emmanuel held up his hand. "Wait, just a minute."

Kaliope stopped crying and looked hopeful.

"I heard another story while I was in hiding. A story about a baron who wanted the king's wife. He couldn't have her because they were both married to others. So the baron set about chasing away his wife and jailing his two children to clear the path for the life he wanted."

The baron stood, turning pale. "Lies."

Perhaps he'd thought he would get away with what he had done and leave Kaliope to shoulder the blame.

Emmanuel strolled closer to the baron. "Demetrius, do you want to tell him or should I?"

Demetrius took Iliana's hand. He needed his wife at his side. "I'm surprised my father doesn't recognize my voice. He was certain nineteen years ago my brother and I were the men who broke into his house to kill him and steal from him."

The baron lunged in Demetrius's direction, but Demetrius deflected the attack. Emmanuel's guards moved forward to intercede.

"I've sent a request to Blackstone Prison that Alexei Drakos be released. He will be taken to Saint Agnes Hospital for treatment, and I will have my guards escort him home when his medical condition is stable," Emmanuel said.

Iliana hugged Demetrius, and he felt the wetness

of her tears on his neck. "Finally, Alexei will be free," she said.

The baron let out a roar of outrage.

"Alexei may want to remain in Valencia, and that will be his choice. I am stripping the baron of Aetos of his title, his powers and all benefits associated with the position. They will be assumed by the next heir, Alexei Drakos."

Demetrius felt the ground shift beneath his feet. Iliana was in his arms and Alexei was free. For the first time in his life, he had everything he needed. His heart had never felt so full.

Under the care of his attentive doctors in Saint Agnes, Alexei looked in far better condition than when Iliana had last seen him in Blackstone Prison. He was clean, his face shaved and, while it would take time for him to heal, he was talking and smiling. The resemblance to Demetrius was stronger. As he gained weight, she guessed it would grow stronger still.

"I don't know how to thank you," Alexei said.

"No thanks are needed. I didn't free you. The king did," Iliana said.

Alexei closed his eyes. Though he was healing, he was still weak and tired easily.

"I'll leave you to rest," she said. She patted his arm and left his room.

Demetrius was standing in the hallway, waiting for her. She had lingered an extra moment to say good-bye to Alexei. Though she hardly knew him, her joy at seeing him was unbound.

She wasn't sure what to say to her husband. Leaving him would be impossible, but he had what he wanted. This is where their paths diverted. Did her love for him matter? Did it mean anything? "Alexei is free and now you are free of me," Iliana said.

Demetrius touched the side of her face. "I do not want to be free of you. I want you in my life. You wanted to choose your path. You wanted to be free to decide. I will give you that option. I want you to choose me, but I won't force you."

If he could let her go so easily, perhaps he didn't care about her the way she wanted to be cared for. "I have work in Valencia. Emmanuel has put me in charge of reform at Blackstone Prison. It's a big job. And I'm going back to school. I will take and pass the bar in Valencia. I want to help people like Alexei."

Demetrius's eyes darkened. "I will never give up on winning you back. I had your love, and I know what a precious and rare gift that is."

She wanted his love in return. Such a simple concept and yet fraught with problems and complexities. She turned to go, but he grabbed her hand and spun her around to face him. "Before you leave, you have to know I can let you out of my life, but I won't let you out of my heart. I love you, Iliana. I've loved you since you first mouthed off to me when I offended the queen."

Iliana felt joy spread through her. "I didn't mouth off."

Demetrius kissed her. "I don't know why it took me so long to place a word on the emotion I feel for you. I've seen some messed-up relationships, and I was afraid you and I would follow in those footsteps. But I know that would be impossible. I love that you're smart and spirited and you follow your heart. I love when you sleep beside me and wake next to me. I love those things so much, I will win them back."

Happiness filled her chest. His love was all she had wanted. "What if you've already won me?"

"Then, I will spend every day trying to make myself worthy of that love. I want to be your family. I want to be your home. I want to be your everything."

Iliana hugged him and kissed his cheek. "I love you, too. Now take me home, Mr. President. To our home."

"Here or in Valencia?"

"I guess we'll have two homes. Can we make it work?" she asked, feeling excited and hopeful about the future.

"We can make anything work. Home is wherever we can be together."

* * * * *

If you loved this suspenseful, sexy thriller,
don't miss these titles from C.J. Miller:

TRAITOROUS ATTRACTION
PROTECTING HIS PRINCESS
SHIELDING THE SUSPECT
TAKEN BY THE CON
UNDER THE SHEIK'S PROTECTION
COLTON HOLIDAY LOCKDOWN
CAPTURING THE HUNTSMAN
THE SECRET KING

Available now from Harlequin Romantic Suspense!

"Did you—" Lizzie broke off, her voice heavy and out of breath as she came through the door.

"He's gone."

"He?"

"I thought." Ethan stopped and turned back toward the window. The figure had vanished, but he conjured up the image in his mind. "He was wearing a thick sweatshirt with the hood up, so I guess it could be anyone. He was too far away to get a sense of height."

"The police will ask what color."

"It was nondescript navy blue." Ethan glanced down at his own sweatshirt, tossed on that morning from a stack of similar clothes in the bottom of his drawer. "Just like I'm wearing. Hell, like half the population wears every weekend."

"It's still something."

Lizzie stood framed inside the doorway, long, curly

waves of hair framing her face, and he stilled. Since he'd seen her the morning before, his emotions had been on a roller coaster through the ups and downs of his new reality.

Yet here she was. Standing in the doorway of their child's room, a warrior goddess prepared to do battle to protect her home. He saw no fear. Instead, all he saw was a ripe, righteous anger, spilling from her in hard, deep breaths.

"Maybe you should sit down?"

"I'm too mad to sit."

"Once again, I'm forced to ask the obvious. Humor me."

He reached for the window, but she stopped him. "Leave it. It's not that cold, and maybe there are fingerprints."

Although he had no doubt the perp had left nothing behind, Ethan did as she requested. She'd already taken a seat in the rocking chair in the corner, and he felt his knees buckle at the image that rose up to replace her in his mind's eye.

Lizzie, rocking in that same chair, their child nestled in her arms, suckling at her breast.

The shock of emotion that burrowed beneath his heart raced through him, and Ethan fought to keep any trace of it from showing. How could he feel so much joy at something so unexpected?

At something he'd never wanted?

Don't miss
COLTON'S SURPRISE HEIR by Addison Fox,
available February 2016 wherever
Harlequin® Romantic Suspense
books and ebooks are sold.

www.Harlequin.com

HRSEXP0116

JUST CAN'T GET ENOUGH?

Join our social communities
and talk to us online.

You will have access to the latest
news on upcoming titles and special
promotions, but most importantly,
you can talk to other fans about your
favorite Harlequin reads.

Harlequin.com/Community

Facebook.com/HarlequinBooks

Twitter.com/HarlequinBooks

Pinterest.com/HarlequinBooks

THE WORLD IS BETTER WITH

Romance

Harlequin has everything from contemporary, passionate and heartwarming to suspenseful and inspirational stories.

Whatever your mood, we have a romance just for you!

Connect with us to find your next great read, special offers and more.

f /HarlequinBooks

🐦 @HarlequinBooks

www.HarlequinBlog.com

www.Harlequin.com/Newsletters

ℍ HARLEQUIN®

A *Romance* FOR EVERY MOOD™

www.Harlequin.com